Also by Jackie Ashenden

ALASKA HOMECOMING
Come Home to Deep River
Deep River Promise
That Deep River Feeling

Find Your Way Home

JACKIE ASHENDEN

sourcebooks
casablanca

Published by Sourcebooks Casablanca, an imprint of Sourcebooks
P.O. Box 4410, Naperville, Illinois 60567–4410
(630) 961-3900
sourcebooks.com

Printed and bound in Canada.
MBP 10 9 8 7 6 5 4 3 2 1

This one's for my Kiwi whanau.

Chapter 1

"STOP! STOP THE CAR RIGHT NOW!"

Isabella Montgomery jammed her foot on the brake, the car skidding slightly on the loose gravel of the road but luckily not too much since they weren't going very fast. There was a hundred-foot drop-off to the left and Izzy had been traveling for nearly three days solid, so to say she was tired would have been an understatement.

"Yes!" Bethany exclaimed excitedly from the passenger seat, apparently uncaring that her abrupt screech had nearly caused them all calamity. "Stop here!"

"Oh my God," Indigo moaned from the back seat. "Are you insane, Beth?"

Beth ignored her, too busy gazing out the window at the lovely valley that had appeared after they'd gone around that last, nerve-wracking hairpin corner.

The guy at the car rental place had asked them if they were planning on driving down a road called Kelly's Canyon, because if so, their insurance wouldn't cover it. The three women had looked at each other with a touch of grimness, because yes, they were planning on driving down Kelly's Canyon. It wasn't the only road into Brightwater Valley, the little town they'd come halfway around the world to New Zealand to visit. There was another that apparently the tour buses used, but it took twice as long and they were all sick of traveling.

Izzy had asked him why their insurance wouldn't cover

it, but he'd just shrugged and said the road could be "a bit tricky."

"A bit" was an understatement. As was "tricky."

The road was gravel for miles, so narrow there was barely any room to pass another car coming in the opposite direction, and then there was the little matter of the hundred-foot drop on one side.

Izzy was jet-lagged, exhausted after three flights—one nearly twelve hours long—and a long car ride, plus driving on the other side of the road was a challenge she hadn't prepared for. Beth's constant excitement and optimism, coupled with Indigo's frantic seat clutching and moaning, were beginning to grate.

"Stop?" She tried not to sound cross since she'd only known Beth and Indigo for approximately twenty-four hours. They were her only link to anything resembling home for the next three months and she didn't want to alienate them. "Stop where?"

"Here." Beth gestured to the side of the road where there was exactly zero room to park. "It's not like there's any traffic."

She was right. And what little of the road ahead that Izzy could see was empty, as was the road behind.

Perhaps they could stop for a moment or two...

Izzy wasn't given a choice, since Beth was already undoing her seat belt and throwing open the door, leaving the paper map spread out over the dash—she'd been navigator since they'd lost cell service twenty minutes ago—and leaping out of the car. She hurtled toward the edge of the road as Indigo moaned in distress again.

"Oh my God, I can't look. She's going to go over the edge."

Izzy flicked a glance at Indigo in the rearview mirror. She

might not have known her two travel companions long, but certainly long enough to figure out that Beth was the eternal optimist, while Indigo leaned more toward the pessimistic.

When Izzy had arrived at Auckland airport after her twelve-hour flight from LA and had approached Beth and Indigo to let them know that she was Georgie's replacement, it had been Beth who'd welcomed her with open arms. Indigo, however, had regarded her with some suspicion, asking a whole lot of questions that Izzy didn't want to answer.

She couldn't blame Indigo for her suspicion though. Leaving Houston for LA, then going on to New Zealand had been a spur-of-the-moment decision she'd made in a second of intense rage, which hadn't left Izzy with a lot of time to let them know to expect her.

Indigo and Beth were from Deep River, Alaska, where Izzy's brother, Zeke, also lived. They were on their way to start a new business in Brightwater Valley, New Zealand. She'd met Beth and Indigo once before while visiting Zeke, and while she didn't actually know them, she'd been able to recognize them at the airport at least.

A third woman, Georgie, was supposed to have joined them, but she'd had to pull out at the last moment, so Izzy had thought to take her place.

Nothing whatsoever to do with the cancelation of her wedding or being ousted from the board of her family's company.

Nothing at all.

"She won't go over the edge," Izzy said with calm reassurance. "Are you sure you don't want to come and look at the view?"

Indigo had one hand over her blue eyes. "Oh, absolutely sure."

"Okay. I'll only be a second."

Izzy undid her seat belt and got out of the car, checking the road once again for any traffic before going over to where Beth stood, right on the very edge of the cliff.

The gravel crunched beneath the soles of the expensive and brand-new hiking boots she'd bought at the last minute in Houston. It was supposed to be midsummer here, but a cool breeze that had to have come directly off the mountains surrounding the valley made her pull her equally expensive, brand-new parka tighter around her.

Beth was in a T-shirt and jeans, her long, white-blond hair blowing around her face. It was clear she did not feel chilly in the slightest.

But she wouldn't. She was from Alaska.

"Isn't this amazing?" Beth held out her arms at the vista before them. "It's soooo beautiful!"

Sharp, snowcapped mountains cloaked in dense, dark green forests ringed the small, deep valley that sat at the bottom, with the most beautiful blue lake glowing like a jewel in the middle of it. The silvery, glittery thread of a river sparkled in the sun as it wound through the open farmland on the valley floor.

Brightwater Valley in New Zealand's South Island. Their new home.

It wasn't where Izzy had planned to be when this year had opened. She'd thought she'd be married, she and Josh shopping for a new home in Houston. She'd thought she'd still be working at Montgomery Oil and Gas, engineering a new direction in green energy for her family's company.

She hadn't known that only a week earlier, the company's board would inform her that while they loved the company's new direction, they couldn't in good conscience keep progressing with the remnants of the "old guard" still at the company. Izzy being the "old guard."

Or that, as she was still reeling from that news, at a gala celebrating Montgomery's new focus that same night, Josh would tell her that he couldn't marry her and that he was in love with someone else.

Which had been when the intense rage had come in.

She'd stood there on the white marble balcony of the gala venue, resplendent in the red designer gown she'd spent half her month's salary on, realizing that she was here to support a company who'd gotten rid of her like she was yesterday's trash. And the man who should have been her support and comfort the way she'd been his had dumped her on the same day.

Izzy wasn't a woman who lost her cool. She was always calm and unflappable. But that night her cool had evaporated into a cloud of hurt and fury, and since hurt wasn't useful, she'd fully embraced fury and a desire to get as far away from Houston as possible.

Zeke had told her in passing a couple of days before about a new Deep River initiative with their sister city of Brightwater Valley, something about starting new businesses to encourage growth. He'd muttered something about people from Deep River volunteering to make the trek down to the bottom of the world but that one of them had pulled out. So that's when she'd decided.

She needed a fresh start.

She needed to go to New Zealand.

Usually an eternal planner and organizer, she'd given herself no time to plan and had organized nothing. Not wanting to have to explain everything to Zeke, she'd contacted Astrid James, Deep River's mayor, to get the expedition details, at the same time making sure Astrid didn't know Izzy was planning on joining it herself. Then, propelled by anger, she'd packed up her apartment, put her stuff into storage, chucked whatever came to hand into a suitcase, stopped to get boots and a jacket at a local outdoor-gear store, then had gotten straight on the plane.

And now she was actually here. And she hadn't realized it would be so...beautiful.

"Yes," Izzy said, staring out over the valley below, ignoring the thick tangle of emotion that had lodged under her breastbone ever since she'd left Houston. "Yes, it is."

And with the sun shining down from a clear blue sky and the chill breeze clearing away some of her jet lag, it even felt hopeful.

Beth glanced back at the car. "Do you think we should drag Indigo out here? I'd hate for her to miss out on this."

"Uh, no." Izzy remembered the misery in the other woman's voice. "I think she's happy in the car. She'll probably be even happier once we get there."

"True." Beth looked back over the valley again, green eyes sparkling with excitement. "Oh, this is going to turn out to be so good, I just know it. Look at all that inspiration!" She waved a hand at the mountains. "And it's really not that different from home. Mountains, water, and no cell phone coverage. It's also so much warmer." Beth gave a delighted little shiver. "Can you imagine wearing a T-shirt in February?"

Izzy, who'd worn T-shirts in February in Houston, didn't

live surrounded by mountains, and always had cell phone coverage, tried not to let her growing trepidation that she'd made a terrible mistake in coming here show.

She forced a grin. "I know, right? If it gets any warmer, I'll have to take my parka off."

Beth gave her a look that was familiar from Izzy's visit to Deep River. The "poor city girl, too soft to deal with the harshness of the remote Alaskan landscape" look.

Sadly, Beth wasn't wrong. Izzy *was* a poor city girl, though years of being in the male-dominated oil industry had given her a tough skin and a cool reserve. She could deal with difficult people—she'd been dealing with them her entire life. Three months in an isolated New Zealand small town helping get a new business up off the ground would be nothing.

Certainly it couldn't be any worse than what she'd left behind in Texas.

"I guess it is colder than Houston," Beth allowed generously. "So you might want to keep it on."

Izzy had told the other two a little about why she'd suddenly turned up at Auckland airport in Georgie's stead, mentioning the end of her career at Montgomery Oil and Gas and how she'd been wanting to "explore new opportunities."

She hadn't mentioned Josh. The less said about him the better.

Beth had accepted it all without a flicker. Indigo, apparently, was still reserving judgment. Not that Izzy blamed her. All the two women knew about her was that she was Zeke's sister who used to run the oil company that had once tried to lay claim to the oil reserves under Deep River. Skepticism about her motives was par for the course.

Izzy shifted on her feet, impatient. Standing still gave her brain time to go over whether the decision she'd made to come here was actually a good thing, and not the definition of insanity she had a horrible suspicion it might be. She did not want to play the second-guessing game.

"Come on," Izzy said briskly. "The sooner we get going, the sooner we can get off this damn road."

They piled back into the car and continued on, winding down the horrible, narrow road until finally it opened onto the rolling green farmland Izzy and Beth had spotted from higher up.

The road was still narrow though, the unsealed surface vile to drive on. Because Izzy wasn't comfortable going too fast, it took another hour before they finally saw a plank of wood with *Welcome to Brightwater Valley* painted haphazardly on it, hammered to two struts on the side of the road.

"Well," Beth announced unnecessarily, looking down at her map. "We're nearly there. Finally!"

Yes, finally.

A tension that Izzy refused to call anxiety crawled through her, making her wish she still had the rage that had driven her from Houston to hold on to. But that had receded over the course of her journey, leaving her uncertain and full of unfamiliar doubt.

She hadn't told Zeke she'd decided to take Georgie's place. She hadn't told him about the canceled wedding or about how she wasn't working at the family company anymore. She hadn't told anyone. She'd been too angry and upset and hadn't wanted to explain.

Once she was settled in though, she'd give him a call. She didn't want him to worry.

Anyway, she shouldn't be feeling anxious. She should

concentrate on feeling excited instead. She'd wanted to get out of Houston and she had.

This would be her new start, a place where she could make her mark in a way that didn't have anything to do with her family. Where she wasn't the boss's obedient daughter, working in his company and engaged to the son of one of his good friends.

Where she was her own woman.

The road became asphalt again, to Izzy's relief, skimming the side of the lake, which had sun glinting off the water, making Bethany sigh in delight. At last they came to a small cluster of buildings lining the road opposite the water. One was wooden and two-storied, painted a faded red, with a sign on the front proclaiming it THE ROSE HOTEL. Next to the hotel was an old, long stone building that had perhaps once housed several stores but now the only sign on it read BRIGHTWATER VALLEY GENERAL STORE. BAIT AND TACKLE! PIES!

There was only one other building. It stood on the other side of the hotel, also wooden and two-storied, but it was much newer. The sign on the front was much more professionally done and read PURE ADVENTURE NZ. KIWI OWNED AND OPERATED. NOT YOUR DAD'S ADVENTURES.

Izzy stopped the car in the parking area beside the lake and the three of them looked at the buildings in silence.

"Is…that it?" Bethany sounded uncertain for the first time.

"Well, we knew it was small," Indigo said. "Remember?"

On the trip from Auckland to Queenstown, where they'd rented their car, Izzy had looked a few things up on the internet but hadn't been able to find much about Brightwater

Valley online. Nothing except Pure Adventure NZ's website, which quite frankly needed some work done to it, since there was nothing about the town on it.

Automatically, Izzy reached into the pocket of her parka to get her phone, mainly to double-check the info she *had* found, but of course there was no service. Just like there hadn't been for the past four hours.

She gritted her teeth. It didn't matter. She didn't need the internet for every little thing. She could manage very well without it.

On the drive from Queenstown, Bethany and Indigo had shared a little of their plans for Brightwater Valley with her. Bethany designed and made jewelry and was hoping to set up a craft store with Indigo, who spun and dyed yarn for all kinds of fiber arts. Georgie was a wood turner who would have completed their little creative triumvirate, but a family situation had caused her to pull out.

Izzy wasn't creative, but years spent in her father's company had given her a hardheaded business brain, so she'd told Beth and Indigo that while she couldn't do any wood turning, she'd be happy to take over an admin role.

Starting a small craft business from scratch couldn't be any harder than running an oil company, surely?

Except…well…the town *was* tiny.

And apparently deserted.

The hotel had a wide veranda with a couple of benches, but nobody was sitting on them. Another long bench was outside of the general store, but there was no one sitting there either.

A dog trotted out from behind the general store. It was black, of an indeterminate breed, and it stood there in the middle of the road staring at them. Then after a moment, it turned and loped off back the way it had come, leaving behind it nothing but silence, broken only by the low, insistent buzz of cicadas.

Izzy had to stop herself from making a noise just to be sure she hadn't gone deaf.

"Was someone supposed to meet us?" she asked instead, staring at the deserted-looking town.

"Yeah," Beth said. "Some guy called Kelly."

Abruptly the door of the Pure Adventure NZ place banged open and a man with the kind of build that uncomfortably reminded Izzy of her brother and his two friends strode out. Tall, muscular, wide shoulders, narrow waist, and long, powerful legs. Dressed in jeans and a dark green T-shirt. Black hair in a short, military-style buzz cut. A face with the kind of aristocratic features that had probably graced coins in ancient Roman times. A blade of a nose. Strong jaw. High cheekbones. Intensely charismatic, compelling…

Drop-dead gorgeous.

"Oh my," Bethany murmured.

"Wow," Indigo breathed from the back seat. "I didn't think…"

Izzy wasn't thinking at all.

Every word had gone clean out of her head as the man headed straight for their car.

"Oh," Bethany said. "He looks annoyed. Did anyone—"

But before Beth could finish her question, the man reached for Izzy's door, pulled it open, and a pair of gunmetal-gray eyes gave them all an intense, fierce stare.

"I hope you're the lot from Deep River," he said in a deep, rough voice. "If so, where the bloody hell have you been?"

Chase Kelly was royally pissed. He didn't allow his temper to get the better of him often, but today had been an exception.

First, his brother, Finn, part owner of Pure Adventure NZ, had forgotten to leave a message at Queenstown airport for the Deep River contingent letting them know that one of the Pure Adventure team would chopper them back to the valley so they didn't have to drive down Kelly's Canyon. Second, Levi, the third owner, was supposed to have been the one doing the choppering, but he'd gotten sidetracked at a Queenstown bar the night before—usual story for Levi—and had slept in that morning. Third, the number Chase had for the main Deep River contact wasn't working, which meant he couldn't call her himself to tell her to stay put in Queenstown.

Fourth, by the time he'd finally managed to figure all of this out and had rung around to all the car rental firms in Queenstown on the assumption that the Deep River ladies would have rented a car, he'd realized that it was too late to retrieve them and there was nothing he could do to stop them from probably killing themselves on the drive down the narrow and twisting gravel road.

Not only would the women be jet-lagged, but they'd also be driving on what was, for them, the wrong side of the road. Having the first batch of Deep River arrivals drive off the side of a cliff and into a canyon was *not* how he'd hoped his new initiative would go.

So he'd waited around, finally tracking down Finn and Levi and giving them each a piece of his by now heartily pissed off mind. Then wondering why on earth it was taking the Deep River women four hours to complete a two-hour drive and debating whether or not he should take his truck and drive up the road to find them.

Then finally, he'd heard a car and glanced out the window, recognizing the rental firm's cheerful purple-and-green paint job, and unfortunately, relief had only added fuel to the fire of his already-smoldering temper.

He organized everything in his life, from his business to his town to his friends to the women he dated, so it could run like clockwork. It was an old military habit he'd never gotten out of, and he was *not* happy when that clockwork refused to function.

People were the problem. People who weren't him. He'd found them to be unreliable, which was why he preferred to do everything himself.

His mood was also not enhanced by the fact that the woman sitting in the driver's seat of the rental car was also the prettiest woman he'd ever seen in his life.

Pretty, in his experience, did not do well in Brightwater Valley.

Her eyes were dark, like bittersweet chocolate; her features delicate, pale, and porcelain smooth. She had long black hair, glossy as a raven's feathers, and dark eyebrows that winged up at the ends, giving her a vaguely feline look, and the kind of mouth that—

"Excuse me?" The woman's voice was sweet, with the most delicious, syrupy drawl. "What do you mean 'where have we been'?" One of those delicate brows arched as if that was the stupidest question she'd ever heard.

At that moment, the woman in the passenger seat leaned straight across her friend and stuck her hand out. "Hi! I'm

Bethany Grant." She had long, white-blond hair in a loose ponytail and bright green eyes, a pretty, open face and the widest, most generous smile Chase had seen in a long while. "And you are?"

A third woman sitting in the back seat said nothing, blue eyes watching him guardedly, a wealth of brown hair in a loose braid down her back.

He made a mental note to remind himself not to chew Levi out too badly because it was a good thing he hadn't been there to greet them. Levi had an eye for the ladies and the last thing Chase needed was for him to create a situation with Brightwater Valley's new recruits.

"Chase Kelly," Chase said, still annoyed. "You're from Deep River, right?"

"Yes, that's right. I think we're supposed to meet you." The dark-eyed, beautiful woman pushed at the blond's shoulder. "Um, sorry, Beth, but can you move?"

Beth pulled back with obvious reluctance.

"Then who is the contact and why weren't they answering their phone?"

The woman in the driver's seat blinked, then gave the other two a glance. "Is that a trick question? Because there's no service—"

"I'm not talking about here," he interrupted impatiently. "I tried calling you last night and this morning and there was no answer."

"Calling who?" the dark-eyed woman asked.

"Oh," the blond—Beth—said suddenly. "You were trying to call Georgie's number, weren't you?"

Chase didn't know whose number he had, and he didn't care. It hadn't been answered. "I called the number that was given to me and no one picked up. So which of you was it?"

"None of us actually," the dark-eyed woman said, giving him a cool look that he found oddly challenging. "If you could give me some room so I could get out of the car, I'll explain."

Chase realized he was standing rather close, preventing her from getting out. Further irritated by a very real desire not to move just to see what she'd do, he ignored his baser self and took a step back, eyeing her as she undid her seat belt and got out.

She wore the most ridiculous outfit, like some fashion designer's idea of what rugged outdoor clothing should look like without ever having been outdoors.

Expensive-looking hiking boots straight out of the box, a deep-blue fleece with a black-and-silver rain jacket over the top, despite the fact that it wasn't raining nor was it forecasted for the next week. About the only thing he approved of were her tight-fitting designer jeans, since they showed off her beautifully proportioned legs, curvy thighs, and rounded butt to perfection.

She looked like a city princess playing at being in the great outdoors, definitely not the kind of rugged individual he'd been hoping for when he'd gotten in touch with the folks in Deep River, a long-shot chance at saving his dying town. And he couldn't say he wasn't disappointed about that.

City princesses, in his experience, didn't last long out here.

However, he liked to give people the opportunity to prove themselves, plus there was a certain…cool speculation in her gaze, hinting that there was more to her than met the eye.

It stirred something in him that he did not want stirring.

Get a grip, Kelly, for God's sake.

Firmly leashing his temper, Chase said, "Well? I wanted to tell you that I was going to chopper you all over the ranges, so you didn't have to drive down Kelly's Canyon." He crossed his arms and surveyed her. "That road is very dangerous for people not used to it."

"There was a mix-up," the woman said levelly. "The person you were trying to call pulled out at the last minute. I'm her replacement and obviously you wouldn't have had my number."

That made sense. It didn't help his temper, though.

"Right, so someone couldn't have called me to let me know that?"

"I would have if I'd had your number." That delicate brow arched higher. "But I didn't."

Something inside of Chase stirred again.

Goddammit.

The urge to stand there and keep eyeballing her was a temptation he didn't need right now, so he flicked a glance at the car. Beth was already getting out and coming around the side. The other woman hadn't moved from her place in the back seat.

"I thought something might have happened to you all," he said gruffly. "There's no cell service and—"

"No, I know," the woman interrupted. "And I drove at twenty miles an hour the whole way."

That explained why it had taken them four hours.

Beth had now come to stand beside the dark-eyed woman. She grinned at him and elbowed her friend in the side. "Introduce yourself, Izzy. Come on, don't be rude."

An expression of irritation briefly flickered through Izzy's dark eyes then was gone. "Fine. I'm Isabella Montgomery, Georgie's...uh...replacement." She extended a delicate, long-fingered hand. "You can call me Isabella."

Perhaps if he'd been in a better mood he might have found her haughtiness amusing. Now though, having spent his morning watching his carefully laid plans fall to pieces and worrying over whether his new recruits would die in a fiery car crash, he didn't find *anything* amusing. Most especially not a delicate city princess who obviously found him as irritating as he found her.

Still, they'd come a long way and he didn't want to frighten them off immediately, so he forced a smile. "Nice to meet you, Isabella," he said, taking her hand.

A mistake.

Her skin was warm against his, the touch of her fingers sending a small electric charge through him. And he didn't miss the flare of awareness in her dark eyes; obviously she felt it too.

Shit.

This was not what he wanted. At all.

"Oh my God," Bethany murmured to Isabella in an aside he probably wasn't supposed to hear. "His accent..."

He decided to ignore that, glancing yet again at the third woman who still remained in the car. "Who's in the back seat?"

"That's Indigo," Bethany said cheerfully. "She's still a little carsick. Wow, is this your town? It's beautiful!"

Chase was used to people rhapsodizing over the scenery around Brightwater Valley, but not so much about the town. He gave her a narrow glance, but it was clear she was nothing but genuine.

"Is it similar to Deep River?" he asked curiously.

Deep River and Brightwater Valley had become sister towns back in the forties, after some American GIs had found refuge here when mining had been the town's main industry. Chase had always meant to visit at some point since Alaska sounded like his kind of place, but he'd never quite gotten around to it. Instead, he'd joined the army and become an SAS paratrooper.

An overachiever some would say.

Chase preferred to think of it as always striving for excellence.

"Yeah, it kind of is," Bethany was saying. "The mountains and the bush definitely. We don't have a lake and we're more coastal, and I think a little…" She paused, looking around. "Bigger."

More irritation twisted in Chase's gut.

He'd told Bill in the general store and old Jim in the Rose that the new people would be arriving and would appreciate a welcome. And where the hell was Finn? He was supposed to be here too, not to mention Levi. Cait, Jim's daughter, should be here at the very least…

You know why they're not here.

Yeah, he did. They hadn't been too enthusiastic about his idea to get some new blood into the town. In fact, some of them had been downright grumpy about it.

But Chase wasn't here for their grumpiness. Brightwater was dying and if something wasn't done, it was going to turn into the ghost town it had nearly become after the gold rush had ended over a hundred years earlier.

And that couldn't happen. It had some of the most beautiful scenery in New Zealand, if not the entire damn world, and he wanted people to see it. He wanted people to protect it.

People would bring money. Money that would bring jobs, that in turn would bring more people. People to stay. People to start families. People to bring Brightwater back to life…

Isabella coughed delicately into her hand. "As lovely as it is standing around admiring the town, it's taken us pretty much three days of constant travel to get here, not to mention spending the last four hours in the car. So if it's all the same to you, I think we'd all really like to find our accommodations and get unpacked."

Of course they would.

Not only had they had a hell of a drive over the ranges and down Kelly's, but he also hadn't exactly been friendly when they'd gotten here. Now he'd kept them all waiting around in the hot sun.

So much for the warm welcome he'd planned.

Chase tried very hard not to scowl and failed. "Follow me," he said with as much friendliness as he could muster, turning and stalking off toward the Rose before any of them could say a word.

Chapter 2

"OH. MY. GOD," BETH SIGHED AS THE UNFRIENDLY KIWI stranger turned and strode off toward the hotel. "That man is *stunning.*"

Izzy disagreed. For some reason, she'd taken an instant and irrational dislike to Mr. Chase Kelly.

She didn't often have such a strong reaction to people, not without good reason, but he'd gotten her back up the moment he'd stormed over to their car, electric gray eyes staring at her with irritation, as if it had somehow been her fault that they were late. She hadn't even realized they were on a schedule, but he went on about his call not being answered. Fair enough if he'd been calling Georgie's number, but still…

Perhaps it was him being a man and her having little patience with men in general. Or perhaps it was because she was more tired than she thought.

That's not the reason.

But Izzy didn't want to think about that other reason right now. The one about how the fabric of his T-shirt had pulled over his broad chest as he'd straightened up and folded his arms. About the fit of his worn jeans, hanging low on his lean hips—

"He's a bit like your brother," Beth went on. "All kinds of tall, dark, and brooding."

Yes, like her brother, that was good. That should stop her thinking about all those…other things.

"Tall, dark, and extremely rude, you mean," Izzy murmured, trying to take no notice of how she could still feel his big hand nearly swallowing hers as he'd taken it, warm and very strong, the slight roughness of work calluses brushing against her skin.

Not like Josh.

No, very not like Josh. Josh was a lawyer, the son of one of her father's good friends, and his hands were uncallused. He wore sharp suits most of the time and when he did put on a pair of jeans, they definitely were not of the worn variety. He liked to look good. *Dress for success* was his motto. Her mother had always told her that they made such a handsome couple...

Not anymore though, right?

Ugh. Why was she thinking about Josh? He was the very last person she wanted in her head right now.

Izzy shoved that thought away, that tangle of emotions in her chest aching harder.

Anyway, she'd seen plenty of Chase Kelly's type in Houston. The take-charge-and-order-everyone-around type. Confident, arrogant, thinking they were God's gift. Her father had been exactly the same.

Wow, snap judgment much?

So? She'd been traveling virtually nonstop for days, and she was bone-weary. All her judgments were snap ones at this point.

"He wasn't that rude," Beth said. "He was sweet, being all worried for us."

"Sweet?" Izzy shot a glare in his direction. "I wouldn't call that sweet."

Beth shrugged. "Maybe he's having a bad day. Come on,

let's go check out this hotel. This is where we're supposed to be staying, I think."

Beth and Indigo had mentioned that they'd booked rooms at the local hotel until they'd settled in and figured out where they were going to live for the next three months or so.

Izzy stared at the hotel, fighting her slowly growing feeling of dismay, as Beth hurried back to the car to get Indigo.

The hotel looked old, and not in a sensitively-restored-with-all-the-modern-conveniences kind of way but in a hadn't-been-touched-since-the-turn-of-the-previous-century kind of way.

So it's not the Four Seasons. This is what you signed on for.

True. Far away and isolated had seemed like paradise to her back in Houston, and this was as far away and isolated as it got. Sure, she liked comfort and a few everyday luxury things. A high thread count on her sheets and expensive bath oil. High-quality coffee and good food. A decent hair straightener and nice clothes. Not *that* much to ask for in the greater scheme of things.

She wasn't going to get most of those things here, but if they had a coffee maker in her room at the very least, she'd be happy. It didn't have to be one of those pod coffee machines. Filter would be fine. She'd settle for sachet creamer too.

"Not exactly friendly, was he?" Indigo commented, pausing beside her as Beth went up the wooden stairs of the hotel. "What was his problem?"

"He was worried about us, at least that's what Beth thinks. Or he could just be rude." Izzy didn't want to give him any credit, not when she could still feel the brush of his fingertips over her skin.

"I hope this isn't going to turn into a disaster," Indigo muttered gloomily.

"It won't." Automatically Izzy fell back into her most familiar role, mediator and general pourer of oil on troubled waters. "It might take some adjustment, but I think if we give this some time, it'll turn out great."

"Now you sound like Beth," Indigo muttered.

Izzy decided to let that slide and continued up the stairs that led onto the wide veranda, Indigo following behind.

Inside was a wide hallway with a set of grand-looking stairs leading up to the second story. The wooden floors were clean, but the carpet runners looked worn and there was a vaguely musty smell in the air.

On the right was a door with a sign on it that just said BAR. On the left another door led into what looked like the dining room of a restaurant.

The whole place gave off an atmosphere of comfortable neglect that wasn't nearly as off-putting as Izzy thought it would be.

Beth was already pushing open the door to the bar, so Izzy and Indigo followed her.

The bar was...interesting.

Every square inch of the walls was covered with stuff: framed photos, beer coasters, old newspaper clippings, street signs, place signs, various paper currency from different countries, old farm implements, someone's rain jacket, an old boot, a set of antlers, and more than a couple of ancient firearms. The ceiling was just as crowded as the walls, with antique headlamps, rusty lanterns, a couple of buoys, a fishing net, and some stuffed birds hanging from it.

It looked like someone had decided that the contents of

their attic would make great decor and attached everything in it to the wall or ceiling.

A big wooden bar top ran down one side, with a huge glass shelf full of bottles that extended up to the ceiling, while the rest of the room was full of mismatched tables and chairs clustered around in groups.

Chase Kelly was at the bar, his muscular arms crossed, arguing with the tall, cadaverous-looking old man standing behind it. He broke off as they all trooped in, both men staring at them.

"Oh, wow!" Beth wandered into the middle of the room, staring at the crowded walls with intense delight. Izzy was beginning to suspect that purely existing caused Beth intense delight. "This place is so awesome! Like the Moose only with less dead animals."

"Great," Chase said. "Glad you like it. Ladies, this is Jim O'Halloran." He nodded at the old man. "He owns this hotel and he's got the rooms you booked ready, haven't you, Jim?"

Jim had a shock of white hair, bushy white eyebrows, and a dark, suspicious gaze. He wore a loose red T-shirt that revealed faded tattoos crawling up both arms; his craggy features revealed nothing.

"Might have," he said laconically, his voice sounding cracked. "Check-in's at four."

"Jim." There was an unmistakable warning in Chase's voice. "You're not full. In fact there have been no guests for five days. You can stand to check them in now."

"Huh." Jim picked up a cloth and gave the already-spotless bar top a good wipe-down, pointedly ignoring the younger man shooting daggers at him.

An awkward silence fell.

Beth was still staring around in wonder, while Indigo had gone over to look at something on the wall more closely. Neither of them was going to handle this situation and it needed handling, that much was obvious to Izzy.

She wasn't a fan of letting things get difficult if they didn't need to be, especially if she could do something about it.

Moving over to the bar, she held out her hand. "I'm Isabella Montgomery. Pleased to meet you, Jim." Sometimes you could force a little politeness on someone if you were scrupulously polite yourself.

The old man sniffed, gazing at her for a second before dropping the cloth he'd been holding and reluctantly shaking her hand. "Gidday."

Izzy was used to using her femininity to charm—it worked a treat in the oil business, so there wasn't any reason it wouldn't work on one grumpy old man.

"We're all really excited to be here." She turned her smile on full blast. "It's such a beautiful place."

"Uh-huh." Jim's face remained expressionless.

Okay, so either a smile didn't work on him or he was one of those types who took a bit of time to warm up. Or maybe he was trying to scare them away? Whatever, she wasn't done yet.

"This is also Beth Grant and Indigo Jameson." She gestured to the others. Beth waved, while Indigo gave a nod. "If the rooms aren't ready, we can wait. Perhaps you'd like to give us a tour of the hotel? Or maybe we could have a look around on our own?"

"The rooms are ready," Chase said flatly, turning his laser-focused gaze on her as if she were the one arguing with him. "Aren't they, Jim?"

Another burst of irritation went through her. She could soften up the old guy, but how was she expected to do that with this idiot getting in the way and making everything worse?

"Like I said." She kept her voice calm, adding a little honey to her drawl, pointedly not looking at Chase. "We're really happy to wait until four."

Chase stared at her very fixedly.

She ignored him.

Jim glanced at Chase and then back at her, a shrewd glint in his eyes. As if he knew something she didn't.

A thread of discomfort wound through her, though she wasn't sure why.

"Could make an exception," Jim said. "Maybe."

It seemed that not everyone here was on board with a bunch of new arrivals from the States coming into their town and stirring up stuff.

Great. This whole situation was a little more complicated than she'd initially thought.

"Jim." Chase's deep voice with that tantalizing accent—Beth was right about that: it *was* hot—was flat with a certain authority. "These ladies have come halfway around the world. They've been traveling for days. They're tired and jet-lagged, and they just spent four hours driving down Kelly's. The very last thing they should be doing is standing here waiting until you decide you're ready to check them in to their rooms. So yes, make a bloody exception."

Izzy resisted the urge to tell him to be quiet and stop interfering because he wasn't helping their cause.

Instead, she caught Jim's gaze and rolled her eyes slightly.

The old man snorted in what sounded like amusement.

"Yeah, okay," he allowed. "Maybe I will." Then he turned and glowered at Chase. "But not for you, Kelly. You go get Cait."

A muscle ticked in Chase's strong jaw. He was not pleased, but he nodded once, then turned and, without a word, vanished through the door back into the hallway.

"I'm sorry if we put you out," Izzy said, feeling rather pleased with herself. "Like I said, we can wait if it's an issue."

"No issue." There was a wicked glint in Jim's eyes. "Worth it to see Kelly lose his cool."

"Does he often lose his cool?" She wasn't curious, not at all. She was simply making conversation.

"No," Jim replied. "Not since he was a kid."

Well, that was…interesting.

Izzy wanted to ask more questions, but the door opened again and Chase strode back in followed by a short, round woman in her late forties or early fifties, with curly, silver-streaked black hair and strong, handsome features. She was in practical jeans and a blue checked button-down, and unlike both Chase and Jim, she gave all three women a wide, welcome smile.

"Hi," she said. "I'm Caitlin O'Halloran. The daughter of that grumpy bugger behind the bar. You can call me Cait."

The grumpy bugger behind the bar snorted again and went back to wiping the bar top, leaving his daughter to deal with the new arrivals.

Indigo stopped her study of the wall, while Beth, who'd been staring out the front window, turned and all three of them went over to introduce themselves.

Chase stood grimly behind Cait as they all exchanged pleasantries, watching the interactions like an overprotective father.

Izzy found herself irritatingly aware of him, even though she tried very hard not to be.

"Right, ladies," Cait was saying. "Let's get you settled."

At that moment, the door to the bar opened again, and a tall, slender girl dressed in dusty jeans and an oversized T-shirt came in. She had shoulder-length black hair, strong features that would one day be beautiful and right now possessed what suddenly struck Izzy as a very familiar scowl.

"Dad," the girl said crossly. "Did you lock the front door again? I can't get in. Finn's not there and neither is Levi."

For a second Izzy wasn't sure who she was talking to.

Then she stared in surprise as Chase Kelly's stern, aristocratic features abruptly softened and he gave the girl a brief but utterly gorgeous smile. "Hey, sweet pea. Key's under the mat, where it always is."

Sweet pea? Dad?

Izzy felt Beth's elbow jab her in the side. "He's a dad. Oh my God, Izzy. *Irresistible.*"

———

Chase ignored Beth's muttered comment and the very interested attention of the three Deep River women as Gus rolled her eyes, something of which he was not a fan that his daughter had been doing more and more of these days.

"It's *not* under the mat," she insisted. "That's why I came here." She glanced curiously at the three women, then looked at him. "Who are they?"

"You go deal with that," Cait said to him, nodding at Gus, since clearly he wasn't doing a good enough job of hiding his annoyance. "I'll handle the check-in stuff."

Managing yet another problem wasn't what Chase particularly wanted to do. What he wanted to do was introduce the new arrivals around Brightwater, tell them where they could find certain things, see them settled into their accommodations, and then let them know what was on the schedule for the next couple of days so that everything ran to plan. He also wanted to know what had happened to the third woman and why Isabella Montgomery had turned up in her place.

But Gus always went to the Pure Adventure NZ HQ after school to wait for him until he'd finished work, and if it was locked—which it shouldn't be and he had no idea why it was—then he had to open it up for her. And if he was around to open it up for her, then he needed to stay and chat to her about her day, see what homework she had.

Gus, at nearly thirteen, was a very self-contained and independent kid, but she was also on the cusp of adolescence with a mother who'd abandoned her, so Chase liked to be there for her as often as he could.

His day was royally screwed schedule-wise anyway, and since the Deep River contingent would be fine in Cait's capable hands, he could make some time for his kid today.

Plus he was overly conscious of Isabella Montgomery's cool gaze, and after that minor battle with Jim near the bar, it was a good idea to take a break to get his temper under control.

He nodded his thanks to Cait, then gave the others a sweeping glance. "I'll let Cait get you settled in. We're planning a welcome barbecue for you all tomorrow night, but I'll get you more details this afternoon. Excuse me."

He could feel them all watching as he strode to the door, putting an arm around Gus and ushering her from the room.

"Are those the Americans?" his daughter asked as they stepped out. "From Alaska?"

"Yeah." He gave her a glance as they crunched over the gravel to the Pure Adventure HQ next door. "You're out early. How was school?"

Gus shrugged. "Miss Bennet let us go because it was a nice day. And it was okay."

Chase scanned his daughter's angular features—or at least the bits he could see that hadn't been concealed by her hair.

She had her shoulders hunched, her gaze on the ground, kicking a stone with her dusty sneakers.

He frowned. Something was going on with her, he could sense it. In fact, he'd been able to sense it for the past few weeks, but every time he asked her what was up, Gus would only give that same irritating shrug and say, "Nothing."

He didn't like it. Once, she'd told him everything. Every feeling she had, every thought that went through her head. But lately he'd gotten the sense that there were things she was keeping to herself.

Are you surprised? She'll be thirteen next year. A teenager...

The thought hit Chase uncomfortably hard. Bringing her up on his own after Olivia had left had been difficult, but he'd managed. He'd made sure Gus hadn't wanted for a single goddamn thing.

Apart from a mother, of course.

A thread of tension wound through him. Perhaps that was the problem. Perhaps now she was getting older and approaching young-womanhood, the lack of a mother figure in her life was a problem for her.

Sadly, there was nothing he could do about that. Being

furious with his ex-wife for abandoning her husband and young child, while privately satisfying, wasn't helpful for Gus. Her mother's lack of interest in her was a wound that Chase couldn't heal. All he could do was try and be there for her whenever and however he could.

"Just okay?" he asked, hoping she might say more.

She kicked another stone. "Yeah."

"Nothing's up?"

"No."

"You know you can tell me—"

"Anything," she finished for him, not looking up. "Yeah, I know that, Dad."

His instinct, as ever, was to push, but he knew that when he did, she clammed up even more, so he left it.

But it was tough. Chase could deal with most problems life threw at him—being in the SAS for five years had honed more than a few skills—but being a single father to a nearly teenage girl was not something the special forces had trained him for. More's the pity.

Approaching Pure Adventure NZ HQ, Chase went around the side of the building, where the front door to the second story and the apartment above was located. He had a house ten minutes down the road where he and Gus actually lived, but since the school bus dropped the kids off outside the Rose, whenever Gus finished school she came straight to HQ.

Which shouldn't be locked and yet was. And no, the key was *not* under the mat.

"I told you so," Gus said after Chase had checked. "I looked."

The lack of key was a minor irritation but didn't help his annoyance any.

"Finn probably took it." He pulled his spare key out of his pocket and unlocked the door. "Or maybe Levi did. I'll remind them again that they have to leave it for you for when you get home from school."

Gus, clearly eager to get inside, pushed past him and started up the stairs. "So did those ladies come today?" she asked. "How long are they going to be here for?"

"Yeah, they came today," Chase answered, following behind her. "And they're here for about three months initially, then—" He broke off as he nearly walked into his daughter who'd come to a dead stop at the top of the stairs.

"Why aren't you wearing undies, Uncle Levi?" Gus said curiously.

Chase blinked.

Then came the sound of a muffled curse, some scrabbling, a breathless giggle, and Chase's brain finally caught up with what was happening. Because after all, it was Levi, wasn't it? And there was only one reason Levi King wasn't wearing undies, in the middle of the day, in Pure Adventure's HQ.

By God, Chase was going to kill him.

Pushing past his daughter and shoving her protectively behind him, he stormed into the little living area.

It was furnished sparsely but comfortably with a couch against one wall, a wood burner against the other, and several old bookshelves piled high with books, board games, old hunting and fishing magazines, photos, and other bits and pieces.

Through the window overlooking the road and out toward the brilliant blue of Brightwater Lake, the early afternoon sunlight fell, illuminating the man hastily grabbing at the throw draped over the arm of the couch to cover himself.

A naked woman dashed down the small hallway toward the bathroom, the door slamming after her.

Chase's day went from bad to extremely shitty in seconds flat as his anger, which he'd thought he'd successfully leashed, escaped entirely.

He let out a stream of expletives, totally forgetting that his daughter was standing behind him, and advanced on Levi King, complete and utter asshole who could not control his nether regions and was now sitting on Chase's couch, in front of Chase's twelve-year-old daughter, bare assed.

"Wait, wait, wait!" Levi held up a staying hand, trying to keep the throw in place with the other. "I can explain."

Chase stopped right in front of the couch, his hands fisted, desperately wanting to plant one in the other man's face. This day had become a complete shitshow, so why not end it with a good old-fashioned punch-up?

"Explain? Why the hell would I wait for an explanation while you're sitting there with your balls hanging out in front of my twelve-year-old daughter?"

Levi, who now looked decently shamefaced, shoved his messy, dark brown hair off his face. "Yeah, look, sorry about that." He leaned to the side and shouted around Chase's solid figure, "Sorry, Gussie! Didn't mean for you to see that."

"It's okay!" Gus shouted back. "I don't care."

"Stay downstairs," Chase growled at her, not looking behind him. Gus was sensible. She'd know that now was *not* the time to argue.

"Listen, I locked the damn door." Levi's hazel eyes were wary, as they should be, since although Levi could fly anything with a propeller, blades, and an engine, the last time he'd taken a swing at Chase he'd ended up with a black eye.

"And I took the key away," Levi added. "And, shit, it's only two in the afternoon. How was I to know she'd finish school early?"

But Chase was in no mood for excuses. "This is a family establishment, asshole. You know that much. Also I gave you a goddamn job yesterday that I expected you to do, not to get drunk at a bar then bring some complete stranger back here for some fun the next day."

Levi raised a finger. "About that. I had a—"

"Not a single word," Chase ground out. "And if I catch you bringing women back here again, I'll kick your ass from here to Auckland, are we clear?"

Chase had befriended Levi in the SAS and Levi'd followed him back to Brightwater Valley after they'd left the forces because, as he'd told Chase, he "had nothing better to do."

Levi was easygoing, charming, a genuinely good guy despite his tendency to let his groin do his thinking for him. But one of his most endearing characteristics was that he knew when he'd screwed up and took ownership of it.

He did that now, giving Chase an ironic salute before he slipped off the couch, grabbed his clothes, and vanished down the hall.

Chase stood there a moment, taking a couple of deep breaths to get his fury under control, by which time Gus had walked past him into the little kitchen off the living area.

Really, all he needed now was for Finn to do something stupid and his day would be complete.

"You shouldn't yell at Uncle Levi." Gus's comment was punctuated by the sound of cupboards opening. "He wasn't doing anything."

"Oh, he was most definitely doing something."

"Only a sex thing."

Chase shut his eyes, pinched the bridge of his nose, and prayed for patience. "Gus, please don't tell me that you—"

"Chill out, Dad. I'm not dumb. I know all about *that*." He heard the sound of the fridge door opening. "There's nothing to eat."

Chill out? *Chill out?*

For a second, Chase debated whether or not his head was going to explode, because it seemed his day hadn't reached its low point after all.

He'd thought Levi and his bullshit was the nadir, but apparently his young daughter not being bothered about said bullshit was the nadir.

Since when had she become so blasé about a sex thing? Since when did she even know about sex anyway?

What do you expect? She's been brought up by three men, with very little feminine influence in her life.

It was true. Olivia had abandoned them when Gus had been five, and he'd been left to bring her up alone. The town had rallied around him, as had Finn and Levi, the pair of them looking after her when Chase was out with clients on an expedition or having to make business or promotional visits to the city. And when the two of them weren't around, Gus went next door to the Rose, where either Caitlin or Jim looked out for her.

It wasn't ideal. Gus needed more female oversight, but that was the whole issue with Brightwater. The population skewed male and older, and so poor Gus had grown up with a certain...outlook.

She loved hiking and fishing and spending time out in

the bush. She was more interested in lures and hunting game than she was in boy bands or clothes, and she didn't do a lot of reading. She was a doer, like he was, and adored spending time with him and her uncles and had displayed no interest whatsoever in anything girlish so far.

But that didn't mean she wouldn't.

It also didn't mean that being exposed to Levi and his idiocy was right.

She needs a mother and you know it.

Oh yes, he was well aware. But that was a tricky problem and required the right solution, and he hadn't found that solution.

It wasn't through lack of trying. He'd been keeping his eye out, but he hadn't found anyone who'd make a suitable mother figure for Gus. Of course he kept his "searches" discreet, since unlike Levi, he did have half a brain, but it was still…tricky.

He wasn't going to rush into anything. The woman he eventually brought home to meet Gus would have to be the right one. She'd have to love his daughter as much as he did, be practical, down-to-earth, and tough. She'd enjoy living in an isolated place, love the great outdoors, be able to learn new skills quickly and not complain. Also, she'd have to like him too, and they'd definitely need to be compatible in bed.

Not too much to ask, surely?

Gus came out of the kitchen and paused in the doorway. "Dad, didn't you hear me?" There was a plaintive note in her voice. "I'm hungry and there's nothing to eat."

Chase sighed. "We've got eggs though, right?"

Immediately her expression brightened. "Oh, can I have an omelet? With ham? And lots of cheese?"

Chase could only smile. "Sure. Why not?"

Gus launched herself at him, wrapping her narrow arms around his waist. "Yay. Thanks, Dad. You're the greatest!"

Well, he couldn't fix everything for Gus, but there was one thing at least he could fix: her hunger.

Chase firmly put away his anger and went to make his daughter some food.

Chapter 3

IZZY'S EYES POPPED OPEN SUDDENLY, AS IF SHE HADN'T been deeply asleep only moments before, and she found herself staring at an unfamiliar ceiling.

This one was all curving lines and graceful ridges, reminding her of flowering vines.

Weird. If she wasn't in her bedroom—and it didn't look like the ceiling in Josh's bedroom either—then where on earth was she?

Then memory filtered through, of heartbreak, of rage-fueled snap decisions, of long flights and long drives, of rugged landscapes and mountains...

She wasn't in Houston.

She wasn't even in America.

She was in Brightwater Valley, New Zealand.

Izzy shut her eyes, let out a long breath, then opened them again.

It was dim in the room, which meant it was probably early. She turned over, grabbing for her phone on the rickety wooden nightstand to check the time.

Five a.m. Wonderful.

Jet lag had sent her upstairs just after six the night before, leaving Beth and Indigo down in the bar. She'd fallen asleep almost as soon as her head had hit the pillow and slept nearly twelve hours. No wonder she was wide-awake now.

Izzy wasn't a morning person, but there wasn't much

point staying in bed since she knew she wasn't going to be able to get back to sleep.

Automatically, she checked her emails and texts, only to remember there wasn't any service here. *Great.*

Reluctantly, she got out of bed.

The room was small and very basic yet scrupulously clean. It contained a double bed, a nightstand, an old wooden dresser, and one chair near the window. The carpet was worn, the sheets and quilt cover mismatched, and the towels a little threadbare.

Since she'd gone to sleep so quickly, she hadn't had a chance to explore properly. Now she poked around, searching desperately for some kind of coffee-making device, before coming to the sad conclusion that the room didn't have one. An outrage.

Never mind, she'd just go to a café and—

But there wasn't a café, was there?

Again, this was what you signed on for.

Yes, yes. And she wasn't going to die because she couldn't check her email and have a coffee to start her day.

Annoyed, and annoyed with herself for being annoyed, Izzy took a shower in the tiny bathroom, then got dressed in a pair of jeans, her new hiking boots, a T-shirt, and her new parka.

She didn't like wearing the same clothes two days in a row, but when she'd packed her bag, she'd hurled into it whatever had come to hand, which irritatingly seemed to be a couple of her favorite blouses, one with a bow, two tailored skirts, five lacy bras, two pairs of panties, and three pairs of tailored pants. All of which, bar the panties and bras, were not useful. What had possessed her to bring only two pairs of panties for a three-month stay anyway?

Izzy made a note to find a store and buy more, then remembered that of the couple of buildings that were here in town, neither seemed like they sold women's underwear.

Wonderful. She'd have to go further afield then. Not that they'd passed any big towns on the way to Brightwater Valley yesterday. In fact, the closest place was Queenstown, which had taken them four hours to drive from.

Suddenly feeling tired again, Izzy put the issue of her clothes into the find-a-solution-to-later-preferably-after-coffee basket, and hunted around for her hair straightener and hair dryer. She had those at least, which was good—until she realized that she'd neglected to buy an adapter and couldn't plug them in.

Crap. Her hair went curly if she didn't straighten it and she hated it curly.

Ugh.

Left with no choice, Izzy brushed her wet hair as flat to her head as possible, then ventured out into the little hallway that stretched the length of the building.

Everything was silent.

She walked quietly down the hall, glancing at the photographs on the walls and the old news clippings of a time decades past when Brightwater Valley was a bustling tourist town.

Idly, she wondered where all the tourists had gone, especially since the nature hadn't left. It was still beautiful here.

Downstairs, everything was as quiet as it had been upstairs, though she could hear sounds of someone moving about drifting from the back of the hotel.

Briefly she debated asking about coffee, but then decided she didn't want to bother anyone, creeping out of the front door and stepping outside instead.

The morning was crisp and clear, the sky overhead already getting light, turning from black into a deep lapis blue. Directly across the road was the stillness of the lake, with the mountains beyond tall, serrated, and capped with white. The air was cool and damp, with a vague spiciness to it that reminded her of a pine forest.

Slowly, Izzy sat on the front steps of the hotel and took a couple of deep breaths.

No traffic noise. No city pollution. No people rushing to get wherever they were going to on time. Just…silence and peace.

That tight tangle of emotion lodged just behind her breastbone eased slightly. As if peace was part of the air and she'd inhaled it.

Perhaps her spur-of-the-moment decision to come halfway around the world hadn't been a bad idea after all. Sure, she might have to give up a few of her usual luxuries, and certainly get some more underwear and clothes, but there was something good here, she could feel it.

And at least you're not sitting on the couch at home, weeping into a tub of ice cream after losing your fiancé and career in one fell swoop.

Pain ached inside her, the betrayal of it still raw, but since anger was easier, she made a grab for that instead.

When her brother had left Houston for the army rather than cave to their father's demands of staying to head the company, she'd told herself that if Zeke couldn't turn himself into the kind of yes-man his father wanted, then she would. But her goal had been to take her father's place, turn the company around, and give it a moral compass. Shift the emphasis off oil and into more sustainable energy sources.

She'd done exactly that and had been ready to guide it into the future too…until the board had decided that it would be better for all concerned if all links with the Montgomery name were severed. Including her.

How dare they! All that work, all the loyalty she'd poured into it, and they'd thrown her away like she was nothing. But really, that was *their* loss, not hers. She didn't need them. Oil was a horrible industry anyway and she was glad to be out of it and away from her father's influence.

As for Josh, well, she sadly knew what the deal there was. She hadn't been the ticket to success he'd been hoping for and so he'd found someone else. Someone with better connections, who wasn't as married to their job as she'd been. Someone who was happy to take a back seat so he could shine, supporting his career while bringing up his children…

Not that she'd been aware that's what he'd been aiming for at the time. She'd just wanted to make her parents happy by marrying someone they approved of and who'd seemed on the surface to love her.

Except he hadn't.

Then her parents had blamed her for the breakup, insisting that they would cancel the wedding so "poor Josh" didn't have to.

That hurt too, but she hadn't cried about it. Crying would have been pointless. She'd coped by leaving, and now that she'd left, she wasn't going to think about Josh again.

She could think about her brother though, because he'd done the same thing, escaping Houston and starting a different life in Alaska. And he'd found himself there, falling in love with a lovely woman and building a home and family.

She'd understood why he'd had to leave—he and their father did *not* get along—but less why he'd had to bury himself in an isolated Alaskan settlement. Zeke was a committed outdoorsman and the environment was one of his passions, so it made sense from that perspective. But she'd never seen the appeal of the isolation.

Until now. Now, she kind of got it.

You should probably call him to tell him what you're doing and where you are.

Yes, she probably should.

But she didn't move. She sat enjoying the peace of the early morning, and just when she was considering going in search of coffee, the sound of pounding feet caught her attention and the figure of a man running along the foreshore of the lake came into view.

Then he suddenly veered toward the water, running straight into it and diving beneath the surface. He came up a second later, shaking his head and scattering water droplets everywhere, before swimming powerfully back to shore.

He waded out, pulling off his T-shirt and wringing it out, dawn's light gleaming on his damp skin, highlighting broad shoulders, the hard planes of his chest, and the sharp, chiseled lines of his abs.

Izzy's mouth went dry, her cheeks a trifle warm. She'd never been so conscious of a man's body before, but this man was something else. She couldn't take her eyes off him.

He came closer, water still glistening on his skin, as he raised a powerful arm, pushing one hand through his short black hair. And as he did, she realized it was Chase Kelly.

A full-on blush washed over her. Oh hell, she did *not* want to be caught gawking at him. Her fiancé of two years had just dumped her, so she shouldn't be getting hot under the collar for a complete stranger already.

She definitely didn't want him to know she'd been watching him and didn't want to talk to him either. Especially after he'd been so gruff the day before.

Quickly, Izzy got to her feet and started along the gravel sidewalk that ran beside the hotel.

"Hey," Chase called, "where are you going?"

Izzy kept walking.

"There's nothing down that way except Brightwater Vineyard and they're not open for another five hours."

Izzy took another couple of steps.

"I'm talking to you, Miss Montgomery."

She stopped, her heart beating uncomfortably fast. So what if he'd seen her staring at him? He'd dashed suddenly into the water, and she'd been worried. Yes, that's why she'd watched him. She was concerned. Nothing whatsoever to do with how fine he looked without a shirt.

Izzy ignored her heartbeat, put on her cool, serene expression, and turned around.

Chase had followed her, standing not far away with his sodden T-shirt in one hand.

He was...magnificent. Like a statue of a god rendered into hard muscle, strong sinew, and smooth olive skin. Rugged and powerful and...

Very much not like Josh.

The thought came out of nowhere, winding painfully through her, making her resent Chase Kelly even more. She'd been telling herself constantly she did not want to think of Josh, and yet there was something about Chase that brought Josh to mind in an uncomfortable way.

It was stupid and she didn't like it. She was here to forget what'd happened, not to be constantly reminded of it.

What she really wanted was to ignore Chase and keep on walking, but she was someone who helped solve troubles, not stir them up.

Shoving her hands into the pockets of her parka since she wasn't sure what else to do with them, Izzy gave him what she hoped was a cool smile. "Oh, hi. Didn't see you there."

His gray eyes glinted in the dawn light as he looked at her. "Sure you didn't. That's why you were sitting on the steps watching me as I came out of the lake. Because you didn't see me."

Izzy hoped desperately that she wasn't blushing, but she had a horrible feeling she was and that it was noticeable.

Deciding to ignore it, she lifted a shoulder. "I only wondered if you might need help. You rushed into the water so quickly."

Chase gave her a long, enigmatic look. "I might need help," he echoed. "Right."

There was so much disbelief in his voice that Izzy found herself adding hurriedly, "Well, you were alone. And drowning can happen in a matter of seconds."

"I see." Amusement glittered in his eyes. "And, what? You were ready to leap in and rescue me?"

Izzy bristled, though she tried very hard not to. "Yes. If there was a need."

"Uh-huh. So I guess you can swim?"

"Of course I can swim." She hoped that didn't sound as snappish as she suspected it did, but his questions were irritating. "Your point being?"

"What about surf lifesaver training?" he persisted. "Have

you had experience with CPR? Know all the appropriate holds to use so you can drag a man three times your size out of the water by yourself?"

Izzy prided herself on never causing a fuss. She was always cool and calm and perfectly in control because that's what difficult situations required. So she had no idea why all Chase's questions felt like small needles pricking her. Perhaps it was jet lag or the remains of her rage, or maybe it was the fact that even though she'd been telling herself that coming here had been the right decision, she couldn't shake the doubt that all she'd done was run away.

Whatever the reason, she could feel her patience wearing thin, and she didn't like it. If she was going to remain here in Brightwater Valley and help get this new business venture up and running, alienating one of the inhabitants was a very bad idea.

So she shoved her irritation down and gave him another smile. "No, actually, I don't know any of those things. Good thing you didn't need my help then, isn't it?"

His eyes glinted again, making something inside her twist as a certain awareness crept over her skin.

Oh, she didn't like this. She didn't like this at all.

"Anyway," she said quickly, wanting to get away from him, "I don't want to hold you up."

"I'm sorry," he said in an abrupt tone. "About yesterday, I mean. I shouldn't have snapped at you."

An apology was the last thing Izzy expected and she stared at him in surprise. "Oh...I...I mean, it's fine."

"It's not fine." His dark brows lowered. "You came a long way and didn't deserve the kind of welcome I gave you."

She wasn't quite sure what to say. Apologies from men

like this one were rare in her experience, and now that he'd apologized, it was difficult to be mad at him. At least before, when he'd been rude, she'd been justified.

A deep part of her wanted to snap at him that no, she hadn't deserved it, and she was tired of people not finding her acceptable in some way, and if he was that rude to everyone who visited Brightwater Valley, then no wonder it was deserted.

But difficult Izzy was in the past and would not be resurrected, so all she said was, "Thank you. I appreciate it."

He nodded. "Good. So seriously, there's nothing up that way except the vineyard. There are other trails I can show you if you're after a hike."

"No, I'm not after a hike. I..." She stopped, wondering how stupid it would look to ask about coffee and how much she cared about looking stupid. Deciding she didn't care, she said, "Actually, I was after coffee. There's no machine in my room at the hotel and no one was up, so..."

Chase's expression was hard to read. "You won't be able to get coffee here. But I've got a machine at HQ. I'll make you one if you like."

Again, Izzy was surprised. He looked rugged and tough, definitely not the kind of man who'd have a coffee machine stashed away in his "HQ," wherever that was.

"Don't look so shocked." The hard lines of his face relaxed slightly, the slight glimmer of amusement back in his eyes. "Believe it or not, I appreciate a good coffee."

Didn't you want to get away from him?

Yes, she did. His presence was discomforting and she didn't think she could handle any more discomfort.

But she desperately wanted a coffee. And her options on that front were limited. It was either his coffee or no coffee.

Perhaps she could deal with his company in the name of caffeine. It would be useful to get to know him, anyway, since this business-venture thing was his idea.

"Okay," she said, forcing a smile. "In that case I'd love one."

———

Isabella Montgomery's smile was forced, no doubt about it. And it was obvious that coming to HQ for a coffee was not something she wanted to do. Chase wondered why she'd agreed.

It had to be the lure of coffee.

Not that he cared, he'd just felt compelled to offer something by way of an apology for his previous rudeness. Plus he was curious. He wanted to know what had happened to the third member of the Deep River party who'd pulled out at the last minute and why Isabella had filled in instead.

Isabella was definitely *not* from Deep River. Not wearing those expensive designer jeans, that overengineered parka, or the fresh-out-of-the-box hiking boots. Or with that gorgeous, syrupy drawl.

She looked like a pretty doll in comparison to the other two women, who seemed comfortable in the tough, nononsense clothing they'd been wearing. Isabella did not seem comfortable, radiating a clear unease that reminded him of things he'd rather forget.

Such as how uncomfortable Olivia had been when she'd first come from the city to live with him in Brightwater. How she'd tried to pretend that she liked living here.

This pretty woman wasn't going to last two seconds, he could tell.

You still liked her looking at your chest though.

That was bullshit. He didn't like it. He hadn't even noticed.

Ignoring the very male part of him that insisted he was wrong about that, Chase gave her a nod and then turned toward the Pure Adventure NZ HQ.

"So," she asked as they walked over to the building, "do you often go swimming in the lake with all your clothes on?"

"Would you have preferred me to take them off beforehand?"

She opened her mouth, then closed it, her cheeks going pink. "That's not what I meant."

Inexplicably pleased with himself, he relented. "Sometimes I take a dip in the lake because it's bloody cold and I'm usually hot after a run."

"That makes sense." She kicked a stone, reminding him of Gus doing the same thing the day before.

There was a moment of awkward silence.

He was inclined to start asking her questions now, but she'd probably be more forthcoming—not to mention more pleasant—with a coffee.

Not that she let the silence sit for long, saying a little too quickly, "So, I didn't know you had a daughter."

He smiled as he did whenever his daughter was mentioned. "Yeah. Gus is nearly thirteen. She's a great kid."

Isabella gave him a curious glance. "She seems like it. I take it she found the key?"

His smile faltered, remembering Levi. "Eventually, yes."

"Oh…good." She kicked another stone and winced.

Chase noticed. "You okay?"

"Oh, a blister on my heel," she said dismissively. "It's nothing."

He glanced down at the fancy hiking boots on her feet. "New boots, huh?"

"Yes."

"Did you get them fitted properly?"

An expression he couldn't name flickered over her delicate features. "Not exactly."

"What do you mean, not exactly?"

"Does it matter? You always get blisters with new shoes. It's fine."

"Yes, it matters," he felt compelled to point out. "Having the right gear is important. Your equipment can be the only thing standing between you and dying of exposure."

She rolled her eyes. "Do I look like I'm dying of exposure right now?"

Chase took his job seriously. He took everything seriously. And a pretty woman in overpriced, ill-fitting gear being dismissive about something that could save her life irritated him.

He was aware that his irritation had more to do with memories of Olivia and her attitude than any real issue with Isabella Montgomery.

But he still couldn't help himself.

He, Finn, and Levi did a lot of search and rescue, mainly of idiot tourists who'd wandered into the mountains without preparation or proper gear and had gotten themselves into trouble. The weather could turn so quickly out here and it caught many people off guard.

"You're hiking on a trail," he said. "Snow is setting in even though it was hot when you started out, and then your hiking partner breaks an ankle. You have to go for help because if you don't, you'll both die of hypothermia. But you can't walk either, because your feet are a mass of blisters due to your badly fitting boots."

Isabella stared at him. "Okay," she said slowly. "I'll keep that in mind next time I'm hiking in bad weather."

Let it go, idiot.

He narrowed his gaze. "Please tell me you didn't get them off the internet."

"No," she said coolly. "I did not."

That was something.

He narrowed his gaze further. "Did you even try them on?"

This time there was no mistaking the expression on her face: extreme irritation. "No, I didn't, okay?" Her voice was right on the edge of a snap. "I didn't have time."

"No wonder you have a blister," he said, even though he knew he was being a dick about this. "They're probably a really crappy fit."

"Maybe, but—"

"I'll run you over to Queenstown," he said as they approached the front door of HQ. "Get a mate of mine to find you a decent pair and you can try them on, see how they fit."

She'd stopped in front of the door, a very pissed-off look on her face and her hands in the pockets of the expensive parka that she probably also hadn't tried on since it swamped her and was way too heavy duty for wandering around the lake on a summer day.

Clearly, she didn't find his offer to her liking.

Are you surprised? You're being an asshole.

Olivia had found his managing of every tiny detail annoying too, though he'd tried hard to loosen his grip on his need to control everything. It was an old army habit, cemented by having to bring up his younger brother after their mother had died and his father had stopped caring about anything but his own grief.

People were important though, even ones you didn't know, so why wouldn't you do everything in your power to keep them safe?

"What?" He pulled open the door. "I'm trying to be helpful."

"Thank you." Her tone was very measured. "It's appreciated."

She was placating him. Which did not help his mood *at all*.

"If you don't get better boots," he said, apparently unable to quit even when his own brain was telling him not to be a complete asshole, "you'll only get more blisters and eventually you'll stop wearing them." He bit down on the rest of the lecture he wanted to give her, gesturing at the stairs instead. "After you."

She gave him a look, then turned without a word and went up the stairs.

Being a pushy dick is not the way to endear yourself.

He'd made his point, though; he wouldn't keep on at her about it. Especially when this coffee was supposed to be an apology, not an in-depth, three-day workshop on the importance of having the right gear.

Chase followed her up the stairs, his gaze going automatically to her ass, that very male part of him noting that while her boots might not fit, her expensive blue jeans certainly did. Then he gave himself a mental kicking.

These women were here to start businesses, not for any other reason. If he needed feminine company, he could take himself off to Queenstown and find someone there; no need to make life even more difficult for himself than it already was.

Chase forced his gaze away and concentrated on how his wet clothes were sticking to him and how unpleasant that felt instead.

At the top of the stairs—mercifully there was no Levi being inappropriate with yet another woman—Isabella moved into the room and then stopped, looking around.

"This is very...tidy," she said.

Her tone was neutral, so perhaps she wasn't holding his criticism of her hiking boots against him.

"Old army habit," he said shortly.

"You were in the army?" She wandered over to the bookcase, studying the spines.

"Yeah. Special forces."

"My brother was in the army for a while too." She glanced at him. "That does explain a few things though."

Chase frowned. "What things?"

"Just a general..." She gestured vaguely at him. "Attitude."

Conscious that he was dripping on the carpet and really needed to go take a shower, Chase stayed where he was, oddly needled all over again.

"Attitude?" He could feel his frown deepening. "What attitude?"

The expression on her delicate features smoothed. "Nothing. Forget I said anything."

He should.

Except he didn't.

"Too late," he said before he could stop himself. "I'm curious now."

She shifted on her feet, her gaze dropping to his chest, then jerking back up to his face again. Her expression remained neutral but a trace of pink washed through her cheeks once more.

And for a second, tension hummed in the space between them, a familiar kind of electricity that he hadn't felt in a long time.

Goddammit.

"I'm going to have a shower," he said abruptly. Without waiting for her to respond, he turned and stalked off down the hall.

Chapter 4

Izzy stared after Chase's tall, broad figure as he disappeared down the hall, her heart beating too fast and cheeks feeling too hot.

She turned quickly to the window that looked out across the lake, the intense blue of the water magical against the white-capped peaks of the mountains.

A beautiful view. Except Izzy wasn't thinking about the view.

She'd been an idiot, letting herself get distracted by Chase Kelly's magnificent chest and, even worse, letting him notice her distraction.

Embarrassing. Especially after the way he'd lectured her about her boots.

He'd been so uptight about it, and she already knew she'd come here unprepared and didn't need him rubbing it in.

Annoyance at Chase built inside her, but she forced it away. No point being difficult. Being friendly to the locals was important, especially considering yesterday and Jim's obvious hostility. She was sure there were others who weren't too happy with her, Beth, and Indigo's arrival, so the sooner she allayed everyone's wariness, the better.

So Chase was uptight. She could deal with that. She just had to be calm and measured and not let him annoy her.

Easy.

It'd be worth it for the coffee. She'd drink it, then go back to the hotel and start planning to get this new craft store up and running.

Feeling more in control, Izzy turned from the window and looked around the room. It was a pleasant living area, with a big wood burner in one corner and a worn but very comfortable-looking couch against one wall. A rag-rolled rug lay on the floor and there were a couple of mismatched armchairs near the wood burner.

Tourism posters of soaring mountains and glittering waterfalls adorned the walls. Of people skiing, jet-boating, and bungee-jumping.

Everything was, as she'd pointed out to Chase earlier, very, *very* tidy. The cushions on the couch were straight, the tiled area around the wood burner spotless, every little knickknack on the bookshelves lined up.

Even the piles of clutter—letters and pens, various electrical cords, safety pins, rubber bands—were neatly placed.

If this was all Chase's doing, then uptight was a massive understatement.

He wasn't uptight when he came out of that lake.

Izzy decided it would be best if she ignored that thought completely.

Chase came back a couple of minutes later, now dressed in jeans and a black T-shirt with the Pure Adventure NZ logo on the front of it.

It was an improvement, though not by much. Not given how the cotton of his T-shirt stretched over his broad shoulders and chest, lovingly outlining all the hard muscle Izzy had seen unclothed only ten minutes earlier.

She muttered a curse, then took a deep, silent breath before exhaling, getting rid of her irritation, letting calm fill her.

Chase went into the little kitchen and she followed,

standing in the doorway as he moved over to the very expensive-looking espresso machine on the counter.

Well, this was more like it.

"You really *are* serious about your coffee," she said, staring at the machine.

"Yeah, since you can't get a good long black anywhere here, I decided it was worth the investment." He ground some beans in an equally expensive-looking grinder, before flicking a few switches on the machine. "What'll it be? Flat white? Long black? Cappuccino?"

Izzy didn't know what a 'long black' was, but she could really do with something milky. "Uh, can you do a latte?"

"Sure." He began the process of making the coffee, his movements fluid and sure.

Izzy leaned against the doorframe. "You look like a professional," she observed, feeling the need to fill the silence.

"I did a barista course."

"That's dedicated."

He shrugged. "I like good coffee. And no one else here knows how to do it."

"So…there isn't anywhere else here that does coffee?"

Chase glanced at her, gray eyes glinting. "Did it look like the place was littered with cafés just waiting to make your latte for you?"

"Well, no. But—"

"Do you know anything about this town, Miss Montgomery? Anything at all?"

Izzy could feel herself coloring yet again. How did he do that? He immediately seemed to know exactly what to say to get under her skin, and not in a good way.

He kept making her feel acutely underprepared and

disorganized, and she didn't want to go into all the reasons for it with him.

It was clear that he'd been managing this project and he deserved to at least know what had happened to the other woman and why Izzy had turned up in her place.

"Honestly?" she said, laying it out for him. "No. I was a last-minute replacement for Georgie. And I came from Houston, not Deep River."

Chase stopped what he was doing and gave her another of those stern, drill-sergeant-like looks that made his army background obvious.

"I'm going to need a little more explanation than that," he said.

Izzy resisted the urge to shift against the doorframe. "So my brother lives in Deep River. We were having a conversation and he told me in passing that some Deep River people were going to New Zealand to start businesses here as a kind of revitalization project and that one of them had to pull out. My career in Houston was coming to a... natural end and I'd been looking for...uh...other opportunities. This seemed perfect. They needed someone with some business experience, which I have, so I thought I'd tag along."

"As simple as that, huh?" The look on his face was skepticism itself.

Not quite, but she wasn't going to tell him that.

"Yes," she said coolly. "As simple as that."

Chase's gaze was disturbingly direct. "So, what? You chucked everything into a suitcase, stopped to get some boots and a parka, then jumped on a plane to spend three months in New Zealand?"

"Yes," she repeated, since that's exactly what she had done. "Why is that so difficult to believe?"

"It's not difficult." There was an odd note in his voice that she couldn't quite read. "Lots of people make decisions like that. They come here without preparing, without thinking, without knowing anything about the place and cause a whole lot of problems in the interim."

It was clear he included her in that group and it made her hackles rise.

"I'm not a tourist, Mr. Kelly," she said coolly. "I came here with the expectation of starting a business with Beth and Indigo. And while I obviously haven't got the right clothing, I do know what I'm doing, believe me. Also, as an aside, your website could use some work."

Chase said nothing, continuing to stare at her. Abruptly, he turned to go heat the milk and get out some mugs.

Izzy cursed silently. *So much for trying not to be difficult.* Why on earth was her instinct to argue with him every time he opened his mouth?

Hadn't she decided she needed to be measured and calm to deal with his grumpiness? She was supposed to defuse the situation, not make it worse.

"Look," she said at last, trying to moderate her tone, "I'm jet-lagged and it's early, and I haven't had my coffee yet. I didn't prepare as well as I should have. But…I'm going to remedy that today." She paused. "I'm not one of those people, okay? I'm not here to cause problems. I'm here to fix them."

If Chase was impressed with this little speech, he gave no sign. "Good," he said without pausing with the coffee making. "Because that's why you and the other two are here. To fix Brightwater's main problem."

Beth had told her a little bit about why Brightwater Valley needed some Deep River residents. Faced with a dwindling population, the citizens of Brightwater Valley were hoping to draw more visitors by inviting people to set up businesses in town. Particularly entrepreneurs who were used to living in rugged places and wouldn't mind either the isolation or the harsh elements of Brightwater Valley, in particular.

"Beth told me about how you need new businesses to revive the town," Izzy said.

"That's right." He picked up a metal jug and steamed the milk. "We tried getting interest from Queenstown and other cities, but no one was interested in coming down here, so we had to go farther afield. Deep River is a sister town from way back in the forties and we thought if we got a few interested people from there, the culture shock wouldn't be as bad." With surprising delicacy, Chase carefully poured the milk into a big mug, finishing it up with a strange twist. Then he handed the mug to her with a very direct gaze. "City folk get restless. There's no Wi-Fi. No cafés. No fancy restaurants. No takeout. No department stores or nightclubs or movie theaters. Just the great outdoors. We need people who can handle that."

Izzy reached out to take the mug from him, but he didn't let it go, his silver eyes burning with an odd intensity.

"Can you handle that, Miss Montgomery?"

A bolt of electricity shot down Izzy's spine; it was clear that Chase Kelly had just issued her a challenge.

The spiky and difficult part of her stirred as determination hardened inside her.

She met his gaze squarely. "Yes, I can handle that."

And she meant it.

She *would* handle it. This was her chance to create something without her family's uncomfortable oil industry history getting in the way and ruining things for her. Something of her own that she hadn't been given or inherited.

Something she'd done for herself.

She would make it work, and Josh, Montgomery Oil and Gas, and her parents could all go to hell.

Chase gave one sharp nod, then he released the mug.

It wasn't until Izzy had taken it back into the living area that she realized the swirl in the froth of the milk looked a lot like a fern frond.

———

Chase made his usual morning long black and took his time about it, mainly to give himself a few moments to settle the hell down.

He normally wasn't this grumpy, but Isabella Montgomery seemed to be hell-bent on pushing every one of his buttons. And she didn't even realize she was doing it.

Learning she was from Houston and not Deep River, as he'd previously assumed, explained that gorgeous drawl, yet it had annoyed him.

She was on a break from her career and thought she'd come to New Zealand, to Brightwater Valley, for three months. That simple, she'd said.

Bullshit.

This new initiative was an idea he'd brought to the monthly Brightwater community meeting at the Rose. People were scared of change, so they thought it was ridiculous, but Chase had been persistent.

No one had wanted to come to the ass end of the South Island to a tiny town in the middle of nowhere.

Then—he had to give credit where credit was due—Cait unearthed some old newspaper clippings and documents about a sister-city agreement with an Alaskan town called Deep River.

A few months of renewing ties ensued and then Chase had broached the topic of Brightwater Valley's revitalization project with Deep River's mayor, Astrid James. He hadn't been laughed at, as expected. In fact, she'd sounded intrigued and had promised to bring the offer to the people of Deep River to gauge interest.

A contingent of three Deep River women were set to come out to Brightwater Valley a few months later for a three-month trial period.

For Chase, it had been a particular triumph. Not because he wanted to prove himself to the people here, but because he cared about this little town and he didn't want to see it disappear. He wanted to restore the town to its old glory, the glory it'd had first during the gold rush and then during the tourism boom in the seventies and eighties. He wanted more people here, more tourists, more stores, more people coming and staying. More life.

A future for Gus. A future for the people already here.

Of course, not everyone was happy with his idea and he understood that. They liked their quiet, simple way of life, where nobody was a stranger. But if Brightwater Valley got any quieter it was going to die, so something had to be done.

And he was the man who stepped up to do it.

Finishing his coffee, he cleaned up the machine then grabbed his tiny cup and carried it into the living area.

Isabella was sitting on the very edge of the couch, sipping at the latte he'd made her.

She looked tired. There were dark circles under her eyes and she was pale, which was probably part and parcel of jet lag. Had she eaten this morning? Probably not, since the dining room at the Rose wouldn't be open for another couple of hours.

"Are you hungry?" he asked.

She glanced up at him, startled. "Oh…I…hadn't thought."

"Well, think about it. I'm going to make myself some breakfast and I can make you some too."

A little crease appeared between her delicate dark brows. "I don't normally eat this early in the morning, but I didn't have any dinner last night."

Chase frowned. "Did Cait not feed you all last night?" Cait did all the cooking at the Rose when there were guests, and she was usually pretty reliable at doing it. Surely she would have made something for the three women? There weren't any other places they could get food, apart from Bill's general store, and he'd closed early yesterday to go fishing.

"Oh, yes, she did," Isabella said. "At least, I think she did. I went to bed early and must have slept through it."

"Then you'll need something," he said decisively. "Eggs, bacon, and toast. How does that sound?"

She blinked. "You want to make me breakfast?"

But Chase was already turning back to the kitchen. "That's what I said. You need to eat, and a good lot of protein should help with the jet lag."

It didn't take him long since he made a cooked breakfast fairly frequently—Finn and Levi were fans—and within ten minutes he was bringing out food, plates, and cutlery, setting them down on the small table near the window.

Isabella hadn't moved from the couch and was still savoring her latte. She stared at him as if he'd grown a second head. Then her fixed expression wavered.

"Oh," she said suddenly. "Oh, you know, I think I might be hungry."

Chase put down the toast and butter, the sense of satisfaction he always got when he looked after people glowing warmly inside him. And when she glanced down longingly at her by now empty mug, the sense of satisfaction became even stronger.

"You want another?" He had no idea why he was *quite* so pleased but refused to let it show.

"Oh, yes, that would be great." She gave him her mug and a smile so full of gratefulness that his breath caught.

She really did have the most beautiful smile.

You should not be taking any notice of her smile. Get her coffee and then find out more about her and what she's intending to do here.

Good point.

Chase went back into the kitchen, made her another coffee, and then came back out again to find her sitting at the table, wolfing down the bacon, eggs, and toast he'd put on a plate.

He put the fresh coffee down beside her, then sat opposite, starting his own breakfast.

"Oh my God, this is really good," she muttered, clearly relishing her bacon. "You can really cook."

Chase knew he shouldn't enjoy her praise, but he certainly enjoyed watching her get pleasure from the food he'd cooked.

"I often do breakfast for the rest of the team," he said. "They like a fry-up."

"I can see why." She paused in her eating to take a sip of her coffee, letting out a soft little moan. "Oh, wow, your coffee is sensational too. Those barista lessons sure paid off."

There was no reason on earth why the sound of that soft moan should have caused something inside of him to shift and tighten.

He cleared his throat. "So I meant to come over to the Rose yesterday to see how you were all fitting in, but I got sidetracked. I've arranged a little welcome to Brightwater barbecue this evening on the lakeshore across from the Rose. You can meet the rest of the town."

"Okay, I think you mentioned that yesterday. Sounds good."

"I'm also going to show you the space I'm thinking you can use for your new businesses. It's next to Bill's. Requires a little work, but not too much. There're a few people around here handy with a hammer and a paintbrush who can pitch in to help. I can do electrical work, as can Finn, but any certification will have to come from a sparkie. We'll have to get one in from Queenstown. Plumbing the same. You'll probably have to sit down and draw up a list of materials you're going to need and then we'll have to figure out where we can get them. I'm assuming you've handled all the banking arrangements already, but I'm happy to help if you need it getting that set up. You're booked into the Rose for the next two weeks, but after that you might want to think about your own accommodation. There's a house up the road near the vineyard that's vacant at the moment and I've been thinking you lot can move in there when you're ready. It's in a pretty decent state, livable at least. We can help you get sorted with groceries and other things…" He trailed off, realizing all of a sudden that Isabella was staring at him as if he'd started speaking in tongues.

"What?" he asked, irritated that she hadn't produced paper and a pen to take down notes because he had a lot of information to impart and he didn't fancy going over it twice.

It's six in the morning. You do realize that, don't you?

"Nothing. It's just…" She picked up her mug and took a healthy sip of her coffee. "Well, you've…ah…really organized this quite thoroughly, haven't you?"

"Of course. If you want something to succeed, thoroughly is the only way to organize it."

"You're right." She took another gulp of coffee. "It's good. I just…"

He frowned, noting the slightly overwhelmed look on her face. "You just what?"

"Nothing." The overwhelmed look disappeared and she gave him a very fake-looking smile. "This is all very informative. I'll have to talk with the other two and we can go from there."

Chase studied her, a nagging suspicion settling itself in his brain. "Exactly how much of a last-minute replacement are you?"

"Quite last-minute." She took the last swallow of her coffee, then pushed her chair back. "Thank you for the breakfast and especially for the coffee. It was great. But I'd probably better get back to the hotel."

She was running away. Had it been his list of things to do or his question about her being a replacement? Very definitely the latter, he decided, and that made him want to know why.

Why do you care? The only thing that matters is that they stay and make a go of it.

That was true. But if Miss Isabella Montgomery had decided to come here so suddenly, she could decide to go back equally as suddenly. Which might prompt the others to have second thoughts. And if that happened, he'd be back at square one.

He could *not* let his town die.

However, pushing her now was a bad idea. He'd cooked her breakfast and given her coffee, which was a good start. He didn't want to jeopardize the hopefully positive impression he'd made on her after his grumpiness of the day before.

So perhaps he'd let her run this time. There was always tonight at the barbecue. He could ask her more questions then.

He leaned back in his chair and returned her fake smile with one of his own that told her he didn't believe her. "No problem," he said easily. "I'll catch you later."

Chapter 5

Izzy stalked back toward the Rose from Pure Adventure NZ feeling extremely annoyed—and annoyed that she was annoyed.

She was well caffeinated, had had a great breakfast, and since Chase had very kindly listed all the things that needed to be done to get this new business venture off the ground, she should be feeling excited and ready to tackle the day.

Except she wasn't excited and didn't feel ready to tackle any days, let alone this one.

What she felt was overwhelmed, unsettled, and yes, annoyed.

Because she was still letting him get to her and she shouldn't. She should have stayed sitting at the table for another five minutes or so, not left so precipitously. Doing so gave far too much away and she'd already given enough away as it was—such as how he affected her physically, which she did *not* appreciate.

It was still early, so to calm herself down, she stalked about the tiny town before stopping outside the low, stone building Chase had mentioned would house their new business.

The black dog from the day before appeared out of seemingly nowhere and trotted over to her. She didn't know much about dogs, but this one didn't seem dangerous so she stayed where she was and let it give her a cursory sniff. Then she proffered a hand which the dog greeted by sneezing before abruptly running off.

Strange animal.

Dismissing the dog, she turned back to the building.

The big windows were dusty, and when Izzy peered inside she got an impression of a large open space with exposed brick walls and high, exposed roof beams.

Seemed like he wasn't wrong—there was clearly going to be a lot of work involved.

Can you really do this?

Izzy let out a breath and stepped back from the windows, turning resolutely back to the Rose. Of course she could do this, not that she had any other option. It was either making a go of this, or going back to Houston where there was exactly nothing for her anymore.

No, she couldn't go back. She was here now, and by God, she was going to make it work.

Back in the Rose, she put her head around the door of the little dining room to see Beth sitting at one of the wooden tables looking bright-eyed and bushy-tailed, while Indigo sat opposite, arms folded on the table and her forehead resting on top of them.

"Hey," Beth said, spotting Izzy. "You're up!"

"Sadly." Izzy stepped into the dining room and walked over to where Beth and Indigo were sitting, pulling out a chair and sitting down. "I woke up at five and went for a walk." She glanced at Indigo, who did not raise her head. "You okay, Indigo?"

"No," Indigo said in muffled tones. "Jet lag is horrible."

Beth reached over the table and patted Indigo's arm. "It'll be okay. Cait's cooking us some bacon and eggs." She looked at Izzy. "You want some?"

"No, thank you."

"Oh? But you missed dinner last night."

Much to her continued irritation, Izzy felt her cheeks heat. Which was ridiculous since there was no reason for it. So she'd run into Chase and he'd cooked her breakfast. Big deal.

"I already ate," she said steadily. "I met Chase this morning and had breakfast with him."

Beth's green eyes went very round. "Chase as in Chase Kelly Chase? Hot dad Chase?"

Izzy willed her blush to die down. "Unless there are other Chases in Brightwater Valley that I don't know about, then yes, him."

Beth leaned her elbows on the table and put her chin in her hands. "What happened? Do tell."

At that moment, Indigo lifted her head and looked at Izzy, bloodshot blue eyes narrowing. "Yeah, what happened?"

"Nothing," Izzy said calmly. "We chatted about the new business and what work needs to be done on the building to get it ready."

"Lame," Beth muttered. "I was hoping for something more interesting."

Izzy decided to ignore that. "We should sit down and figure out what we need and get a list of materials together, that kind of thing."

"Ugh." Indigo put her head back down on her folded arms. "I was hoping I could go back to bed."

"There, there." Beth patted her friend's arm again. "There'll be plenty of time to rest later. Oh, by the way…" She gave Izzy a glance. "Have you called Zeke to let him know you're here yet?"

Izzy tried to ignore the guilt that tightened inside her, along with a very real reluctance. She'd had to tell the other two that Zeke didn't know she'd volunteered herself as Georgie's replacement, which Beth was concerned about. He was a good guy, she'd said to Izzy. And she didn't want him to worry. And fair enough. Izzy didn't want to worry him either, which meant she had to get over her reluctance and tell him she was here.

"No. But I will today. Promise." Deciding it was time the attention came off her, Izzy gave the other two a curious look. "What about you guys? You have anyone in Deep River you want to contact?"

Beth shrugged. "Just my folks."

"No one," Indigo said.

It struck Izzy in that moment that while the other two knew a bit about her, since she'd told them, she really didn't know anything about them...since she hadn't exactly asked.

"They okay with you coming all the way to New Zealand?" She directed this at Beth. "I mean, why did you?"

"Come here, you mean? For a change of scene." Beth gave her a smile that was just a touch too wide. "A fresh perspective, different inspiration, that kind of thing."

Izzy had the impression that while that very well might have been the truth, there was something deeper going on there. But since she didn't know Beth well enough to push, she only nodded.

"And I'm here because my grandma died," Indigo offered, her voice still muffled by her arms.

Izzy gave her a concerned look. "Oh, I'm so sorry to hear that."

"Thanks. It was a few months ago though." Her shoulders lifted in a shrug, though she still didn't look up. "Like Beth, I'm here for a change of scene."

Beth patted her again and then mouthed *don't ask* at Izzy.

Izzy nodded. More details would be a discussion for another day, when they all knew each other better. In the meantime, they had other things to talk about.

The three of them spent the rest of the day sitting around, generally recovering from their journey, taking a couple of forays to the lakeshore and a brief visit to the general store. The owner, another grumpy old man called Bill, had determinedly rebuffed all their efforts at conversation and so they'd given up.

Later that afternoon, after she'd put it off as long as she could, Izzy finally went to call Zeke.

She wished there was somewhere more private to talk, but the only option for calls was a landline, and the guest phone was in the lounge/library situated just off the bar in the hotel. It wouldn't have been a problem if the room had been empty, but an old man was snoozing in an armchair near the window. As much as Izzy had wanted to, she couldn't wake him to ask him to leave.

"You're where?" Zeke demanded down the phone after she'd managed to get ahold of him. He sounded exceedingly annoyed.

Clutching the receiver and trying to keep her voice down, Izzy turned her back to the old man. "I'm in Brightwater Valley with Beth and Indigo. I thought you'd have found out by now."

"I've been taking an expedition out in the bush. I only got back today. So no, I didn't find out."

Izzy was not looking forward to telling Zeke about her canceled wedding, mainly because the *I told you so*s would be a whole thing.

Her brother had met Josh a couple of times and hadn't much liked him and had told Izzy so in no uncertain terms. At the time, she'd defended Josh because he'd seemed like a good choice of husband for her and her parents had liked him very much.

Now she wished she hadn't. She didn't want to admit that she'd been wrong.

Perhaps if she didn't mention Josh at all, Zeke would forget all about him.

"I'm sorry," she said, keeping her voice level. "I know I should have left you a message at least. But it was too good an opportunity to pass up."

"So...what? You just left the company and Houston? What did Josh think? Is he there with you?"

Damn.

"No, he's not. The company is doing great with the green energy direction. There're some good people managing it now." Zeke didn't need to know they'd kicked her out due to their family's patchy history and how hurt she'd been by that. That was her problem to deal with, not his.

"Anyway," she rushed on, "Josh is fine with me taking some time away. Don't worry about him."

But Zeke was clearly not going to leave it at that. "He was okay with you staying for three months?" Zeke's tone was laced with his particular brand of flat skepticism.

"Oh, damn, I'm being called," Izzy lied smoothly. "We're having a welcome barbecue so I have to go. Sorry."

"Izzy—" Zeke began.

"Love you," she said before hanging up.

Then she stared at the phone for a long moment, and that tight knot of emotion inside her—the one made up of so many threads she was never going to be able to unravel them all—pulled even tighter.

She didn't want to talk about Josh. She didn't want to think about him or about the gala on the same day the board had told her they were letting her go. Everyone had told her she looked like a million dollars, while she'd stood there feeling like an old quarter lost for decades underneath someone's couch cushions.

All she'd wanted was some support and a shoulder to cry on.

Instead, she'd gotten Josh telling her that he couldn't marry her. That he was in love with some other woman and he hoped she understood.

In that moment, pain had bloomed behind her breastbone because she loved him, while he'd just been so…matter-of-fact about it. As if the two years they'd spent together had meant nothing.

Which had been when she'd ignored the pain and gone for rage instead.

But it wasn't the place or the time for anger, and besides, that would only make things worse. So she'd swallowed all those violent, sharp emotions and smiled, nodded, and said that yes, she understood. And of course the wedding would have to be canceled.

Her parents had canceled the whole thing and she'd had to listen to her father complain about losing deposits, while her mother kept asking her what she'd done to chase Josh away. Because it had to be her fault. A good man like that wouldn't fall for someone else if he was happy at home, right?

Izzy's chest ached and she rubbed at it. Ridiculous to be wallowing. She'd done her duty, told Zeke what was happening…mostly. She'd inform him about Josh later since he and their parents didn't speak.

Now, though, she had a barbecue to go to.

She glanced behind her to check on the old man. He was still sleeping, bless him.

Izzy left the library and went out to the wide veranda where Indigo and Beth sat on one of the long, wide wooden seats. They were looking over to the lakeshore where a few industrious people were setting up a big, expensive-looking grill, along with a large folding table.

A few tourists were milling about too.

Quite a few cars had been parked along the lakefront earlier that day, with people going swimming in the lake, getting ice creams from the general store, and more than a few wandering into Pure Adventure NZ.

Izzy had found herself watching them, assessing them from a market perspective. If people came for the nature, then perhaps they could be persuaded to stay for a few other things.

Most of them had gone now though, since the food options around here were severely limited. The Rose had a dining room, but with their lack of a set menu, she assumed people decided to find food elsewhere.

"What's happening?" she asked, sitting down beside Indigo.

"Looks like our barbecue is ready to go," Indigo replied.

She squinted at the crowd on the lakeshore. She could see Chase among them, standing at the grill, talking to another tall man with dark hair. "Do they need help, do you think?"

"Well," Beth said, "I asked and was told very definitely no."

At that moment, Cait came out the front door of the

Rose carrying a big platter of different meats. She didn't pause, going straight down the steps and across the road to the lakeshore.

As the three of them watched, a dusty green truck pulled up and a tall and muscular man got out, the early-evening sun catching on the gold strands of his dark-brown hair. He was in jeans and a black T-shirt with a familiar logo on the front.

"Oooh," Beth murmured. "Now *who* is that?"

The man went around to the back of the truck and hauled a big white cooler from the bed. Someone else ran to help him and the two of them carried it over to the grass beside the folding table.

"What is it with you and men?" Indigo muttered.

Beth grinned. "Hey, I'm young. I'm single. I'm going to spend three months here, and if there are some attractive men around, I don't see why I shouldn't get to meet them."

"That's not what I'm here for," Indigo said. "If there's a choice between yarn and men, I'll take yarn any day of the week."

"Agreed," Izzy said without thinking.

There was silence as a prickly sensation ran up the back of Izzy's neck.

She gave the other two a sidelong glance and, sure enough, found two sets of eyes—one blue and one green—staring back at her.

"What?" she asked, hoping it didn't sound too defensive.

"That was very…emphatic of you." Beth's expression was curious. "Sounds like there's a story there."

"Uh, no, there's not." Izzy kept her voice neutral. "And hey, Indigo was the one who brought up yarn being better than men."

"But I know Indigo's story," Beth said as if it was perfectly obvious. "I don't know yours."

"Neither do I," Indigo added.

Great. Well, she couldn't say she hadn't expected this, especially given their conversation earlier that day. She'd thrown herself at these two women, inviting herself along on their journey. Yes, they'd both been welcoming, but they were always going to want—and deserved—more of an explanation for her sudden appearance.

She couldn't face telling them about Josh though.

Luckily, at that moment she was saved by Cait coming back up the stairs.

"Cait." Izzy quickly pushed herself up from the chair. "Do you need some help?"

Cait paused. "Oh, don't you worry. You're the guests of honor. You get to sit and watch everyone else do the work tonight."

"Please," Izzy said insistently. "You must have a lot of other things to take out. Let me at least carry some of them."

Cait's features softened into a smile. "Well now, that would be lovely."

"We'll help too." Beth got to her feet, Indigo following. "Don't think I didn't notice that," she murmured in Izzy's ear as they all trooped after Cait. "We're going to want the full story eventually."

Izzy sighed, feeling guilty. "You'll get it. Promise. Just… not tonight."

The three of them helped Cait bring out various cooking implements, plus a stack of paper plates, plastic utensils, and some disposable cups, and by the time everything had been brought outside, more people had arrived.

For such a tiny town, it felt like quite a crowd. Or maybe

she'd been expecting it to be just Chase, Cait, and Jim from the bar. There had to be a good twenty or thirty people all milling around and chatting now.

Chase had gotten the grill going and the smell of cooked meat drifted in the air, along with a biting, fresh chill coming down from the mountains and across the lake.

It was beautiful, and Izzy found herself admiring the scenery—the deep, intense blue of the lake mirroring the darkening sky, highlighting the green slopes of the hills and the snow-white of the mountaintops.

"They weren't kidding about the population," Indigo murmured as she put the last of the salads down on the big folding table, interrupting Izzy's scenery admiration fest.

Izzy looked out at the assembled crowd.

Folding chairs had been arranged on the bank in front of the lake's little beach, and indeed, most of them were occupied by a number of older people. The crowd standing and chatting were mostly older too, heading toward the *late fifties, early sixties, and above* age group.

Interesting. What had happened to all the young people? Had they all gone to the city due to lack of opportunities? Or was there some other reason?

"Hey," a deep, rough male voice said from behind her. "Deep River ladies."

Izzy started and turned around to find Chase standing there, along with the dark-haired man he'd been talking to earlier and the tawny-haired guy Beth had cooed over.

"Oh hey, Chase." Beth's bright smile encompassed the three men. "Good to see you again."

Izzy felt her cheeks get warm for no apparent reason, her heart beating a little faster than it had before.

How ridiculous. Chase had cooked her a lovely breakfast this morning, had made her an even better coffee, and if she'd rushed out precipitately, with only the most cursory of thanks, she hoped he hadn't noticed.

Like Beth, he'd started asking questions that she didn't want to answer. Beth deserved to have the story at some stage, but Chase was a stranger with whom she'd wanted to have a heart-to-heart discussion about as much as she wanted a lobotomy.

Given his general level of driven intensity, she'd half expected him to come over to the Rose at some point to continue the discussion, or at least bring over that long checklist of things he'd overwhelmed her with at breakfast, but he hadn't. Which was good.

Except the way he was intently looking at her now made it clear that he hadn't forgotten how she'd rushed out and would no doubt be talking to her about it at some stage.

Lucky her.

"Good to see you too," Chase said, his stern, aristocratic features relaxing. "I thought I'd introduce you all to the rest of the Pure Adventure NZ team. This is my brother, Finn."

The dark-haired man, who was a shade shorter than Chase, nodded but didn't smile. He had the same strong features as his brother, but his eyes were deeper set and dark brown, and his black hair was longer. And while Chase radiated an intense, almost kinetic energy, this man was quieter and much more reserved—still, like the surface of the lake behind them.

"And this," Chase went on, indicating the tawny-haired man, "is Levi."

Levi, in stark contrast to Finn, gave them a slow-burn

smile that was the most ridiculously charming thing Izzy had seen all day. He was sinfully handsome, with the face of a fallen angel, the wicked humor dancing in his hazel eyes making them gleam gold in the evening light.

Clearly he knew exactly how handsome he was and was quite prepared to use it to good effect.

"Good evening, ladies." Levi's voice was rich, deep, and warm as melted chocolate. "Very pleased to meet you." He held out one long-fingered hand.

Beth took it instantly. "I'm Beth."

"Hi, Beth." Levi grinned.

"Izzy." Izzy stuck out her hand for a handshake too.

"Nice to meet you, Izzy," Levi said, giving Chase a side-long glance as he shook her hand.

Indigo said nothing.

Izzy caught Beth elbowing her discreetly.

Indigo sniffed. "I'm Indigo."

"Indigo." Levi drew out her name, making it sound lush and exotic. "I like it. Hello, Indigo." He held his hand out to her.

She ignored it.

Izzy had no idea what was going on with the other woman, but she could sense things getting awkward, so she said quickly, "Nice to meet you too, Finn."

"Likewise," Finn said, laconic, his dark gaze taking in the three of them, his handsome face utterly unreadable.

"Well, don't just stand there," Chase said, glancing at the other two men. "Get these ladies a drink. They'll probably need it after I finish all the introductions."

"Yes, sir. Drill sergeant, sir." Levi grinned. "Would you like me to distribute pens and papers, sir? So they can take notes?"

Remembering the lecture Chase had given her at break-fast, Izzy suppressed a grin of her own.

Chase scowled and opened his mouth. But whatever he'd been going to say was lost as the tall, lanky girl from yester-day materialized at his side. "Dad," she said breathlessly, "Jim said I could have a shandy, but Cait said only if I ask you first."

Instantly, Chase's stern features softened the way they had yesterday. "First I want you to meet some people," he said. "This is Isabella, Beth, and Indigo from Deep River. Ladies, this is my daughter Augusta." He grinned then. "Except apparently you have to call her Gus on pain of death."

Gus peered curiously at them from behind a lock of dark hair. "Augusta's a horrible name," she pronounced. "I don't like it."

Izzy couldn't help smiling at the firmness in the girl's voice. Clearly she was going to be a woman who knew her own mind, much like her father.

"I don't much like my name either," Izzy said. "So please, call me Izzy."

Gus stared at her for a long moment and Izzy had the uncomfortable feeling she was being inventoried very thoroughly.

"Nice to meet you, Gus," Beth said with her customary enthusiasm.

"Same," Indigo offered, breaking out of her reserve. "But what's a shandy?"

"Half beer, half lemonade." This from Levi, who gave Indigo that slow, ridiculously charming smile again. "It's great for hot days. Would you like one?"

Indigo pulled a face. "No, thank you," she said primly.

"Well, I would," Beth said. "Sounds delicious."

"Yeah, tell Jim it's fine." Chase ruffled his daughter's hair affectionately, causing her to dodge his hand, squirming in embarrassment. He laughed, the warm and amused sound grazing across Izzy's skin, making a small pulse of electricity slide down her spine.

"Thanks, Dad," Gus said and dashed off.

"Tell Jim to go easy on the beer," Chase called after her, still grinning.

And Izzy found herself staring at his mouth. At the way it curved, giving his full bottom lip a kind of lazy sensuality that made her want to shiver.

Then Chase turned his head, his gray gaze catching hers, and she felt all the blood rush into her face.

Hell. He'd seen her staring at his mouth like a fool, hadn't he?

"Well, Miss Montgomery?" His eyes glinted silver, making it very obvious that yes, indeed, he had seen her staring. "Are you ready for your introductions?"

———

Isabella had gone very pink, which satisfied him immensely for some reason.

She'd been looking at his mouth and they both knew it.

Yeah, you weren't going to go there, remember?

Oh, he did remember. And no, he wasn't going to go there. But he could also enjoy the fact that a very pretty, albeit irritating, woman was obviously attracted to him and also was obviously annoyed about it.

And she *was* annoyed. She didn't look away, merely arching one of those delicate brows. "Yes, of course, Mr. Kelly."

Chase was conscious of Finn's suddenly sharpened attention and Levi's eyes widening at the very pointed "mister," but he ignored them.

He'd already decided, after she'd told Gus that she could call her Izzy, that he was now never going to. She would always be Miss Montgomery or, if she was very lucky, Isabella. Because if she was basically going to turn this into a thing by letting everyone else call her Izzy, then bring it on.

"Mr. Kelly?" Finn muttered from beside him. "What the hell did you do?"

Chase ignored him. No doubt he'd have to put up with bullshit from Finn and Levi later, but right now he had better things to do.

"Let's go, ladies," he said and led them into the assembled crowd.

Introductions didn't take long, since there weren't that many people to introduce them to. He wondered if Bill Preston, who owned the general store, would be difficult, since he'd argued the most vociferously against "strangers coming in and taking over." Chase knew he was worried about competition, but no amount of telling him that any new business would *not* be any sort competition for him would change his mind. It was probably something the old man would have to see for himself.

But Bill wasn't overly friendly nor overtly rude, giving the Deep River women a laconic "gidday" and a nod.

Correction, the two Deep River women and the one Texan.

On the other hand, everyone else Chase introduced them to at least made an effort.

Shirley Bell, who helped Bill out on occasion, gave them a

smile. Clive and Teddy Grange, a couple of youngish retirees from the city who owned the vineyard, were very interested in what kind of store the women were going to be setting up.

Evan McCahon, a reclusive, eccentric artist who lived farther up the valley even turned up to say hello, which was surprising given that he'd been one of Bill's supporters in the whole "say no to strangers" debate.

Perhaps it was the fact that the three women were very friendly. Or maybe it was just that they were young and therefore a novelty.

Chase found himself pleased that the town had made an effort and hadn't actively tried to scare the women away.

He let the three of them circulate for an hour or so, keeping an eye on them just in case someone was less than polite, making sure they had drinks and knew they could help themselves to food.

Then, when he saw Cait go off to deal with some drama in the hotel kitchen, leaving Isabella sitting on her own, he saw his opportunity to resume the discussion they'd begun that morning at HQ.

This time he was not going to let her walk away until she'd told him exactly what her deal was. The future of his town was too important.

Yet before he could even take a step in her direction, Gus wandered up to where Isabella was sitting.

Chase stopped, staring as his daughter abruptly sat down beside Isabella and started talking to her.

Gus was a friendly kid and never had any problems talking to adults, mainly because there weren't any kids in Brightwater, so most of the people she interacted with on a daily basis were adults. So he shouldn't have been surprised that she might want to talk to at least one of the three new-comers, especially given that they were female and Gus hadn't had a lot of female input in her life so far.

However, Chase would have thought Gus might be drawn to friendly, down-to-earth Beth or serious Indigo, not delicate, cool, and very feminine Isabella.

Apparently he was wrong.

"So what's the deal between you and her?" Finn said, coming up beside him.

Chase worked not to scowl automatically. "There's no deal. What are you talking about?"

"Don't give me that." Finn held out one of the beers he was holding. "The 'Mr. Kelly' stuff is a dead giveaway."

Chase took the beer, giving his brother a look. Finn had never been the outgoing, friendly type, growing even more reserved and quiet over the past few years since his wife, Sheri, had died, but he'd not lost his powers of observation. Damn him.

Telling Finn that he'd decided not to call Isabella anything but Miss Montgomery since she wouldn't let him call her Izzy made him sound like a petty dick. And to be fair, he *was* being a petty dick. But he wasn't in any hurry for his brother to know that.

"I was being polite."

"Bullshit." Finn raised his own bottle and took a sip. "There's some tension there. Anyone with eyes can see it."

"Then I'd appreciate it if you kept your eyes elsewhere."

"You made her coffee *and* breakfast this morning. I haven't seen you do that for a woman since..." He paused and looked at the sky, making a big show of thinking about it. "Oh, I don't know, since Olivia."

Chase resisted the sudden and familiar urge to strangle his brother. "If you must know," he growled, since Finn wouldn't get off his back unless he gave him something, "there's something a little…off about her. She was up early this morning looking for a coffee, so I thought I'd make her one and see what her deal was."

"Uh-huh." Finn took another sip, the expression on his face neutral. "What do you mean by 'off'?"

"She's a last-minute replacement for some other woman. And she's not from Deep River, she's from Houston."

"That's generally not a hanging offense."

"No, but she shows up here in boots that don't fit and a parka better suited to the Arctic, looked surprised when I said there were no cafés, and appeared to know nothing about the businesses she's supposed to be helping set up."

Finn was silent a moment. "She's not Olivia," he said quietly. "You do know that, right?"

Chase couldn't stop himself from scowling now. "This has got nothing to do with Olivia. I don't want some city chick coming in here unprepared, not knowing what she's getting herself into and not particularly caring about it either. If she came here at the last minute, she can leave at the last minute too."

Finn shook his head. "Nope, nothing to do with Olivia at all."

Chase decided he didn't want to talk about this anymore. "Where the hell is Levi?"

"Over there." Finn nodded toward Beth and Indigo on the lakeshore, helping Levi construct the usual beach bonfire that ended most town barbecues.

Or at least Beth was helping, while Indigo stood there frowning.

It did not improve Chase's mood. "He bloody better not—"

"Relax," Finn interrupted. "Beth is just being friendly, but I think Indigo would like to cut his balls off."

That was not an uncommon reaction to Levi, though admittedly usually from men.

"Good," Chase said. "As long as he can still fly, I don't care what she does with his balls."

Finn winced. "Yeah, priorities, right? You want me to supervise?"

"Might be a good idea."

"What about you?"

"Me?" Chase glanced back at where Gus was still sitting with Isabella. "I think I might go supervise my daughter."

Ignoring Finn's raised eyebrow, he walked over to where Gus sat with her legs crossed, an avid look on her face. "So do people really wear cowboy hats?" she asked. "Like, at the mall and stuff?"

"Oh yes," Isabella replied in that drawl he found so unbearably sexy. "They really do."

"And does everyone have a gun? Like, can you just carry them around?"

"Well, you have to have a permit and—" She broke off, suddenly noticing him standing there.

Gus did too, twisting around to look up at him. She scowled as if he'd interrupted something very important. "Dad, what?"

He decided to ignore her tone. "I need to steal Miss Montgomery away for a couple of minutes."

Gus was not pleased. "But we're having an important conversation."

"About guns, yes. It'll keep." He glanced at Isabella. "I need to know how you're going to want to proceed with getting these businesses off the ground."

Her gaze flickered as if she knew that was just a smoke-screen.

Still, to her credit, she didn't try to get out of it.

Instead, she smiled at Gus and said, "I'll come and find you after I've finished, okay?"

For a second it looked like his daughter might protest—like him, she could be damn stubborn about some things—then she sighed. "Okay, I guess."

"Go help Cait with the marshmallows," Chase suggested. "You know she always gives you extra if you help out."

Gus's features brightened. "Good point." She leapt to her feet and ran off.

"She's a sweet kid," Isabella said, getting up from the grass.

"I know." He didn't care if that sounded smug. He was well aware of how sweet Gus was. "I hope she didn't pester you with too many questions."

"Only about as many as her father," Isabella said. "Though don't tell me: you don't want to talk about business, you want to ask me about cowboy hats and guns too."

Chase was almost surprised into a grin. "Funnily enough, no. But you already know what I want to ask you about."

She absently brushed off the back of her jeans. Then she bent to pick up the tall glass she'd balanced on the grass next to her, a movement that made him far too aware of the shape of her ass.

"These are really good," she said, waving the glass at him. "The shandy, I mean."

"Does that mean you want another?"

"I mean, if you're offering."

"Sure," he said easily. "I'll go get you one after you answer the question I asked you earlier today."

She turned to face the lake, crossing her arms.

The sun was going down, sending bright fingers of orange light across the deep blue of the sky, the stars already twinkling.

"You're very persistent, you know that?" She sounded irritated. "Why does my background matter to you so much?"

"I told you why. The whole reason I encouraged this project was to get committed people who want to stay here, not come in for a couple of weeks, decide they don't like it, then bugger off again."

"What makes you think I'm one of those people?"

"You're clearly underprepared and joined the other two at the last minute, which to me indicates a certain lack of commitment," Chase informed her. "I'm not here for fly-by-nighters. This town's future is at stake. I hope you understand that."

"Okay, okay," she muttered. "I get it."

He gave her a direct look because she needed to know he wasn't going to be screwed around with. "Do you? Brightwater Valley is dying, Miss Montgomery. I have to bring it back to life and not only for the sake of my business and the other businesses here, but for my daughter too." This wasn't simply a business decision. While his own childhood here after his mother had died hadn't exactly been a bed of roses, he'd made sure that Gus's was a happy one. And that she loved Brightwater Valley as much as he did. "Someone needs to stay here and guard the environment for future generations. Gus will do that. But she can't do it on her own."

Isabella's dark eyes widened as she stared at him and he realized his voice had become a touch more emphatic than it should have been, a thread of anger running through it.

He *was* angry, because this was important. The town's importance wasn't so much about the success of its businesses as it was about the environment—the mountains and the lake and the bush. The isolation. A place given wholly over to the planet and not to humanity and giant cities.

Someone had to guard it, look after it. Make sure it stayed untouched. And perhaps it was arrogant of him, but he'd taken it on since no one else had stepped up. And he wanted Gus to feel like she could do the same.

"That's…quite the goal," Isabella said after a moment. "I mean, for an adventure company."

"It's not just an adventure company," he said. "It's getting people out into the environment. Getting them to see what's out here, the beauty of it. Showing them something greater than themselves and their small city lives. Something precious that needs to be preserved." Conviction had crept into his voice exposing a deeper truth that he normally kept close.

She stared at him, an odd expression on her face, but he wasn't ashamed of how much this mattered to him and so he stared back, letting her see his belief.

Softly, she let out a breath. "My job in Houston ended rather abruptly, and I had some…personal issues that I wanted to get away from." She glanced out over the lake again. "Yes, it was last minute. Yes, I'm underprepared. Those things aren't usual for me." She was silent another moment, then she turned and looked at him, the same thing glowing in her eyes that he'd seen that morning when she'd told him she could handle it, her own kind of intensity, a steely determination that he suspected would match his. "I don't want to talk about the details of why I left. But I swear to you that I'm here for the three months that was promised and that I'm serious about it. We'll get the business we've got planned up and running, and at the end of three months, we'll decide where to go from there."

He couldn't ask for more, he understood that. She'd given him what he wanted—a promise to stay.

He'd been serious with her and so she'd been serious with him, and he respected that.

Yet he could feel the tug of curiosity that wanted more. That wanted to know what "personal" reasons made her leave Houston and why she didn't want to talk about them.

But of course those reasons were none of his business.

So all he did was nod his head as if they'd sealed a deal. "Understood. Better get that shandy you wanted, then."

Chapter 6

THE NEXT DAY IZZY STOOD IN THE BIG, EMPTY, DUSTY shop space next to Bill Preston's general store and squinted at the cobwebs up in the high raftered ceiling. Those would be easy enough to get rid of, but the rest…

"It's wonderful." Beth ran her fingers across the dusty exposed stone of the walls and looked around the rest of the large space. "Absolutely perfect."

"It needs heavy-duty cleaning." Indigo paused beside one of the windows that faced the road and tried to wipe some of the dust off, pulling a face as she did so. "And perfect it is not."

"Definitely has potential though," Izzy said, taking the middle ground.

But it really did. The stone building was old and had wonderful character. While the space was big and echoing with that ceiling, it had lots of windows that let in light, giving it an airy feel.

Izzy could see the scuffed, dusty wooden floor all sanded and varnished and gleaming like melted honey, the exposed stone walls dust free. Shelves could be fixed on the walls, and some cabinets. Or even some antique furniture brought in to be used as display cases. A hutch dresser maybe, displaying linens or pottery…

A thread of excitement wound through her.

This would make a wonderful gallery space. Beth and Indigo had already thought about selling jewelry and yarn, but why not think bigger? Why not use this wonderful space to display all kinds of things? Jewelry, yarn, pottery, crafts... Maybe there were people who made honey around here, and soaps, and...hadn't there been a painter at the barbecue last night? Perhaps he might like to display his paintings.

It wasn't the kind of high-powered-executive thing she'd been doing in Houston, and her father would have curled his lip at what he would have termed "the smallness of her vision," but Izzy didn't care.

This was a business that could contribute to a community, a business dealing in pretty things and little luxuries, souvenirs for eager tourists...things that made people happy.

The oil business had been far too exploitative for her liking, too much about the money. But this? This was about people and she so wanted to be a part of it.

"Hey, listen," Izzy began excitedly. "I've got a great idea."

The others looked at her, but then the door opened and Chase strode in, a manila folder in one hand and a mug full of some steaming brew in the other.

He was dressed in his usual uniform of jeans and his black Pure Adventure NZ T-shirt, and the expression on his handsome face was irritated; he'd been meant to meet them here ten minutes earlier but had clearly been delayed.

Something inside Izzy fluttered, reminding her of Chase last night, standing on the bank by the lakeshore, his gunmetal-gray eyes gone silvery with conviction as he told her about his purpose to protect the land and keep it safe for future generations.

The strength of his belief hadn't surprised her. He was clearly a man of deeply felt, strongly held passions, and looking at him had made her realize just how empty her father's emphasis on making money and Josh's on success really were.

Oh, she'd been uncomfortable with it for a while now—basically after Zeke had left and she'd come into contact with the Deep River community—but it hadn't been until Josh had left her standing there at the gala that she'd truly understood.

Her father and Josh only thought about themselves. But Chase didn't. He was all about his daughter, and the land he protected and the people of his town.

He reminded her of Zeke in a lot of ways, because her brother too loved the land with a single-minded fervor and wanted nothing more than to protect it.

Chase wants to protect this place, his community, and his daughter, and what have you been doing? Running away and hiding.

That had not been a comfortable thought because while she might have run away, she wasn't hiding. This was all about a fresh start in a new place.

Still, it had made her realize that she'd been thinking quite selfishly, about what *she* wanted for herself rather than what was right for the community.

So of course she'd had to give him back her own vow that she'd stay for three months, that she'd commit to this business. And the moment she'd promised him she would, she'd felt the ghost of a conviction she hadn't even realized she'd lost shift inside her.

The same sense of purpose she'd once had when she'd helped Deep River resist her father's efforts to get their oil reserves.

A sense of purpose that, somehow, one bossy, supremely

irritating man's quiet intensity about his own town had given right back to her.

"I had an idea on a direction," Izzy said before Chase could open his mouth. "For this store, I mean."

Indigo turned from the window, frowning. "What do you mean, 'I'? 'We' also matters."

Chase had paused in the middle of the room, giving her one of those assessing looks. It made her feel self-conscious, mainly because she'd gotten mud on her jeans the night before and Cait had washed them for her. But they weren't dry, so she'd had to wear the only other clothes she'd brought with her—a pencil skirt and blouse combo, which probably looked bizarre given their location.

But all he said was, "Right. Let's hear it, then."

"An art gallery." Izzy folded her arms. "Or craft gallery, whatever you'd prefer. Beth can display her jewelry. Indigo, you can have your yarn for sale or whatever other fiber stuff you want. We could get the community involved to sell other things too, like honey, natural skincare, pottery—"

"An art gallery?" Chase interrupted, his tone suspiciously neutral. "Are you serious?"

"Of course I'm serious." Izzy met his gaze. "You wanted to showcase the scenery, or at least that's what you told me was important last night. But how about we also showcase the people here too?"

"Oh, well, I *love* that idea," Beth said, enthusiastic as ever. She looked over at Indigo. "You could sell yarn and hand-knitted pieces. Hey, I could even make some nice accessories for you! Stitch markers and buttons and stuff."

Indigo's frown became one of contemplation. "Hmm. Actually, that doesn't sound like a half-bad idea."

"What about that artist guy I met last night?" Beth glanced at Izzy. "We could ask him—"

"No," said Chase curtly. "You won't get Evan on board. We tried something similar in the past and he steadfastly refused."

Beth shrugged. "If he doesn't want to, that's fine. No skin off our nose."

"Except that the tourists coming here are here for the scenery, not souvenirs." There was a sharp edge to Chase's voice, his expression set in hard lines.

What was his problem with an art gallery? Because it was clear he didn't like the idea.

A deafening rumble sounded from outside along with the squeal of air brakes.

Beth joined Indigo near the window and Izzy went over too, curious.

Outside in the parking area by the lake opposite the Rose were several giant tour buses. The doors opened and a stream of people exited, milling around in the middle of the road and wandering down toward the lakeshore.

The excitement inside Izzy gathered tighter. Because while many of them were heading toward Pure Adventure NZ HQ, others were simply standing, looking around— others who weren't dressed in outdoor gear. Others wearing expensive items of clothing and carrying expensive purses and bags.

Others with money to spend and nowhere to spend it.

"Wow, that's a whole lot of people," she said.

Chase came to stand beside her, looking out the window with the rest of them. "Yes. It's an initiative I've been trying to get off the ground for the past couple of years. Finally got a couple of tour companies on board and they've been coming twice a week this summer."

"So what do they do here?"

"Most of them come into HQ. We hire out kayaks, guide them on nature walks. Take them up the Bright River in the boat. Heli-tours. A fair few also do horse riding up at Clint's."

"What about the others who don't want to do anything too adventurous?"

"They go and sit in the Rose."

"What? And that's it?"

Chase looked irritated. "Yes, that's it. And it's also why you lot are here. To give them something else to do that isn't sitting in the Rose."

"Well then," Izzy said, "I don't know why you wouldn't want an art gallery or at least some kind of craft shop. Look at all those expensive clothes and the labels on the purses those women are carrying. Those people have money and I bet they'd love to spend it on something nice."

"Now *that* is true," Beth replied. "Deep River is a stop for cruise ships and we've got a couple of markets up and running to cater to the tourists. They *love* browsing and they *spend*."

Izzy glanced up at Chase standing beside her. His features were hard, his mouth set in a grim line as he looked out at the milling tourists. Yes, it was *very* clear he did not like the sound of an art gallery one bit.

The scent of coffee hit Izzy's nostrils, coming from the mug Chase had in his hand, making her abruptly aware that she hadn't had a coffee this morning and was in desperate need of one.

"A coffee cart," she muttered. "That's what this place needs."

He looked down at her all of a sudden, his gaze catching hers, and once more she felt that odd jolt, like the one last night at the barbecue. It was starting to get very annoying.

"This is for you." Unexpectedly, he held out the mug. "I thought you might need one."

Izzy stared at him in surprise, that feeling in her stomach fluttering harder.

"Wow," Beth murmured. "Two coffees in a row, this is getting serious."

Izzy blushed, but Chase just glanced at Beth. "Tell me how you like yours and I'll make you one too."

"Aw, that's sweet of you, but I'm not a coffee drinker," Beth replied, then added meaningfully, "unlike Izzy."

Great. This was the last thing she needed, Beth glancing at her and Chase and making pointed comments.

"I don't want one either," Indigo said, still squinting at the crowd through the window. "In case you were going to offer."

Izzy decided that this was getting out of hand. "You're late, you know," she pointed out, meeting Chase's gaze. "By ten minutes."

He continued to hold out the coffee mug. "Are you sure, Indigo?" He kept his attention on Izzy. "Looks like I'll have one going spare."

The challenge in his voice was loud and clear.

"Using drinks against me is getting old," she said levelly. "I suggest escalating, using chocolate."

He lifted one powerful shoulder. "Guess I'll have to drink it myself then."

"Oh for God's sake," Izzy muttered. "Give it to me."

"Too late." Chase lifted the mug and took a slow sip,

watching her, a definite silver flicker in his eyes. "If you don't take it, you lose it."

"You know," Beth announced, "I might go outside and talk to some of those people. Coming, Indigo?"

Indigo turned from her view out the window. "What? What do you mean—" But Beth had already grabbed her by the arm, dragging her out of the store and the door slamming shut behind them.

Izzy gritted her teeth. No prizes for guessing why Beth had left so suddenly. She must have thought Izzy and Chase needed to be alone, which was the last thing Izzy wanted.

"You should have just taken the coffee," Chase murmured.

She glared at him. "And you should have been a bit nicer about the art gallery."

"I didn't say a word."

"But that expression on your face sure did. What have you got against the gallery idea anyway? You must have known what businesses Beth and Indigo are interested in starting up before we got here, so an art-orientated space surely must have occurred to you."

His gaze narrowed. "Do I look like the type of guy an 'art-orientated space' would occur to?"

No, he didn't. He looked big, tough, and rugged. Like he wrestled lions in his spare time rather than wandering around art galleries sipping delicately at glasses of white wine.

"Then what did occur to you?" Izzy demanded. "Bait and tackle? Outdoor gear? A bookshop? What?"

He scowled. "Something useful. Something that would educate people on the importance of the environment. Something that would—"

"Art can do that, you know," Izzy interrupted, on a roll

now. "Everything we sell could be made out of or be reflections of the scenery here. Something of this place that people could take home with them and remember, that aren't just pictures on their phones they never look at. It could be a favorite pair of earrings or a sweater made here or a painting they can hang on the wall. And if you charge appropriately, then the money that will flow back into the community could be valuable for financing other environmental projects."

He said nothing, but a muscle flicked in his jaw.

"What exactly is the problem?" Izzy went on. "You told me last night how important the success of this venture with Deep River is to you and the town, so why are you getting annoyed about something I suspect you actually agree with? Is it me? Because I meant what I said—"

"It's not you." He let out a short, frustrated-sounding breath, then thrust the mug at her again. "Would you take the damn coffee?"

"I thought it was too late?"

Chase glowered. "I don't like lattes."

Unwilling amusement tugged at her. She wasn't sure why, but she was starting to find his irritated glower rather endearing.

"Guess I better take it then." She reached for the mug only for her hand to jerk slightly as their fingers brushed and a small bolt of electricity leapt between them.

A spark glittered in his eyes, and for a second the ever-present tension that seemed to ebb and flow around them whenever they met pulled tight yet again.

She gripped the mug and looked away, taking a hurried sip and mentally telling her own ridiculous heartbeat to slow down and stop acting stupid in his presence. And why it was doing so was anyone's guess.

No mystery. You're attracted to him.

She was not. She perhaps liked challenging him far too much for her own good, and maybe respected what he was trying to do here, but attracted to him? As if.

And as for that little bolt of electricity? Static. That's all.

She took another sip, calming herself, then glanced at him. "So if I'm not the problem, then what is?"

———————

That was a very good question Chase didn't have the answer to. Or at least not an answer that would satisfy her.

Because he'd lied when he'd told her that she wasn't the problem.

She was absolutely the problem and he'd known it the minute he'd walked in.

For some reason she wasn't in the jeans and T-shirt she'd been wearing for the past couple of days, but a form-fitting knee-length skirt in sky blue and a filmy white blouse with a little bow at the throat.

She looked like she should be going to work in some city office, not inspecting a dusty, dirty, abandoned stone building. What the hell did she think she was doing, strutting around dressed like that? She was ridiculous.

Sadly though, although his brain insisted she was ridiculous, other parts of him very much liked the way the skirt hugged her hips and the soft-looking curves of her ass. And that little bow at her throat, the way the ties kind of hung down just begging to be tugged…

Damn, that annoyed him. He'd been late meeting them due to some booking snafu, and then to come in and see her wearing *that* and recognizing that the attraction he'd been hoping would disappear hadn't? It had gotten even worse when she'd started talking about her idea to turn this into some kind of art gallery, and her eyes had started to glow with excitement, her cheeks getting pink. She'd looked as beautiful as she had the previous night, promising him that she was committed to making this work, nothing but steely determination in her expression.

He didn't want to find her beautiful or be attracted to her in any way, so like a petulant little boy, he'd taken his irritation out on her idea instead.

Yeah, real good move that was, dick.

Teasing her about the coffee had also been a stupid move. Especially when he knew damn well that it hadn't been so much teasing as it had been flirting.

"Your art gallery idea is fine," he said, still staring out the window. "I've just got a lot on my plate at the moment."

"Oh?" She sounded curious. "I guess it's not easy running a business and…apparently the entire town, as well as being a dad."

"I'm not running the entire town." He tried not to sound grumpy about the assumption. "This place is a democracy, not a dictatorship. I'm not—"

"I know," she interrupted quietly, coming to stand beside him. "Sorry, I didn't mean it like that. I just meant that it can't be easy being a dad while you're doing all these other things too."

She was standing very close and he caught her scent, something unexpectedly sweet, like honeysuckle. It surprised him, since he'd expected something more sophisticated and cool.

Unfortunately, he also liked it very much.

If he pulled that bow on her blouse and bent to nuzzle at her throat—

Bloody hell. He needed to stop thinking about her. Now.

"Yeah, it's not easy." His voice was rougher than it should have been.

"What about Gus's mother?" Isabella asked. "Is she around—"

"No, she's not around." This time it was his turn to interrupt. He didn't want to talk about Olivia right now and quite frankly, standing here and continuing to talk to Isabella with that sweet scent of hers clouding his senses wasn't a great idea. Especially given that he hadn't been lying when he'd said he had a lot on his plate. He did. And he couldn't afford to stand around, getting distracted by one pretty American.

"So we need to go through some logistics." He pushed himself away from the window frame and turned to face her. "We have a lot to sort through, so we may as well get started."

The sun shone through the dusty pane of the window, illuminating her face as she looked back at him. She really did have the loveliest skin, smooth and pale and silky. A stark contrast to her black hair and dark eyes and the thick sable of her lashes. He could see the pulse at the base of her throat, beneath that white bow, beating faster and faster.

Was that him? Was he making her heartbeat quicken?

"Why are you wearing that?" he heard himself ask, even though he hadn't meant to.

She blinked. "Wearing what?"

"That blouse and that…skirt." It sounded accusing and he hadn't meant that either.

"Oh, uh…" She looked down at herself, and the way

the sunlight was shining abruptly made him aware that her blouse was a lot more see-through than he'd thought. In fact, he could see the bra she wore underneath, something white and lacy and...

Shit.

He needed not to be looking.

"I didn't bring a lot of clothes with me," she was saying. "I know, you were right, I didn't come prepared. I only brought a couple of changes of clothing with me and I got some mud on my jeans last night. Cait washed them for me, but yeah...I brought some skirts and some blouses and..." She ran her hands over the soft blue material of her skirt, obviously smoothing it and yet only drawing attention to the shape of her thighs beneath it. "I probably need to go somewhere to get some more clothes because wearing this is a little ridiculous, but..." She shrugged. "It was either that or nothing. And I couldn't wear nothing. So I had to find something else and..."

He didn't catch the rest, the sudden and startling image of Isabella Montgomery wearing nothing imprinting itself without warning in his brain.

It was not an image that should be there. At all.

"Here," he said gruffly and thrust the manila folder at her. "I've drawn up a plan and given you a list of materials. Go through it and see what you think. We'll meet up later." He turned for the door. "I have to go back to HQ."

"Wait," she said.

But he was already at the door.

"What about your mug?" she called after him.

"Leave it at the front desk."

He stepped out of the store and strode back through the milling crowd.

Clearly he was going to have to get a handle on this inconvenient attraction somehow, especially as he was going to be helping get this new business venture off the ground. He couldn't be spending that time admiring the shape of her ass in her jeans or the glow in her pretty eyes. He couldn't be standing around feeling the tension grow between them and wanting to push it harder, make it more intense so that one of them would break. Her, perhaps. She would step forward, put her hands on his chest, and then—

Goddammit. This really needed to stop.

Stepping into HQ, he found there was already a queue of people waiting.

It was a nice little space, with a counter made from a good solid hunk of macrocarpa. On the walls were various photographs of the scenery around Brightwater: the snowcapped Southern Alps, the bush, a pretty alpine valley, Brightwater Lake in all its brilliant blue glory. The majesty of Glitter Falls. There was also a big whiteboard with the most recent weather report, plus any tips, tricks, and recommendations that occurred to them. Racks of pamphlets advertising Pure Adventure's facilities and services stood near the counter, along with a small selection of outdoor gear that people could buy.

Okay, so yes, he'd been disappointed that the Deep River ladies hadn't thought that stocking more outdoor clothing and equipment might be a good move. He didn't have the room for a lot of stock, and while Bill had a few extra things in the general store, he'd been hoping that the three women might want to stock a few more brands and products than he was able to.

But no. It was to be an "art-orientated space."

Which was fine. He got Isabella's explanation about why jewelry and stuff was a good idea, and hell, when it came down to it, he agreed. Still, though, some people came here badly prepared, and it would be nice to offer them something more than any parka they had in stock and a bottle of sunscreen.

Finn was behind the counter doing customer service, Levi was no doubt off getting kayaks ready since he was down to do that, so Chase joined his brother, helping out with questions and taking bookings. It was shaping up to be a busy day—actually a busy week, since it was high summer— which made him happy. He'd never had the slightest doubt about the success of Pure Adventure NZ, though there had been some naysayers in the town when he'd floated the idea, but it was always nice to have proof that confidence hadn't been misplaced.

Half an hour later, the rush had subsided.

Chase and Finn went out to help Levi get the kayaks out, since a lot of the tour bus people were interested and it really was a beautiful day to be out on the water. Finn would take a few more people up to Clint's stables later for some horse riding, and Chase had a small crowd who wanted to go on the nature walk up to Glitter Falls.

Finn finished helping one tourist into one of the kayaks— the man was wearing jeans, Chase noted with disapproval, which was hardly good clothing for kayaking—and then came up the little beach to where Chase was standing.

"What's up?" Finn asked. "You've been in a foul mood all morning."

"Nothing," Chase said flatly. "Will Levi be okay to keep an eye on Gus when she finishes school?"

"Yes and bullshit it's nothing." His brother gave him an assessing look. "I know. It's that pretty Texan, isn't it?"

"Piss off," Chase said grumpily.

Finn gave him one of his rare grins. "What's the big deal? I'm pretty sure she likes you, if that's the issue."

"I'm not talking about this with you, asshole."

"Why not? You never have that problem when you're the one bringing up subjects people don't want to discuss."

Chase didn't dignify that with an answer, mainly because it was true.

"Would you like me to pass her a note?" Finn went on, apparently not caring one bit about Chase's temper. "Tell her that my big brother thinks she's pretty?"

"You do know that I have no problems whatsoever with punching you in the face?"

"Come on, you're an adult and so is she. She's hot. She likes you—"

"She does not."

"Oh, not that kind of like. The other kind of like. The *I hate you but I want to rip your clothes off* kind of like."

Chase wondered what people would do if he turned around and strangled his brother right there on the bank. "Stop talking, Finn."

"Seriously, though."

Finn was like a terrier with a favorite toy—he would *not* let anything go. Probably why he was still grieving his wife five years on, and Chase tended to let things slide with him, but enough was enough.

"Because, asshole, sleeping where you eat is always a bad move."

"Technically," Levi said, coming up behind them, "you

wouldn't actually be sleeping. And surely you'd wipe down the table after—"

"Haven't you got people to supervise?" Chase snapped, rounding on him.

Levi grinned, unrepentant. "They're all in their kayaks and having fun, and I can supervise from here. So…no."

Winding people up, particularly Chase, was Levi's favorite thing to do. Because apparently Chase made it "so easy." He'd been like that in the forces too, and Levi got away with it because there wasn't a better pilot or tour guide, excluding Chase and Finn, in the entire country.

Plus when he wasn't being inappropriate with women in HQ or winding people up, he was an excellent guy to have around, especially in a crisis.

Still, in this moment, Chase could cheerfully have strangled him too.

"We were just discussing a certain pretty Texan," Finn said helpfully. "And Chase being a grumpy asshole whenever she's around."

"Ah." Levi nodded sagely. "My advice—"

"Which I did not ask for."

"My advice," Levi continued, as if Chase hadn't interrupted, "would be to get in there, mate. Before someone else does."

Chase growled, his bad temper returning full force. "If you—"

"Hey, I didn't say me." Levi held up a calming hand. "I mean, far be it from me to poach on another man's turf. But if the lady in question only has eyes—"

"I will kill you. Slowly."

"Go and help that woman, Levi," Finn said in a long-suffering tone. "And leave my poor brother alone."

"Okay, okay. I'm going." Levi strode off, a grin still plastered across his face, making Chase's fingers itch with the urge to slap it right off him.

There was a moment's silence.

Then Finn said, "Basically, the way I see it, you've got two choices."

"Don't you start," Chase growled. "Because I swear to God—"

"You either do something about the attraction or you ignore it. And if you ignore it, you have to find some way of dealing with your temper that doesn't involve pacing around and biting people's heads off."

Chase opened his mouth to tell his brother that was terrible advice, then closed it again. Because it was actually pretty good advice he should be taking.

Because yes, the choice was simple.

He either acted on the attraction between him and Isabella or he ignored it and handled himself. And since acting on the attraction brought too many complications, that left handling himself.

Luckily, he knew a good way of doing just that.

"Fine," he said, trying not to sound grumpy as hell and mostly succeeding. "Looks like I'll be taking a lot more expeditions."

Finn glanced at him, his expression unreadable. "So distance is your answer, then?"

He scowled. "You got a better idea?"

"I do, but you don't want to hear it."

"No, I don't. Because it's not going to happen." Chase held his brother's gaze. "She's only just arrived, she's got a business to start up, a way of life to get used to, and if this is going to work, if they're going to stay, then getting involved with her and potentially screwing all that up is the last thing I want to do, understand?"

"Oh yeah, I understand," Finn said. "But you're both adults. You could probably work something out."

You could. And all those other things…well, they're starting to sound a little like excuses, don't you think?

No, he did not. One thing was for sure, though: he was tired of thinking about it. The whole situation was taking up far too much of his headspace when he had more important things to worry about. Such as the logistics of getting these businesses up and running, what to do about promoting them, where the ladies were eventually going to live…and, of course, Gus.

She still wouldn't tell him what her problem was, maybe for the first time ever. It was…concerning.

"Why are you so up in my face about it?" Chase asked, making an attempt to sound like he wasn't annoyed. "What do you care?"

"I don't care. But you're a grumpy bastard and a pain in the butt when you don't get laid, and I'm just trying to make sure everyone stays happy."

He's not wrong. You are *a grumpy bastard.*

That was true. And it wasn't fair to the others to take his own bad temper out on them.

"I hear you," he said after a moment or two. "I'll deal with it."

And he would. Because he was *not* going to let one small American get the better of him, no matter how pretty she was.

Chapter 7

THE CLOTHES SITUATION WAS IN DIRE NEED OF ADDRESS-
ing, Izzy decided a couple of days later, as she scrabbled
around trying to find a clean pair of underwear.

For the past two days, she'd had to wash her panties in
the sink and dry them on a makeshift line she'd rigged up
in the bathroom and that was getting old. As was having to
wear one of her skirts and blouses whenever her jeans and
T-shirts were in the wash.

Plus she'd taken to wearing the lone pair of pumps she'd
brought with her instead of her hiking boots, since the blister situation was also in dire need of addressing.

The night before, as they'd pored over the list of materials Chase had given them, adding their own and discussing
what other things needed to be done, the three of them had
decided that a trip to Queenstown was necessary.

The rental car had to be returned anyway, and while Beth
and Indigo were curious to see more of the country they'd
make their home in for the next three months, Izzy was just
downright desperate for some civilization.

More investigation into the state of their internet recep-
tion revealed that if you drove up to a certain point in
Kelly's Canyon, you'd get a signal, and that Pure Adventure
HQ had a satellite phone that could also provide a signal,
but since that was hugely expensive, it was only for
emergencies.

Wanting to check her email, her social media, plus

reading her favorite news websites probably didn't constitute an emergency, Izzy guessed.

And it wasn't just decent service she needed, but adapters for her hair appliances as well as a whole lot of practical details for the businesses that needed to be taken care of.

Levi had offered to chopper them back over the ranges after his usual drop-off of sightseers, which was great of him, but Izzy wasn't looking forward to driving back up the canyon again. The alternative was the route the tour buses took that wound up through the valley, but since that added another couple of hours onto an already long drive, she wasn't happy about that either.

Not much she could do about that though. The car had to be returned somehow.

Izzy picked up her jeans, gave them a sniff, pulled a face, then put them back down. No. She wasn't going to be wearing them. Or any of the T-shirts, since one had a coffee stain on it from when Indigo had bumped her arm the day before and the other two were on the clothesline behind the Rose and still not dry.

Sadly, pencil skirt, blouse, and pumps it was to be.

She got dressed, idly wondering if she'd see Gus again today. For the past couple of days, Izzy had noticed the girl hanging around the Rose after school, or wherever she, Beth, and Indigo happened to be. She never said anything, mostly looking like she was deep in the book she was reading, but Izzy knew the kid wasn't actually reading. She was watching them instead.

Izzy wasn't sure why, whether it was because the three of them were new and thus interesting or if there was more to it than that. She wondered if the next time she saw the girl she should say something, though what, she had no idea. She didn't have any experience with kids.

The other two were in the dining room when she went downstairs, and it was a measure of how excited they were about the trip to town that they only made a few cursory teasing comments about Izzy's outfit.

Cait gave them a few recommendations for stores to visit, frowning a little when Izzy told her that no, they weren't taking anyone else with them, and yes, it would be fine. They were grown women. They could figure out some stuff on their own.

She didn't argue though, which should have made Izzy suspicious, especially when the three of them trooped outside to the car to find the entire complement of Pure Adventure NZ standing by their rental.

The guys were all in jeans and the company T-shirt, and it was really too bad they were all extremely annoying, given how good-looking they were. Or maybe it was only Izzy who found them annoying, since Beth grinned and gave them a cheerful wave. "Hey, guys. What's up?"

"Great," Indigo muttered.

Okay, good to know it wasn't just her.

She hadn't seen Chase for a couple of days. After his abrupt departure from the empty store, he seemed to have dropped off the radar completely. Not that she'd noticed or even wanted to know what was going on with him, nope, not at all. Beth, who'd decided the extremely reserved Finn was her latest friend challenge, had mentioned something about Chase doing extra guiding on some of the trails, but Izzy certainly hadn't taken that information on board.

And she definitely didn't feel that little electric shock when his gray gaze met hers.

His handsome features had begun to twist into a fierce scowl, as if he'd felt that shock too and was just as annoyed by it as she was, and then they abruptly smoothed out again.

"We heard you're going into Queenstown today," Chase said, his voice so neutral that Izzy was instantly suspicious.

"We are." She wobbled slightly on the uneven gravel as her heel caught in a small hole.

Chase moved so quickly she barely had time to take it in. One minute he was standing in front of the car with his arms crossed, looking forbidding, the next one large, warm hand was beneath her elbow, steadying her.

He was very strong, she could feel that right away, his grip gentle yet firm, supporting her, and she had the strangest feeling that if a hurricane hit them or the entire world turned upside down, she could hold on to him and everything would be okay. He was like a mountain, rock-solid, unwavering.

Instinctively, she looked up at him and her breath caught. His eyes darkened, something wordless hanging in the air between them, an understanding maybe, or an acknowledgment.

Then Levi coughed ostentatiously into his hand, and Chase's grip shifted and heat rushed into her cheeks.

"Thanks," she muttered ungraciously, feeling ridiculous as she pulled her arm out of his grip. "But that wasn't necessary. Believe it or not I know how to walk in heels."

There was an odd expression on his face. "You need new shoes. As in yesterday."

"Are you done?" Finn was staring pointedly at his brother. "Because we have things to do."

The odd expression shifted into a scowl, while Beth

raised her eyebrows meaningfully at Izzy, which Izzy pretended not to see.

"Yes," Levi said, looking far too amused for Izzy's liking. "Many, many things. Things such as giving you ladies a ride into Queenstown."

Izzy smoothed her skirt down even though it didn't need smoothing, the movement helping settle the stupid fluttering feeling in her stomach. "We don't need a ride, thank you. We have to take the rental car back anyway, so we're going to drive."

There was a silence as the three men all looked at each other.

"No," Chase said in an uncompromising tone. "You will not."

Izzy stared at him. "What do you mean 'no, you will not'? We need to get that—"

"I'll drive it back. That canyon is a killer if you don't know the road, and it took you hours to just drive down. Going back up is worse, especially when you're not used to driving on the other side of the road."

She bristled, his imperious tone rubbing her the wrong way as usual. "If I can drive it down, I can drive it up. There's really no need—"

This time it was Beth's turn to cough loudly. "Can we not have this argument? If there's any way I don't have to sit in a car for four hours, then by all means, I'm happy not to have to drive."

"Me too," Indigo said. "I hate that canyon."

"No worries," Levi said smoothly. "I'll fly you all there."

"Oh yes!" Beth clapped her hands together. "Now that's a great idea. I'd love to see the landscape from the air."

Indigo frowned. "I don't like helicopters."

Levi, who'd been leaning against the car, pushed himself away from it and winked at her. "You'll like mine."

"Good plan," Chase said, ignoring both Levi's comment and Indigo's disgusted look. "Why don't you guys get prepared and take these three over to—"

"I said I'll drive and I meant it." Izzy folded her arms and looked Chase in the eye.

You are being stubborn and ridiculous.

Oh, she was fully aware. But she could still feel the warmth of his palm against her skin, could still feel his strength. And worse, could feel the traitorous urge to lean into that strength, let it hold her up, support her.

She couldn't remember feeling that with Josh. He was so fixated on his own success that he'd never had anything left to give her. She'd told herself for a long time that was a good thing, that she was strong enough on her own and she didn't need him to support her. Yet he certainly expected her to provide it when he needed it.

He admired your strength, but only because it meant he never had to give you any of his.

She didn't like how that thought made her feel stupid, as if she'd been blind to his glaringly obvious faults, so she ignored it.

"No." Chase stared back at her. "I'll take the car. You go in the chopper with the others. You'll be there in twenty minutes."

Izzy opened her mouth to disagree, but then Beth began tugging at her arm. "That's a great idea, come on. Do you really want to be in the car for four hours?"

"Yeah." Levi was grinning. "Or are you arguing just

because Chase is being a tool? Because if so, I get it. He *is* being a tool."

"Well," Izzy said. "Now that you mention it—"

"Come with me, then." Chase's voice was low, a sudden intense note in it that stopped Izzy in her tracks.

She blinked. "What?"

"Come with me." A challenge glinted in his eyes. "I'll drive up the canyon, but you can drive the rest of the way."

Finn glanced at his brother. "Um, bro," he began.

"Let's leave these two to sort it out themselves," Levi said firmly, then took a couple of steps toward Indigo. He shoved his hands in his pockets and nodded his head in the direction of HQ, that slow-burning, charming smile curving his mouth. "Wanna come see my helicopter?"

Indigo went bright red, then scowled ferociously. "I told you, I don't like helicopters."

"*I* would like to see your helicopter," Beth said, grabbing Indigo's arm and pulling her toward HQ. "And Indigo's lying, she loves a helicopter."

Levi laughed, Indigo muttering as the three of them walked off.

Finn gave his brother a look, which Chase did not return, then he shrugged and followed in the others' wake.

"Do you like helicopters?" Chase asked mildly. "I won't stop you if you want to go too."

Izzy could have cheerfully strangled him and Beth and Indigo for leaving her in this position, but there was no help for it. Either she went along on the helicopter trip, or she stuck to her guns and subjected herself to a long car journey with Chase.

You want to go in the car. You know you do.

No. No, she didn't. Except…

That challenge glinted in Chase's gaze and no matter how much that annoyed her, she knew she couldn't resist. And she suspected he knew it too.

"Why do you want me to come?" She folded her arms over her heartbeat in an effort to slow it. "You don't need me there."

He lifted one powerful shoulder, the glint in his eyes changing into something warmer, something that looked suspiciously like amusement.

Which was not a good thing. Because if he was hot when he was grumpy, he was even hotter when he was amused, and that was very, *very* bad for her peace of mind.

"No, I don't," he said. "But perhaps I wanted the simple pleasure of your company."

Oh dear. He could be a serious problem.

As if he wasn't a serious problem already.

Izzy swallowed, her mouth dry. Well, he'd only be a problem if she let him be one. So what if the prospect of a couple of hours in his company didn't actually annoy her as much as she made out? So what if she actually kind of wanted to? It didn't mean anything.

Anyway, continuing to argue with him about it just because she was uncomfortable with her own response to him was silly and pointless. Not to mention she was supposed to be getting the locals on her side, not alienating them.

And besides, she was a grown woman. She could stand to be in the company of a hot guy without losing her head or making it mean something it shouldn't.

The alternative was the helicopter, and while that was an attractive prospect, it did pale in comparison to spending a couple of hours in Chase Kelly's company.

Still, she didn't want to give in too easily. It wouldn't do for him to get too cocky.

"Okay," she said slowly. "But if I have to compromise on this, then you do too."

He raised a brow. "Hey, I did offer to let you drive from the top of the canyon."

"True. But I feel I need something a bit more, since you were so damn officious about it."

Chase gave a reluctant-sounding laugh and glanced away, putting his hands in his pockets. "Yeah, okay. That's fair. How about this, then." He glanced back at her. "If you have any questions you want answered, then ask away. I'll answer them all. Honestly."

Curiosity kicked inside her. "Any questions?" she clarified.

He nodded. "Any questions."

"Hmm. Tempting. You're assuming, of course, that I'd be interested enough to ask."

"That is true." His eyes gleamed. "You might not be interested."

"No, I might not."

"In which case you'd better go check out the helicopter."

Izzy didn't move. And said nothing.

He smiled all of a sudden, brief and brilliant, dazzling her. "Give me the keys, then, Izzy, and let's hit the road."

———

All Chase's good intentions had gone straight out the window the moment Isabella had come out of the Rose, looking so beautiful in her little skirt and blouse, pretty heels on her feet.

He'd always liked a practical woman, but he had to admit that her particular brand of delicate femininity, wrapped around a backbone of pure steel, did it for him like nobody's business.

And then she'd got her heel stuck in a hole in the gravel and she'd wobbled and...well. He'd darted out to grab her before he'd had a chance to think better about it.

Her dark eyes had widened, looking up into his, her mouth opening slightly in surprise, and he'd felt as if someone had punched him in the stomach.

In that moment, he'd known that she'd felt it too and that all the distance in the world wasn't going to work. There was no fighting this pull between them.

Starting something physical with her was a line he shouldn't cross—he had his daughter to think about, after all, and small-town affairs always brought their own issues—but he didn't see why he couldn't spend time with her. Get to know her without this irritation that seemed to spring up between them whenever they met.

He should probably *not* have agreed to answer all her questions. Then again, he'd wanted to offer her something. And perhaps it was arrogant of him, but he thought she might be interested. He certainly had a few questions of his own and maybe by offering to answer hers, he might be able to get a few answers for himself.

She didn't comment on his use of "Izzy," merely rolling her eyes and going over to the driver's side of the car in preparation for getting in.

He grinned. "Wrong side."

She flushed yet again, muttered a curse, then stalked around to the other side.

"It would help if you didn't take quite so much pleasure in my mistakes," she said, pulling open the car door.

"Where's the fun in that? Your mistakes are the best part."

She said something rude under her breath as she got in, which made him grin even more, because she wasn't quite as cool and calm as she made out and catching little glimpses of what lay underneath was unexpectedly fascinating.

He could see now why Levi liked ruffling people. It was very satisfying.

As he started the car and began to turn the wheel, a familiar furry black shape came loping out from behind HQ. It stopped directly in front of the car and looked at them.

Chase sighed and waited for the dog to move, which it would. Eventually.

"Whose dog is that?" Izzy asked curiously. "I've seen it around a couple of times."

"Yeah, that's Mystery," Chase explained. "As in he's a 'mystery dog', because no one knows who he belongs to and no one knows where he came from. Cait usually feeds him."

She frowned. "Has no one adopted him?"

"Oh, people have tried, believe me." He'd tried himself once, because he didn't like the thought of the dog having no one to take care of him even though Chase was away too often to look after pets. "But Mystery isn't having it. We all figure he'll decide for himself when he's ready about who gets to adopt him."

Mystery grinned at them then sat down in the middle of the road. He gave himself a scratch before abruptly getting up and trotting off toward the lake.

"He's cute," Izzy murmured, watching him go.

"Don't go getting ideas," Chase said, grinning at the

thought of pretty, precise Isabella Montgomery trying to entice the town's dusty, scruffy mystery dog. "Levi's been angling to adopt him for months now and he won't like someone muscling in on his territory."

She only sniffed.

A couple of minutes later they were driving up the road and out of the little town. Izzy seemed tense, one hand clutching her seat belt, the other smoothing out the fabric of her skirt in a reflexive motion.

Interesting. Was she tense because of him? His driving? The prospect of a couple of hours in his company? Or did she just not like the road?

"It's okay," he said, breaking the silence that had fallen, wanting to reassure her. "You can relax. I've driven up Kelly's literally thousands of times. I could do it in my sleep."

"Oh, I'm not worried."

"Right. That's why you're clutching at your seat belt like it's the last life preserver on the *Titanic*."

Instantly she let go of the seat belt. "I am not."

"Sure," he said noncommittally, deciding to let her have that one.

There was another moment's silence, as they maneuvered through the green farmland that surrounded the town.

It was another beautiful summer day, the way it so often was in this part of the country, sunlight falling through the window and glossing Izzy's night-black hair.

Not that he was looking at her hair. He was very definitely looking at the road in front of him.

She cleared her throat. "Is Kelly's Canyon named after your family, then?"

So she'd been paying attention. Enough to remember

his surname and the name of the road. He liked that she was interested enough to ask about it too. She'd given him a promise to stay in Brightwater Valley and he'd believed her, but promising to stay and actually making an effort were two different things, as he well knew, and this display of curiosity in the town's history was a good start.

"Yes." He kept his gaze on the road, very conscious of how she was looking at him and that he liked that too. "Mick Kelly was one of the first people here. Came out for the gold around the turn of the last century and became the town mayor. He knew that if he wanted the town to grow, he was going to need a road link to the rest of the country, and so that's what he did: mobilized some guys to start construction. Took them years. The upper part of the road they had to carve out of the rock with pickaxes, and some areas they had to blast with dynamite."

"Wow, that's some commitment."

She sounded awed, which pleased him.

"Yeah, it was a big project. The family has been in the valley ever since, stuck around after the gold ran out, even when the town died."

"Oh? So what did they do after that?"

Chase was proud of his family's history, of the guts it took to settle in such a hard-scrabble environment. Of the commitment they'd all had in order to stay here, even when the going got tough and most everyone else had left.

But the Kellys hadn't. The Kellys had dragged this town back into the land of the living even when most people had given it up for dead.

All except his father, of course. Despite being a Kelly, the old bastard had never had the Kelly fighting spirit. He'd left

Brightwater for Christchurch years ago and good bloody riddance.

"What did they do?" Pride tinged his voice. "They realized the new gold was in the landscape around them, not what was under the ground, and so they made tourism a thing. Everett Kelly kickstarted it by successfully arguing that Brightwater Valley be a stop on a new scenic train route from Christchurch to Queenstown."

He could feel her interest sharpen and realized, only belatedly, that this perhaps wasn't the best topic of conversation, especially considering where it had the potential to lead.

"A scenic train? What happened to it?"

"They closed it down in the eighties." He tried to think of some other topic he could introduce, but the sheer pride he had in his family wouldn't let him. He *wanted* her to know about how the Kellys had fought to keep Brightwater Valley alive and were still fighting to this day. That they would never give up on this town, not while there was a Kelly still alive to fight for it.

"Oh, ugh. Why did they do that?"

"Too expensive to run, apparently. A pity, because when the train stopped running, so did the town."

Except for his mother. Diana Kelly had kept it going singlehandedly, while his father argued for upping sticks and moving back to the city. She'd been the one to insist they stay though. A Kelly never left the land and they never gave up, and she wasn't going to be the first one to do so.

"So what happened to your family?" Izzy asked, that delicious accent of hers sweetening the words. "What did they do?"

What happened? Your mother died and your father decided that meant he could give up, despite having two young boys to raise.

Chase ignored the thought. "Well, times were tough. A lot of people left for better prospects in the city. My father wanted to, but Mum refused. She took over the general store after the owner left and then helped run the Rose. There weren't many tourists around, but she made sure she catered to the ones that came, and that was enough to keep the town going."

Izzy's attention was on him, sharp and interested. Probably catching more of that pride in his voice. Well, and why not? His mother had been a force of nature who'd kept the town running even when everyone else was telling her to give up. How could he not be proud of that?

"She sounds like an interesting woman," Izzy said.

"She was." He stared hard at the road. "She passed away when I was eight. And my dad... Well, let's just say he did his best."

His dad hadn't done his best. His best was telling eight-year-old Chase to get himself and his brother some dinner because he was going to the pub. It had only gone downhill from there.

Another brief silence fell, her sharp gaze boring into him. It wasn't so pleasant now, so he tried to ignore it.

"I'm sorry about your mother," Izzy said. "Your family sounds like the only thing that keeps the town from going under. But you didn't stay, did you?"

Ah, crap. This was the bullshit he didn't want to get into. The personal stuff that went along with his upbringing—or rather his lack of upbringing. He'd brought himself and his brother up, and yeah, it had sucked. He was in no hurry to go into detail about that or why he'd left either.

Then again he'd promised her answers, and he was a man who kept his promises.

"Well," he said, "here's the deal. I love this place. I love the landscape—the bush, the mountains, the lake, the river, all of it. It's a special place and the people here are special too, and at the end of the day, I'm a Kelly. I can't let it die. It's true that I left. Spent a few years in the army. But sometimes you have to leave a place in order to figure out for certain that's where you belong."

She didn't say anything, the rumble of the engine now joined by the sound of tires crunching on gravel as they left the paved part of the road behind.

He glanced at her.

She was looking out the front windshield, an expression on her face that was almost...lost. And all of a sudden, he was very aware that there were things about her he didn't know. That she'd mentioned some "personal" things she'd left behind in Houston and that she didn't want to talk about them.

Which only made him more curious. What kind of personal things was she talking about? Was it a boyfriend? Something to do with her brother? Had someone hurt her? Was it a friend she was upset with? Had the mention of belonging to a place triggered some unhappy memory? Because it was clear that the look on her face wasn't a happy one.

"You don't agree?" he asked, keeping the question casual.

She blinked, then looked down at her lap. "I'm not sure. I've never left home before, so I can't really comment."

"Never?"

"No. I've visited my brother in Deep River, obviously, and traveled around the States, but I've never lived anywhere other than Houston."

"Except for now."

She nodded. "I suppose I shouldn't have said that, should I? You'll probably take that as another indication that I'm not suited to being here and that you don't approve of our businesses—"

"Hey," he interrupted gruffly. "You know I didn't mean what I said about the business. I apologized for that."

She let out a breath. "True. You did."

"And you gave me a promise to stay. I believe you'll keep that promise." Why he felt the need to reassure her, he had no idea. Probably something to do with that lost expression. "With no judgments or assumptions, okay?"

This time he thought he saw amusement flicker over her delicate features. "Is that even possible?"

"Believe it or not, I'm not usually this difficult. Sometimes, yes, but most of the time, no."

"Why? Is having a bunch of Americans here that irritating?"

"No," he said without thinking. "Just you."

"Oh? So *I'm* irritating now?"

Shit. Why had he said that?

He glanced over at her again, but she didn't look offended, a hint of laughter clear in her dark eyes.

God, she was so damn pretty.

Look at the road, fool.

Gritting his teeth, he jerked his gaze back out the front windshield. "I didn't mean it like that."

"You say a lot of things you don't mean, don't you?" The amusement warmed her voice, making melted honey of her accent. "What's up with that?"

And just like that, he was sick of pussyfooting around the issue. Sick of pretending that he wasn't affected by the attraction between them. Besides, it wasn't fair to be inexplicably grumpy with her when it wasn't *her* who was the problem.

"You really want to know?" He kept his eyes forward. "What's up is one extremely pretty Texan."

A silence fell, her surprise almost palpable.

"Me?" she asked after a moment.

"Do you see any other Texans around here?"

"No, but... Well. Care to be a bit more explicit?"

"Not really," he said with total honesty. "I don't think it would help either of us if I were. Then again, clearing the air mightn't be a bad thing. Especially since getting your business up and running is going to involve me."

"It doesn't have to involve you, you know."

He gave her a glance. "It's my town, therefore it *will* involve me."

Her dark eyes met his. "You really don't like me challenging you, do you?"

"Actually, I love it when you challenge me. And that's part of the problem."

"What problem?"

What was he thinking? This was a stupid conversation to have while he was driving. Then again, no, perhaps it was a *great* conversation to have while he was driving, because then he wouldn't be tempted to push and keep pushing, bringing this attraction between them to its natural conclusion: in bed.

"The problem of me being literally unable to think of anything else but taking you to bed and keeping you there for a very long time. That explicit enough for you?"

Chapter 8

Izzy blinked, staring at the aristocratic, angular lines of Chase's handsome face. His attention was firmly on the road ahead, which she was grateful for since it was a hell of a road.

But…he wanted to take her to bed, he'd said. He literally couldn't think of anything else.

She swallowed and turned her head, looking sightlessly out of the window, her brain still trying to process the admission.

You already knew how he felt.

Well, a deep, female part of her had. The part of her that found him fascinating, that couldn't take her eyes off him whenever he was around. That loved his take-charge attitude purely because it gave her such a thrill to challenge it. Because when he looked at her, he *really* looked at her, and not in a way that Josh ever had.

The part that had shivered when he'd taken hold of her elbow just before, wanting to know what it would feel like if he took hold of the rest of her.

That wanted him to…

But no, that was a bad idea. She'd only just come out of a relationship—one she hadn't ended herself—with one man and she wasn't in any hurry to involve herself in another one.

You don't have to have a relationship. You could just sleep with him…

A wave of heat washed over her and she pressed the

button to put the window down, desperate for some air. Except they were still on a gravel road, which made dust pour in too, not to mention some car noise, so she quickly put the window back up again.

Chase continued to say nothing, staring fixedly ahead.

The silence brought tension, making the car feel far too small. She was very conscious of his physical presence.

She didn't look at him, but she didn't need to. She already had a fine image in her head of him driving with one hand on the steering wheel, long fingers wrapped around it in a firm grip, while the other rested on one powerful thigh, his muscular body relaxed back against the seat.

He was almost unspeakably sexy.

She should say something, since it was very obvious that he wasn't going to. Except she couldn't think of what.

"Oh, I see," she said at last. "I mean—"

"You don't have to say anything." Chase's deep voice was firm. "Because I'm not going to do anything about it. I just thought you should know the exact nature of the problem. And that it's not you, it's me."

She should have felt relieved, but she didn't. No, she felt more like...disappointed. Almost as if she wanted him to do something about it, which surely couldn't be true, not so soon after Josh, whom she'd loved and was going to marry.

Are you sure you loved him? *Or did you love the fact that marrying him would please your parents?*

It was an uncomfortable thought. She'd met him at her parents' country club, and when they'd gotten together, her father had been very pleased. His approval was difficult to earn, and Izzy had felt, for the first time in her life, as if she'd done something right.

Except it wasn't right, was it? He was just another mistake you made.

The voice in her head was snide. Izzy determinedly ignored it.

"I... Thank you, I guess?" she said hesitantly. "But... uh...can I ask why you're not going to do anything about it?"

He flicked her a glance, a flash of sudden, brilliant silver that made the breath catch in her throat. "Why? Do you want me to?"

Yes, you so do.

No, she didn't. Casual sex with relative strangers had been something her friends often did, but she'd never seen the attraction. Going to bed with someone you didn't know well had seemed...kind of cold. It had never been a problem anyway, since she'd never really met anyone she'd felt strongly attracted to.

What about Josh?

She'd been attracted to Josh, sure, but...

Not as much as you are to Chase.

Izzy shoved that thought away. "I'm just curious."

They were starting the climb up the canyon, the road narrowing, the first hairpin turn coming up. Chase drove like he knew every dip and hollow and pothole, his handling of the car expert, making her very thankful that she'd let him drive.

"A number of reasons," he said. "You're new here and I don't want to make it difficult by bringing sex into it. Also, Gus is twelve and that's an important age. Casual relationships, I keep away from home, and anything more serious will have to be run by her first."

He'd clearly thought about this, not that it was any surprise. Chase was the kind of man who not only had a plan for every single facet of his life but also had a reason to back it up with.

And Gus was a very good reason.

She liked that he put his daughter first. Not all fathers did that. Her own, for example, had been all about Zeke, even though he and Zeke hadn't gotten along. After Zeke had left for the army, Andrew Montgomery had told her in no uncertain terms that if she wanted anything from him, he expected her to toe the line. And since she hadn't wanted to make things any worse, she had.

Certainly life at home had improved the better behaved she was. Managing her difficult parents was easier if she remained cool, calm, and ready to please. That worked in other aspects of her life as well, and so she'd kept on doing it, always steady, always there to make sure everything ran smoothly...

But it wasn't enough in the end, was it?

Time to stop listening to her stupid head.

Izzy folded her hands in her lap and studied Chase instead. "That makes sense. I suppose this kind of thing is difficult when you have a child to think about as well."

He shrugged. "Not really. I mean, it's worked pretty well so far. But Gus will need some kind of mother figure in her life at some point, and I want to be able to give her that."

That wasn't a surprise either, since it was clear from their discussion that not only was Brightwater Valley important to Chase but so was his family.

It made something in her chest ache unexpectedly, though she wasn't sure why.

"So what happened to Gus's mom?" she asked without thinking.

Chase shifted in the driver's seat, his long, muscular body tensing, the lines of his face hardening. Clearly this was not a subject he wanted to discuss, which she should have remembered, since when she'd asked a few days earlier, he'd been brusque to the point of rude.

"Sorry," Izzy said hurriedly, irritated with herself for introducing a subject that made an already tense situation even more tense. "You don't have to answer if you—"

"Olivia left," he interrupted, his voice hard. "She couldn't hack the isolation here. The valley was too small, the people too unfriendly, the life here too hard. It didn't matter that she had a kid who needed her, she decided she'd had enough and she left. And she never came back."

Izzy heard echoes of fury in his voice loud and clear.

"Do you ever have contact with her?" she asked carefully.

"No." The word was short and sharp, bitten off. "After she first left, I tried to get her to stay in contact with Gus, but she didn't. She sure had a whole lot of excuses as to why not though."

No wonder he was furious. She would be too. Not that she was a mother or anything, or even had any experience with kids, but the idea of simply leaving your daughter...

Her own mother had been too obsessed with her country club friends and her social climbing to pay much attention to Izzy. Or rather, her mother would show her off and be ostentatiously proud of her, but only when it was to her own benefit. Izzy had often thought her mother saw her as more of a social tool than a daughter.

Ugh. So much for not thinking of her parents.

"That sounds awful," she said aloud. "Poor Gus."

Chase shot her a glance, then looked back at the road

again. "Yeah. She's a great kid and she didn't deserve that, especially not from her own mother. So you see why I want to be careful. That kid doesn't need someone else up and leaving on her."

Oh, she could see why. She could see perfectly.

Her heart ached a little more.

"What about you?" She wasn't sure why she was asking this question, but that didn't stop her from asking it. "What do you want?"

"Not that. Not again." An edge crept into his voice. "Don't get me wrong, I'm happy to be a partner to someone, to enjoy their company and keep them well satisfied in bed, but if they want anything more from me than that, then they'll be shit out of luck."

Well, that was...decisive. And an indication that Gus's mother hadn't only hurt Gus, she'd hurt Chase as well.

That bothered her. A lot. Because though he was the kind of man who demanded a lot from people, she also got the feeling that he gave a lot in return. And people who gave a lot could be hurt quite badly, as she well knew.

"I'm sorry," she said impulsively, wanting him to know that she was on his side and that she sympathized. "It sounds like you and Gus had an awful experience."

He gave her another of those brief, glittering looks. "It's okay. It was years ago."

But it wasn't okay—she heard that loud and clear.

"And for future reference," he added, swinging the car hard into the side of the canyon without even batting an eyelid as another car came suddenly around the corner in the opposite direction, "I didn't tell you to warn you off. It's just information."

He might not have intended it as a warning, but it sure sounded like one to her. Which was fine. She didn't need to be warned off, not when what she was in the market for he definitely wasn't selling. Not that she was in the market for anything, but still.

"Well, thanks," she said, deciding that since he'd let her know where he stood, she might as well let him know where she was at. "But when it comes to relationships, I don't do casual."

"Okay."

"And by that I mean I don't sleep with people I don't feel anything for and who don't feel anything for me."

"Got it."

"Good."

Another silence fell.

Izzy resisted the urge to glance at him, dissatisfaction sitting in her gut though she wasn't sure why.

Sure you do. You wanted a bit more of a reaction from him than that.

That was, unfortunately, true.

She gave in to temptation, sliding him a surreptitious glance. His attention was on the road, an unreadable expression on his face, a certain tension to his jaw.

Had the news that she didn't do casual annoyed him? Was he disappointed? If so, good. It wasn't as if he was going to do anything about it anyway, and no, that didn't rankle. At all.

"What?" Chase didn't turn his head.

She flushed at being caught looking. "Nothing."

"We're on the same page, right?"

"Yes, of course."

"Izzy."

The way he said her name shivered down her spine, making goose bumps rise everywhere. "I didn't say you could call me that."

"Too bad." One corner of his beautiful mouth lifted, the hard edge vanishing from his voice, turning it deeper, warmer. "You're annoyed, aren't you?"

Oh, damn, how had he picked up on that?

"No," she lied. "Not at all."

His smile deepened. "Did you want me to take you to bed?"

Heat washed over her, making something quiver deep down inside, and she had to turn away to the window again, even though there was nothing to see but the rocky side of the canyon.

She'd never had any issues talking about sex, but somehow, when it involved Chase, he only had to mention her and bed and she just about went up in flames.

Sure, he was hot, but nothing was going to happen between them and they both had too many good reasons why not.

Still, she didn't like that he could fluster her so easily.

So? Give him a taste of his own medicine.

But what would happen if she did? What would he do? Only one way to find out…

Izzy swallowed. "Maybe I could…be persuaded."

He didn't say anything for a long moment, taking the car around another hairpin turn.

Then he said, "I thought you didn't do casual."

"I don't." She took a breath. "But I could make an exception for you."

Chase gripped the steering wheel, keeping his focus on driving even though every part of him wanted to focus instead on the woman sitting in the passenger seat next to him.

The words vibrated in the air between them, soft and husky and sweet, an admission that gripped him, making him hard and wanting more than he could ever remember wanting in a long time.

Was it her? Or was it simply that he hadn't gotten laid in far too long?

It's her, come on.

Sadly, it was. Their physical chemistry was insane and he found her fascinating, and when she'd gotten adorably flustered by his admission that he wanted her, he hadn't been able to help flirting with her.

It was stupid.

Stupid because, though she might be able to make an exception for him, he couldn't make an exception for her. Not while she lived in Brightwater Valley. And not while Gus lived there too.

Why not? You could scratch the itch in Queenstown. Just once…

Hell, he didn't need that idea in his head. It was far too tempting, not to mention easy. They could get a room in a hotel and—

No. *No.* It wasn't going to happen. Apart from everyone knowing exactly what was going on if he and Izzy decided suddenly to spend the night in Queenstown, there was the issue of the art-gallery thing Izzy was hoping to start.

He could compartmentalize sex very well, thank you very much, but what about her? Could she do that? She said she only slept with people she had feelings for and who felt something for her in return, so possibly not. Which meant it would be very wrong of him to start down that path with her, since she might end up getting hurt and hurting her was the very last thing in the world he wanted to do. It might affect the business she and the others were starting up, and that would in turn affect the rest of the town.

So yeah, not going to happen.

For a moment he was silent, staring hard at the road ahead and trying to get his recalcitrant body to pay attention to his brain. Then at last he said, "Good to know. But it's still not happening."

"Why not? I told you I'd make an exception for you."

"Yeah, but I can't for you." He was gripping the steering wheel rather tightly. "Sex is casual for me, Izzy. It's all pleasure, no commitment. Fun. No strings. That's all I can offer. And if afterward you decide that you want more...well, I can't give it to you."

"I might not want more. You don't know."

He let out a breath. How the hell had he gotten himself into this position? Arguing with a woman he very much wanted about all the reasons they *shouldn't* sleep together. Levi would laugh himself silly.

"Tell me," he said. "How many times have you had casual sex?"

She didn't reply, though he could feel the waves of annoyance radiating from her. He almost grinned, even though it confirmed that his decision not to touch her was the right one.

"I see," he went on. "You haven't, have you?"

"That's beside the point."

She sounded so deliciously cross that he wanted to keep arguing, but that would take things in a direction he didn't want to go in. Which meant it was time to bring this particular topic of discussion to a close.

"It's absolutely the point," he said firmly. "But I have to pay attention to the road and talking about this isn't good for my concentration. Put some music on the stereo if you want some noise."

He could tell that she wanted to argue with him every bit as badly as he wanted to argue with her, but she didn't say anything, only snorting before reaching to poke at the complicated-looking display for the stereo.

It was obviously intended to stream music, which of course was impossible without an internet connection, so Izzy tried to find a radio station.

In the end, they argued about that instead, expending some of their energy fighting about whether to stick with the station playing good old-fashioned rock—his preference—or the country music station—hers.

That kept them happily occupied as they climbed out of the canyon, and then Izzy dove for her phone as a signal returned. His own phone buzzed, but he didn't bother picking it up since it was likely only Levi letting him know that they'd arrived in Queenstown.

Izzy didn't speak the rest of the way, too absorbed with whatever she was doing on her phone, and while he got that she probably had some things to follow up on, he couldn't help feeling slightly miffed at being ignored.

A stupid feeling that he dismissed, though he did turn the music up a tad louder than necessary.

An hour later, they passed through Queenstown's outer suburbs before winding around Lake Wakatipu and into the town itself.

Situated on the shores of the lake with the serrated edges of mountains all around, Queenstown was the perfect, picturesque little alpine town. Chase had always found it far too full of tourists for his liking, but it was quite beautiful, especially on bluebird days like this, with a cloudless sky overhead and the mirrorlike sheen of the lake reflecting that same endless blue.

He enjoyed Izzy's exclamations of delight though—after she finally put down her phone and took a glance out of the window—as they drove into the central part of town to where the car rental place was located. He had a list of errands he had to run and had planned to go do them after the car had been returned, so he wasn't sure why he found himself standing next to her on the sidewalk as she muttered irritably about her friends' lack of response to her texts, not making any move to leave. In fact, his brain was already shoving those errands to the side in favor of giving her a nice tour of the town and perhaps lunch at one of his favorite restaurants on the wharf overlooking the lake.

"Hopeless," Izzy muttered as she bent over her phone yet again. "I think they're used to Deep River service, which is basically nothing, so they don't check their phones."

He wanted to touch her dark hair, slide his fingers through it, see if it was as silky as it looked.

Go do your stupid errands, fool.

He cleared his throat.

"Clothes," Izzy said before he could speak. "I need some decent clothes that aren't office wear." She glanced around the busy street they were standing in. "Where's the best place to go do that?"

Ahem. Errands.

"You need new hiking boots that fit properly too," he heard himself say. "As well as a parka that isn't designed for sub-Antarctic weather."

She looked up at him. "Yes, I guess I do. So where do I start?"

And he couldn't resist. A minute later, he was taking her on a tour of the little town center and its plethora of camping/skiing/hiking shops, helping her choose a decent lightweight jacket, and then finding some boots that wouldn't give her blisters.

He glared the shop assistant away as the guy tried to help Izzy with her boots, kneeling in front of her himself and slipping off her pumps.

"You don't have to do that," she said. Her eyes were dark, especially in contrast to the blush washing over her cheeks.

"Yes, I do." He cupped the back of her heel, the warmth of her skin soaking into his palm. A very bad idea to touch her, but he couldn't stop. "I need to make sure they fit properly."

She didn't move, staring at him, and he could feel their chemistry fizz and snap around them, crackling like a live wire.

"If I'm not going to be an exception," she murmured, "then perhaps you should let me go."

She was right, of course she was right. Yet her skin was warm and he knew that if he stroked his thumb over her ankle bone, she'd shiver.

What the hell are you doing?

He had no idea. Letting her go was exactly what he *should* do.

But…he didn't.

Instead he looked back into those dark eyes of hers and

very deliberately stroked his thumb over the silky bare skin of her ankle.

She shivered, exactly as he thought she would, and her breath caught.

They stared at each other.

This was crazy. He shouldn't do this with her and yet he wanted to. Badly. Which made him no better than Levi, but when was the last time he'd done something he shouldn't? Something that wasn't sensible, that was just a little bit forbidden? Not for years. Not since Gus was born.

It was wrong and it might lead to complications he didn't want or...it could be something sweet and pleasurable that they both enjoyed, then put behind them.

"I changed my mind," he said before he could second-guess himself. "I think I might want to make an exception for you."

More wild color washed through her cheeks, but she didn't look away.

"But it has to be now," he went on, the idea taking on a life of its own and suddenly becoming urgent. "Here in Queenstown, not back in Brightwater."

Her gaze became even darker, drifting down to his mouth for a moment. "I...can handle that."

And everything became very clear.

He forced himself to look down, guiding her foot into the boot she was supposed to be trying on. "Here, try these on for size first." Then he let her ankle go, rose to his feet, and stepped away.

She blushed fiercely as she continued to try the boot on, though he could tell she was distracted. He liked that a lot, adding to her distraction by helping her with the other boot and sneaking in another ankle stroke, then tying the laces once she'd put it on.

The boots were a good fit, and after she'd paid for them, he took her hand in his and lead her out of the store.

"Where are we going?" she asked breathlessly as he led her down the street, heading for the lakefront.

"Where do you think? There are some hotels on the lake where we can get a room for the night."

"Oh, if we're staying the night, then—"

"We're not staying the night." He gave her a meaningful look. "But they don't rent rooms by the hour in Queenstown."

She pulled a face. "I suppose not."

The lakefront was only a couple minutes' walk. There were yet more cafés along it, a couple of little parks, and a wooden boardwalk, plus long jetties that were moorings for private boats, tourist jet boats, and one big old-fashioned steamship.

Chase hurried Izzy along a broad, paved path that wound beside the lake until he came to the entrance to one of the many hotels situated on it.

It was one of the more expensive ones, but he didn't care. Five minutes later, room booked, he unlocked the door and led her inside, letting the door shut with a heavy clunk behind them.

She was still clutching her bags, so he relieved her of them, setting them down on the floor. She looked up at him, hectic color in her cheeks.

"So," he said, because there were a few things he needed to say first. He always had rules when it came to pickups, and even though she wasn't technically a pickup, the same rules applied. "Here's the deal. I don't want this to get back to anyone else in Brightwater, mainly because I can't trust any of them not to let something slip around Gus. So they can't know, okay? Also, this is a one-off. Just to get it out of our systems and then we go on as if nothing happened. And another thing, we can't—"

But he never got to finish, because Izzy laid a delicate hand on his chest, slid the other up around his neck to the back of his head, rose up on her toes, and brought his mouth down on hers.

Chapter 9

Izzy couldn't think of another way to shut Chase up. She didn't want to hear his list of rules, mainly because pausing to listen to them would involve stopping. And stopping led to thinking, which would then lead to doubts, and she didn't want to give in to those doubts.

What she wanted was him and she felt like she'd been wanting him for far too long. Wanting and resisting, giving herself all these reasons why it was a bad idea. Telling herself it was a stupid thing to do so soon after Josh, especially when it involved someone she was going to be seeing every day on a regular basis.

But she was tired of resisting. Tired of telling herself that being attracted to him was wrong. Tired of telling herself that it would make things too difficult. Tired of thinking about Josh and deep down wondering if this thing with Chase was a mistake.

She was always trying to do the right thing, always trying to please other people. But what about her? Who was concerned with pleasing her? Certainly not Josh. She'd been there for him when he'd needed her to be, listening to him talk about his job, his friends, his dreams. Offering him support during professional setbacks and celebrating his successes unreservedly.

Yet he'd never done that for her. He'd never asked her about how her job was going or what her plans for the future were. He'd never asked her about her dreams.

He'd never made her coffee and breakfast or noticed when she had blisters on her feet. He'd never offered to get her new boots nor helped choose them even when she'd been argumentative with him.

Not like Chase had. She mattered to him in some way, and even if that was only in a sexual way, it still meant something to her. And besides, she was tired of trying to make everyone else's life easier. She wanted something for herself, especially after the last couple of weeks, and hey, coming here was supposed to be a new start, so why shouldn't that new start include sex with Chase?

He wasn't a complete stranger. He was drop-dead gorgeous and up front about what he wanted and what he could give her. She would never discover that he'd never loved her in the first place, for example...

His chest beneath her fingers felt hard, the cotton of his T-shirt warm from his body, and his mouth on hers hot and firm.

Had she felt this way with Josh? She couldn't remember. In fact, it was very difficult to think about anything at all except the pressure of Chase's mouth, the hard plane of his chest, and the warm, musky scent that was all him.

He didn't move, as if he was waiting for something, though she wasn't sure what he could possibly be waiting for.

She touched her tongue to his bottom lip, tracing the line of it, leaning into the heat of his hard, muscular body. She wanted to push against his strength, test it, see what would happen if she did and what he'd do.

He was a man who seemed to be always in control, and while she found that incredibly attractive, there was a sneaky part of her that really wanted to make him to lose it.

Yet he still didn't move.

Then just when she was about to pull away and demand to know what he was doing, she felt his hand come to rest in the small of her back, a bright point of heat. Then his fingers traced her spine, moving upward until she felt them tangle in her hair, gathering all the strands together into his fist and then slowly, inexorably, drawing her head back.

She let him, because then his mouth was opening, his tongue beginning to explore, the taste of him hitting her in a hot rush, and suddenly she was drowning in heat and desire, and gripped by a need she hadn't known would be this intense.

She clutched at him, abruptly desperate and trembling though she wasn't sure why, and when he lifted his head, his gray eyes gone silver with intensity, she thought she might ignite on the spot.

"Are you okay?" His voice was soft and rough, the hold he had on her hair firm but not painful in any way, his other hand resting lightly on her hip.

While you're ready to climb him like a tree.

The thought wound through her brain, making her realize that she was clutching handfuls of his T-shirt, her entire body pressing urgently against his, and that she was shaking.

God, how embarrassing. He was such a controlled guy, and here she was trembling like a virgin. Probably not at all the kind of woman he was used to hooking up with. She was supposed to be treating this as a casual thing, like it didn't matter, because wasn't that how you were supposed to approach casual sex? As if it were nothing. Just physical. An itch to scratch that you could scratch with anyone, certainly not just him.

"Yes." Her voice was breathless and she tried to unclench her fingers from his T-shirt. "Of course. I'm fine. Why wouldn't I be?"

His gaze narrowed and his grip on her hair loosened, his hand moving to cup her cheek. "You're shaking, Izzy."

Another wave of embarrassment threatened.

"Can you please stop talking?" she said quickly, hoping he wouldn't notice. "I thought we were—"

"We are. But I need to know you want this."

She let out a breath, trying not to sound irritable, fighting the doubts that she could already feel rising up inside her. "I do want this. Seriously, Chase, I wouldn't be here if I didn't. It's just…been a while for me and I'm a little…desperate, okay?"

She hadn't wanted to admit that part, but it was the truth. And if she told him, he might hurry this along so her stupid brain would stop getting in the way.

He didn't say anything for a long moment, his sharp gaze searching her face. Then his thumb stroked along her jawline before gently sliding beneath her chin, tilting her head back. He bent and brushed his mouth over hers, making her tremble. She went up on her toes, trying to deepen the kiss, wanting more, but he raised his head a fraction, the electric silver of his gaze holding hers.

"We're going to take this slow." He said it with all the authority of a man who knew exactly what he was going to do, come hell or high water. "Because if it's been a while for you, then I'm sure you'd rather I didn't rush it."

Izzy's breathing quickened and she couldn't control it. Her skin felt tight and hot, like she wanted to shrug it off along with her clothes, and there was a deep, aching pulse centered between her thighs.

"You can rush it," she heard herself say. "I don't mind."

"Well, I do." His hand had fallen away from her jaw and had now slipped behind her, his palm pressing lightly between her shoulder blades, his fingers tracing little circles over her back. "If this is a one-off thing, I want to savor it." His gaze held her fast. "I want to savor *you*."

Oh God. The way he was looking at her, as if she were the still point around which the rest of the world turned. As though nothing else in the entire universe was of any interest to him but her.

Josh had never looked at her that way. While he hadn't been exactly selfish when it came to sex, a small piece of her had always wondered whether he'd been as into it as she had. It hadn't been anything he'd done, just a vague sense of... disconnection. As if he'd been holding a piece of himself apart from her.

A feeling that had been correct, as it turned out.

But she didn't have to worry about that now because connection wasn't what this was about. All that mattered was that he wanted her. And it was clear that he did. In fact, she got the sense that all his focus was here in this hotel room, with her. On her.

"Okay," she breathed, shivering at the brush of his fingers circling on her back. "I guess I can handle that."

"Good." Keeping one hand on her hip, he let the fingers of his other hand brush all the way down her spine and then away, before reaching to take hold of one end of the little bow of her blouse. "Now...do you know how long I've spent fantasizing about undoing the bows on your blouses?" He tugged gently on the tie. "Quite a few nights, Izzy."

Her mouth had gone dry, her pulse speeding up. She'd

had no idea that him just tugging on the tie could be quite so erotic, but it was. And God, he'd fantasized about it. He'd fantasized about *her*...

"Oh..." she murmured. "I...uh...had no idea."

"Of course you didn't. Because I didn't tell you." Gently he tugged harder and the bow came apart. His gaze dropped to her throat and he lifted his hand, his fingertips brushing over the sensitive skin there, leaving little trails of heat everywhere. "You're so soft." His voice sounded deeper, with an exciting kind of roughness to it. "Just like I imagined. No... better."

His arm circled her waist, drawing her against him and holding her there as he bent his head and pressed a kiss to the base of her throat.

Izzy's breath caught, all her awareness centered on the feel of his mouth on her bare skin, glowing there like a hot coal, on the feel of his body against hers, hot and hard as iron and so very strong, so very powerful.

Yet for all that power, he'd touched her gently. His hold around her waist was firm but not constricting, and the brush of his lips over her skin was soft.

She wasn't sure why she found that so unspeakably erotic, but she did. It made her feel precious and treasured, and after Josh's abandonment, for all that she could acknowledge what a selfish man he'd been, her soul had been wounded all the same. And Chase's touch was balm to that hurt, soothing it, healing it.

She leaned into him, allowing her head to fall back. She closed her eyes, shivering as his breath ghosted over her bare skin, raising goose bumps.

His mouth was so warm, leisurely mapping a trail of kisses

over her collarbones, unhurried as she felt his fingers move to the buttons of her blouse. He didn't rush or fumble, deftly undoing each one, stroking over the skin that was unveiled. There were calluses on his fingertips and she could feel them graze her flesh, adding a further delicious layer of sensation to the soft brush of his mouth.

Her thoughts strayed to Josh again, unable to help herself. Had he ever done this for her? Had he ever taken his time with her, undoing her buttons slowly and then making sure to touch every inch of skin as he went?

No, you know he didn't.

Josh hadn't liked to hold her, that was true. He'd kiss her and give her a squeeze, and then he'd roll over, putting distance between them.

He'd never behaved as though each bit of her was a delight he couldn't get enough of, not like this. Not like Chase.

Her throat felt strangely tight, weird tears pricking the backs of her eyes, which made no sense at all because the last thing she wanted was for sex with Chase to make her cry.

She swallowed hard, forcing the tears away and concentrating instead on Chase's touch as he finished undoing her blouse, his fingers stroking over her bare stomach and then caressing up again, grazing lightly over the lace of her bra.

He lifted his head from her throat and found her mouth, kissing her deep and slow, his tongue exploring as if he had all the time in the world. He tasted so good, a rich, masculine flavor with the faintest hint of coffee, and she kissed him back, harder, deeper, becoming demanding.

He cupped her breast, stroking her nipple with his thumb over the lace of her bra, sending electric shocks of pleasure rushing through her.

She gasped, arching into his palm, wanting more, *needing* it, but he was clearly in no hurry, keeping the kiss slow and sweet.

Her hands pressed against his chest, feeling hard muscle and heat beneath the cotton of his T-shirt, but it wasn't enough, so she found the hem and slid her fingers beneath it.

His skin was so hot and smooth, the muscles beneath rock-hard, tensing as she began to explore him. This was a body that had been honed by long hikes in the mountains and rock climbing and kayaking in rivers. It wasn't created in a gym, but by hard, physical work, and there was something incredibly attractive about that.

He'd made her mouth go dry the day she'd found him running without a shirt on, and now she felt dry-mouthed all over again, because now she could not only look at him but touch him as well.

She pressed her palms flat to his hard stomach and heard him growl, then suddenly she was being lifted into his arms and carried over to the bed, then laid down on it.

"Stay," he ordered as she tried to push herself upright. "I want to undress you."

She went still, her heart thumping as he leaned over her, one hand beside her head, the other sliding underneath her, finding the catch of her bra and undoing it. The expression in his eyes was intense, and he didn't stop looking as he pulled away her blouse and her bra along with it.

Izzy took a shuddering breath. Sometimes with Josh she'd felt a little uncomfortable, a little vulnerable with being naked, and she realized that she'd been subconsciously waiting for that feeling with Chase. But it didn't come.

His gaze devoured her whole, leaving her in no doubt

about how desirable he found her and it made her feel good in a way she hadn't anticipated.

She'd never realized she could be wanted without having to do something for someone. That she could just…lie there and be desired.

She felt surprisingly unselfconscious looking up into Chase's eyes as he reached down and touched her, his fingers grazing lightly over her bare skin, over her collarbones, and down to the swell of her breast. Tracing the curve of it before cupping it lightly, his palm burning against her flesh.

His thumb brushed over the tight, hard peak of her nipple, sending yet more electric shocks of pleasure through her. She sighed, arching into his hand, letting him see that she liked this and that she wanted more.

"Beautiful," Chase murmured, his gaze sweeping down over her before coming to rest once again on her face. "You're beautiful, Izzy."

The word shocked her, made her ache, but she didn't want him to see how much it had meant to her, so she smiled, shivering as his thumb circled around the aching tip of her breast. "And you're a tease. Do I get to see you without a shirt?"

Wickedness glinted in his eyes. "You've already seen me without a shirt."

"Oh, but that—" She broke off, gasping as he pinched her nipple lightly, sending a lightning strike of sensation through her.

"But that what?" He shifted, going onto his hands and knees above her, looking down at her, his gaze alight with that wicked glint. "You were about to say something important."

"I only meant that—" She gasped and shuddered as he pinched her again, then bent to press his mouth to hers.

"Try again," he whispered against her lips before nuzzling his way down her throat.

Izzy closed her eyes, pleasure gathering tighter and tighter inside her, all her awareness on the feel of his mouth on her skin and those maddening fingers on her breast.

"Chase, you—"

A hot mouth closed on her nipple and she cried out, sensation breaking over her in a wave, hot and bright, so amazingly good.

"'Chase, you' what?" His breath was warm on her skin, his hands stroking over her hips, finding the zipper on her skirt and pulling it down. "You keep trying to say something and never finish your sentence."

Her breathing was sliding out of control, her thoughts fracturing. "Because you keep—"

His mouth closed around her nipple again and he sucked gently, and Izzy forgot every word she'd been going to say.

It felt so good. Everything he was doing felt *so* good.

She sighed, arching helplessly up, wanting more, shivering as he eased her skirt and underwear down at the same time as he licked her nipple, biting gently and then sucking again, bright layers of sensation that made her twist in his hands.

"I keep what?" His mouth trailed kisses down her stomach. "Speak up, Izzy."

He was teasing her, flirting with her, his deep voice rolling over her like rough velvet. There were warm notes of amusement in it and other notes too, hotter and slightly demanding, wicked and a little raw, and she loved the sound of it. That uptight, impatient, and rigorous Chase could do wanton and wicked, could be teasing and sexy and slow.

"You're terrible," she whispered. "Stop doing that to me and I'll finish what I was going to say."

"Stop doing what?" He pressed a kiss to her belly button. "This?" His mouth went lower, brushing over the shivering plane of her lower abdomen. "Or maybe this?" He nuzzled against her, his hands sliding over her hips to stroke her thighs. "Or...perhaps this?" Gently he pressed her legs apart and she couldn't stop the moan that escaped her. Then his mouth was back, brushing over the inside of her thighs, nuzzling against all that sensitive skin.

Izzy screwed her eyes shut tighter, the blackness behind her lids exploding with stars, every sense she had focused on his hot, wicked mouth. She reached for him, her fingers sliding through the soft thickness of his hair.

"You..." she began. "You...s-shouldn't..."

"I shouldn't what?"

But she couldn't think of what she'd been going to say, because he suddenly took her hands and pressed them down onto the mattress, holding them still.

"Tell me, Izzy." His mouth brushed over the sensitive skin at the crease at the top of her leg, and she felt herself begin to go up in flames. "What shouldn't I do?"

She couldn't remember. She couldn't think. There was a hunger inside her and it felt vast, and she wanted him to satisfy it. In fact, it almost felt like he was the only one who could.

"Chase," she said hoarsely. "Please..."

He didn't reply. Instead, his mouth moved between her thighs, the flick of his tongue against her sensitive flesh making her cry out in pleasure. He kept a firm grip on her hands, holding them down, and for some reason the slight feeling of being constricted made the pleasure even sharper, even brighter.

She writhed, unable to keep her desperate moans silent and not particularly caring as he feasted on her. Taking his time the way he promised, savoring her, until all there was was the glory behind her eyes and the pleasure climbing higher and higher until it broke like a storm inside her.

And she was lost.

―――――――

Izzy lay on the bed, naked and beautiful, her eyes closed and her cheeks flushed, utterly abandoned to the pleasure he'd given her. She'd called his name as she'd come and he could still hear the sound of it ringing in his ears, still taste the flavor of her on his tongue, so sweet and hot and delicious...

He'd never felt so desperate in all his life.

He'd thought that continuing with the slow, seductive pace he'd set earlier wouldn't be an issue. She'd been shaking, and even though she'd insisted it was because it had been a while for her, he hadn't wanted to move things along too fast. Partly for his own satisfaction, since he'd been telling the truth when he'd told her he wanted to savor her, and partly because he really hadn't wanted to make her uncomfortable. If casual sex wasn't normally something she did, he wanted to make sure she was okay with everything they did together.

But he hadn't realized how erotic it would be to have her gazing up at him, her eyes wide and dark, looking at him with awe and wonder, as if he was the answer to a mystery she'd been desperate to solve. No one had looked at him that way for a very long time and he loved it. Loved, too, how desperate she was for him and how completely she'd given herself to him.

Olivia had never looked at him that way. She'd never stared at him with wonder. Never shook with desire for him. She'd never given herself over to him so completely the way Izzy had. No, Olivia had wanted something from him and because she'd never been able to articulate what it was, he'd never been able to give it to her.

He'd done everything he could to make their marriage work, and in the end it hadn't been enough.

Nothing you do is ever enough.

The thought slunk through his mind, twisting in his gut, but he ignored it. Pushed it away. Because it was wrong.

Since Olivia had left, he'd poured his heart and his soul into making sure Brightwater Valley survived, into making sure Gus was happy, into making his business work, and nothing else mattered.

And now he had this beautiful, sensual, warm woman beneath him, looking at him like he was the most amazing thing she'd ever seen, and all those old doubts felt so tenuous, misplaced even.

Chase stared back, looking at her the way she was looking at him, because she was amazing too, with her hair trailing over the white quilt cover like spilled ink, and her skin all flushed and pink and delicious.

She wasn't holding back a single thing; he could see it.

She touched his chest, the light pressure of her fingers feeling oddly like a brush against his soul.

"Do I get to see you?" Her voice was husky and soft and full of need. "Please, Chase."

Hell, how could he refuse a request like that?

He couldn't get his clothes off fast enough.

His hands even shook slightly, which was ridiculous and not a problem he'd had since he was fifteen, but there was just something about the way she looked at him, about her simple request that made him desperate.

Perhaps that should have worried him since he'd never felt like this about a hookup before, and it might have if he'd been thinking straight. But he wasn't thinking straight.

He felt like a teenage boy looking at a naked woman for the first time.

Her eyes went large as his clothes came off, which was gratifying on just about every level, especially when he tore off his jeans and underwear, and she flushed an even deeper red than she already was.

Pausing to grab some protection from his wallet took far too long, as did having to roll the condom down, but once that was taken care of, he was back on the bed, stretching himself over her, almost ready.

"Oh wow," she murmured, reaching for him, running long fingers over his chest, stroking him, scattering little sparks of sensation all over his skin. "You're amazing, you know that?"

He settled himself between her thighs. "So are you."

And she was. A pure delight. Warm and soft and silky. Delicate femininity combined with an earthy sensuality that had his heart racing.

Her mouth curved, her gaze roving over him. "I'll take that."

He braced one hand beside her head and reached down to adjust himself, pressing lightly against the slick entrance to her body. She gave the most delicious shiver, her gaze turning smoky as she looked up at him.

"Oh," she breathed. "That's, uh…that's…"

He was desperate, but teasing her was so delightful that he couldn't resist the urge to slide his aching shaft through her slick folds, rubbing against the little bud between her thighs.

She gasped, her nails digging into his skin. "Chase." His name was a plea so husky it satisfied everything male in him. "Oh…you're such a…"

"Such a what?" He shifted against her again, sliding, pressing delicately, watching the glow in her dark eyes become more intense. "Having problems with your sentences again, hmm?"

"You're an awful man," she moaned, scraping her nails down the front of his chest. "A t-tease…"

"It's called anticipation, beautiful." He bent to brush his mouth over hers, tantalizing them both. "Haven't you ever heard of it?"

"No, and I don't like it." She looked adorably flushed and very cross.

He slid his free hand beneath her, tilting her hips so she was pressed even more intimately against him. "Well, we can't have that, can we? Let's see what we can do about it." Slowly he eased forward, pushing into her, unable to tear his gaze from her as her mouth opened and her eyelashes fluttered, pleasure rippling over her pretty face.

"You like that?" It came out as a growl, the hot, slick feel of her around him making him grit his teeth because it felt so good. Too good. If he wasn't careful, she might make him lose it.

"Oh…yes…God, *yes*." Her lashes lifted, her gaze meeting his, full of heat and desire and a kind of wonder that made his heart miss a beat. "You feel amazing." She slid her hands up to his shoulders and then down his back, pulling him closer. "More, please…"

And just like that, he lost his taste for more teasing.

He wanted her. She made him feel powerful, like he could do anything, and *God*, how he wanted her.

Chase bent and covered her mouth with his, kissing her hungrily as he began to move, slow and easy at first, then faster, deeper.

This time her nails dug into his back, her arms tight around him, her hips lifting in time with his, meeting him thrust for thrust. Her teeth sank into his bottom lip, sending shocks of sensation through him, making him growl yet again.

Who knew that beneath her cool and calm exterior she was a tigress with claws and teeth? He loved it.

He slid a hand beneath one of her knees, hauling her leg up and around his waist, letting him slide deeper inside her. She shuddered and gasped against his mouth, her body twisting beneath his.

His own thought processes had shut down, the weight of hunger crushing them flat, his mind full of nothing but her heat and the slick feel of her body squeezing him tight. Of her nails against his skin and the softness of her lips beneath his and the exquisite taste of her on his tongue.

He wanted more, and so he pursued it, the sounds of their frantic breathing loud in the room, her gasps turning into soft cries of pleasure. And he could feel the orgasm building inside him, a tidal wave that was going to crush him.

And in the midst of all that glorious sensation, he had the weirdest thought: sex had never been this way with anyone, not even Olivia, and once wasn't going to be enough.

But then the thought was gone, lost under the tide of pleasure. All he had time for was to slip his hand between them, to stroke her gently until he felt her body clench tight around his, her cry of release in his ears, then he let himself go and joined her as the tide swamped him utterly.

Afterward, he lay there, unable to move, his brain barely able to function. Her body was soft and warm underneath his, the musky scent of sex heavy in the air, and he knew if he stayed like this any longer he wasn't going to want to leave this room. He'd want to keep her here all night, which of course would be a mistake.

Just once, he'd said. A one-off thing. To get it out of their systems.

Famous last words, huh?

He hadn't expected it to be so...intense. He hadn't expected to like teasing her so much or that she'd be so responsive. He hadn't expected her eagerness or her hunger or her honest delight in what he was doing to her.

And he certainly hadn't expected to want more.

Bloody hell.

She made a soft sound, and with an effort he pulled himself together, gathering her close and turning over onto his back, so he wasn't crushing her. She sprawled over his bare chest, silky black hair everywhere, all pretty pink skin and glowing dark eyes.

She was smiling at him as if he'd given her the best present in the entire world and it made him ache. He didn't know why.

Not a good sign. None of this was a good sign.

He lifted a hand, slid it into her hair, and brought her mouth to his in a brief kiss, which he hoped would let her know that while he'd enjoyed what they'd done and he was glad she did too, it was over now. It was time to get dressed and get out of there.

Except when he released her, she didn't move. Instead, she folded her hands on his chest and put her chin on them, looking at him. "You're a dark horse, Chase Kelly," she said after a moment.

Okay, so she wasn't getting the hint.

Are you surprised? She said she didn't do casual sex.

In that case, he needed to be careful. He didn't want to hurt her, not after she'd been so open and willing, so he couldn't just rush her out the door. His instincts might be screaming at him to put some distance between him and the urge to roll her over onto her back once again and continue on with where they left off, but that would probably upset her and he didn't want to do that.

Trying to ignore the urge and relax, he pushed a lock of black hair behind her ear. "How so?"

"Oh, you appear all kind of uptight and impatient and a bit managing. Overly serious and sort of intense." Her smile deepened. "Not that those are bad things. Your intensity in particular is sexy. But what I really, really like is that underneath all of that, you're actually quite wicked."

He shouldn't like the way she said it, her voice warm, her melted-honey accent sweetening everything. He shouldn't like how she'd seen something about him that even Olivia hadn't.

No, for Olivia he'd always been too demanding, too bossy. Had expected too much from her without giving her any support in return, or at least that's what she'd told him. Not that she'd ever been clear about what kind of support she wanted. Whenever there was an issue, she'd simply dissolve into tears and nothing he did helped. Nothing he did would fix it.

He'd gotten tired of feeling like he was in the wrong all the time, tired of her constantly refusing to talk about it or be clear about what she wanted, and in the end, he'd come to the conclusion that what she wanted was not to be married to him. Not to have a child. And not to be "buried in a tinpot little town with no support."

"Wicked, huh?" He wound another strand of her hair around one finger and tugged gently, pushing thoughts of Olivia out of his head. "You're pretty wicked yourself."

"I'm not *that* wicked."

"Sure you are." He found he was smiling too. "You're quite the little sex goddess once your clothes come off."

Izzy flushed, which made warmth unfurl in his chest. He did *so* enjoy flustering her.

"What?" He tugged on her curl again, forgetting he was supposed to be hurrying them both out of the room. "No one ever tell you that? Come on. You must have had hundreds of guys lining up at your door."

A flicker of emotion crossed her delicate features, though he wasn't quite sure what it was. "Oh, no, it wasn't quite like that."

He frowned. There was an odd note in her voice, almost like…hurt. Which made him feel possessive all of a sudden, because the thought of her being hurt by anyone… Yeah, that wasn't happening.

"What was it like, then?" He kept his tone neutral. She probably wouldn't appreciate him going full Neanderthal on her right at this particular moment.

Unexpectedly, she glanced away. "It's nothing. Forget I said anything."

Oh, no, she wasn't doing that. Something he'd said had clearly hurt her, and he wanted to know what it was.

Why? This was only ever about sex and you know it.

Yes, that was true, but if he was the one causing her pain, then he wanted to know why so he could avoid the topic in future.

Letting go of her hair, he reached out to take her delicate chin in his fingers, turning her back to face him so he could see her expression. "Too late," he said gently. "Sounds to me like I hit a nerve. Want to tell me which particular nerve it was?"

Her dark brows drew down, a brief, challenging glitter in her eyes. "I didn't think we were here for heart-to-heart chats. Sex and nothing else, right?"

How strange that it should be him pushing for more and her not wanting to talk when just before it had been vice versa. But he couldn't leave it alone now. She'd sounded hurt and he wanted to know why.

"Yes," he replied. "That's right. But something I said hurt you. And don't bother denying it," he added as her mouth opened to protest. "I heard it in your voice."

She pulled a face, her fingers beginning to trace absent circles on his chest. "It's really nothing, okay? I just had a bad breakup before I came out to New Zealand. He was not... as into me as I was into him and so in the end we went our separate ways." She hesitated then added, "Even me being a sex goddess didn't seem to help."

He should let this go, bring this whole little episode to a close. He shouldn't want to know more about this bad breakup and he definitely shouldn't be feeling a sharp tug of emotion just behind his breastbone. Something possessive and protective, urging him to go find whoever it was who hadn't been into her and instruct him on the error of his ways. With a fist maybe.

"That doesn't sound great. Want to tell me about it?"

Slowly she shook her head, still not looking at him.

He didn't want to let it go. He wanted to know more.

You can't. This is only a hookup and that's how you wanted it.

Something clenched hard inside him, but he ignored the sensation. Because yes, it was true, that's exactly how he wanted it. He didn't want to get tangled up with anyone—not yet, not after Olivia had left.

He'd forgiven her for leaving him, but he'd never forgive her for leaving their daughter. And he'd never forgive himself if he ended up with yet another woman who'd find it easy to walk away from Gus.

The next woman who came to Brightwater Valley with him would stay for life, and until then, it was sex only.

Izzy was beautiful and sexy and made him feel good, but he didn't know her. And he hadn't gotten the feeling from her that she was in this for the long haul. Three months, she'd promised him, and he knew she'd keep that promise, but what about after that? Perhaps she'd hightail it back to Texas.

Until then, while this interlude was nice it had to stay being just that: an interlude. And the quicker they wrapped it up the better.

"Okay," he said slowly when she didn't speak. "But just so you know, if you need a friend or a sympathetic ear, you can come to me."

He wasn't normally a man who left something alone. He pushed if he thought it was important. But pushing had only made everything worse with Olivia and he had the sense that it wouldn't work with Izzy either.

Yet he couldn't leave her with nothing, not after that. Not after she'd been so generous with her body and her pleasure—and her honesty.

She glanced at him. "Thank you. I appreciate that."

It was clear that she did, which satisfied him.

"Good." And then, because he really had to be clear himself: "Okay, I suppose we'd better get moving if we don't want the others to get suspicious about where we are."

Izzy pulled a face, then shifted, grabbing at his wrist and the watch still strapped firmly around it. She looked down at the time and then shot him the sexiest look from beneath her lashes. "Actually, they probably won't get suspicious for at least another half an hour. Just saying."

Everything in Chase tightened.

He should really leave, but…he'd paid for a whole night they wouldn't be using. And he really didn't want to go wandering around Queenstown for half an hour, not when there were other more interesting things to do.

"Half an hour, hmm?" He gripped her, easing her so she was lying directly on top of him. "Seems a shame to waste it just walking around."

Her eyes had gone very dark. "Yes, I agree. What else do you suggest?"

"Oh, I have a few ideas." Chase gave her his wickedest smile. "Let me show you."

Chapter 10

Izzy stood in the dusty store and checked her watch impatiently. The tradesman she'd called a couple of days earlier to start work in the shop was at least half an hour late.

It had taken an entire day to go through the list of local tradespeople in the Rose's big thick phone book, then call them all to find someone who was willing to make the trek to Brightwater to repair the store's windows and then build shelves, not to mention do the electrical work needed. He'd promised her he was good to come out to Brightwater Valley, especially if she paid him extra for mileage, and now she was annoyed.

The whole no-service thing was turning out to be a major hurdle when it came to organizing what needed to be done in the store, since all of this stuff was far easier when you could just look it up on the internet. But unless she wanted to drive for an hour up that hideous road until she could get a signal, it was the good old-fashioned phone book for her.

Cait had spotted her poring over the thing and had made some comment about why didn't she just ask someone for help, but Izzy didn't want to.

She didn't mention that Chase had already offered or that she'd refused. And it had nothing whatsoever to do with what had happened between them in Queenstown a week earlier.

Their little half an hour extra had turned into more, which

then had involved having to rush to meet Indigo and Beth at the bank. They'd gotten a couple of strange looks, but neither woman had said anything then or since, so obviously they hadn't picked up on something untoward happening between her and Chase.

Izzy was grateful. She didn't want to go into detail about it with Beth and Indigo. She didn't want to mention it at all. For the first time in her life, sex had felt like something that she could have for herself, that was about making *her* feel good as opposed to just her partner.

It had been Chase who'd made her feel that way, Chase who'd given that to her, and she didn't want to share that with anyone else yet. It felt too private, too intimate, and somehow too precious.

Not exactly casual, was it?

No, which was a problem when casual was all it was supposed to be. Then again, she couldn't pretend it hadn't mattered to her or that it hadn't been important.

It had made being in his general vicinity difficult, since every time she was, her body kept thinking all its Christmases had come at once. An annoying and distracting issue, and not at all helpful when she was supposed to be organizing a new business.

Chase, on the other hand, acted as if nothing had happened between them at all, treating her exactly the same as he'd treated her before, striding around with schedules and lists of "recommendations" and generally trying to manage things. It annoyed her, which was why she'd refused his help, thinking it would be best if she avoided him altogether.

He hadn't argued. And that had annoyed her even more.

She knew it was unreasonable, that he was only doing

exactly what he'd said and treating their encounter as casual, which meant the problem lay with her and she had to handle it. She needed to get over herself and her attraction to him, put it out of her head, and pay attention to what she was supposed to be doing, which was getting this store up and running.

Not helpful when the man she'd hired to build the shelves didn't turn up.

Irritated, Izzy reached for her phone for the umpteenth time only to remember, for the umpteenth time, that there was no service, and if she wanted to call the guy to see where he was, she'd have to use the landline in the Rose.

You should have accepted Chase's offer of help.

Izzy growled. Sure, she could have, but that would have meant him being around her and she needed some distance. Plus he seemed busy with his business, and anyway he'd made such a big deal about "people" not being able to "hack it" here that she now had a point to prove. She wasn't going to go running to him every time she needed something.

The door to the store opened and Izzy turned, hoping it was her missing tradesman, but it was Beth on the threshold instead.

"Hey, Gus wanted to know…" Beth trailed off and frowned. "You don't look happy. What's up?"

Izzy, whose forced smile was fraying around the edges, let out a breath. "The guy who was supposed to build our shelves is half an hour late and I don't think he's coming."

"That's annoying." Beth sounded casual, clearly having no interest in the whereabouts of the tradesman. "Why don't you come out on a nature walk with Indigo and me instead?"

"A nature walk?" Izzy tried to get a handle on her irritation. "What?"

"Chase is taking a bunch of tourists out to Glitter Falls across the lake and Gus came to ask Indigo and me if we wanted to come along. You too."

That stupid fluttering excitement that occurred whenever Chase's name was mentioned fluttered again, tugging at her.

She ignored it. What she needed was more time away from him, not more time in his presence.

"Well, that would be nice," she said. "But I have to stay here in case this guy turns up."

Beth shrugged. "Why not get Cait to keep an eye out for him?"

"No. I have to be here. I need to tell him what we want."

Beth studied her for a moment. Then she came over to where Izzy stood and took her by the arm. "Come on," she said firmly, tugging her toward the entrance. "You need a break. You've been fussing around with the store all week and it's making you grumpy, don't think I haven't noticed."

It wasn't only the store, but Izzy didn't want Beth to know that, so she let herself be tugged. "Someone's got to do it."

"Sure. But someone also needs to get out into the nature here, talk to the tourists, and maybe also see the hot single dad in action."

They'd stepped out into the bright morning sun, but at the mention of Chase, Izzy stopped dead. "This is not about—"

"Are you coming?" Gus came running up, gray eyes—so like her father's—shining, her black hair tangling down her back in a half-hearted ponytail. "Beth said you would."

Mystery, the black stray, trotted up behind Gus and sat down, his tongue hanging out, black eyes gazing at Izzy as if he too wanted her to go on the expedition.

How annoying.

Izzy silently cursed Beth, the tradesman, the dog, and Chase Kelly. Because of course now she couldn't refuse, not with Gus looking at her like that.

Plus Beth was right. It would be good to go on one of the Pure Adventure trips, to see why the tourists came here and to get a taste of the area's nature.

The hot single dad is also a draw, come on.

No, he was not. Not in any way, and she wouldn't let him be. She couldn't afford to.

"Yes." Izzy forced away her bad temper. "Of course I'm coming."

"Oh, cool!" Gus grinned, her enthusiasm infectious.

"Shouldn't you be in school though?"

"It's a teacher-only day today. So I'm helping Dad with the trip." She turned toward the lake. "Come on, Dad hates it when we're late."

Mystery leaped to his feet and loped off around the side of the Rose, clearly considering his job here done.

"Cute dog," Beth said as she went off after Gus. "I'll see you down there, Izzy."

Izzy only just resisted the urge to roll her eyes.

She made a quick detour to the Rose to tell Cait to keep an eye out for her missing tradesman, but by the time she arrived at the little jetty where the Pure Adventure NZ boat was tied up, most of the tourists were already aboard.

Chase was at the helm, tall and broad and imposing, and he gave Izzy a frowning glance as she quickly got on, no doubt irritated with her lateness.

Her stomach dipped, her body recognizing him and helpfully reminding her about everything they'd done together and how great it would be to have it again, the way it had been doing all week.

She ignored it, throwing him a hopefully apologetic smile before quickly finding a seat with Beth and Indigo and putting on the life jacket Beth handed her.

A couple of minutes later, they were motoring across the lake, the hot sun glinting off the water and making the almost mineral blue of the lake seem even more intense.

In front of them were the snow-capped mountains of the ranges, sharp peaks edging the sky, the slopes clad in dark green native bush.

It all would have been wonderful and relaxing if she hadn't been so conscious of the man standing at the helm, with Gus at his side, chatting easily to another tourist who'd also come to stand beside him.

He was in full outdoor gear today, forest-green utility pants that hugged his lean hips and powerful thighs and the black Pure Adventure NZ T-shirt that made the most of his broad chest. He wore a bright yellow life jacket over the top, as did everyone else in the boat, and it was in no way detrimental to his sexiness which was already at insane levels.

He smiled as Gus interjected something, reaching out to ruffle her hair, making her scowl, much to his amusement and that of the tourist.

Izzy's heart gave a little pulse behind her breastbone.

Once was enough, huh?

Yes, of course it was. She didn't need to revisit their encounter and she wasn't thinking about it, not in any way.

"So the builder guy didn't turn up, huh?" Indigo brushed her hair out of her eyes.

Both she and Beth had spent the past week since their

Queenstown trip investigating getting the equipment and supplies they needed so they could start producing items for the shop. They both had brought some stock with them so they had something to start with, but Indigo had been desperate to start dyeing, while Beth had been making frantic sketches of new designs in her sketchbook. The pair of them had clearly been inspired by the natural beauty of their surroundings, which was understandable.

"No," Izzy said. "I'll give him the benefit of the doubt, though. It's a long way for him to come and maybe he got held up."

Indigo looked annoyed. "I'm not giving him the benefit of the doubt. We should ask around Brightwater. Get a local to help." She frowned. "Didn't Chase offer?"

Izzy shifted uncomfortably on her seat. "Yes, but I thought we could handle it ourselves."

"But don't we—"

"And there're a few other things we have to sort out," Izzy rushed on, not wanting to get into the particulars of why she'd refused Chase's offer. "Sourcing some more items, promotion, and oh yes, finding a name."

"Oh, I know!" The fresh breeze on the lake blew Beth's white-blond ponytail out behind her like a plume of snow from a mountaintop. "How about Brightwater Gallery?"

Indigo shrugged. "Isn't that kind of…obvious? Look, I don't really care about names, but what I will say is that we institute a 'no men allowed' policy."

Beth, taking no apparent offense to the lack of enthusiasm for her store name, looked interestedly at her. "Oh? Why is that? Is a certain person annoying you?"

The "certain person" being Levi, whom Indigo had taken

an irrational dislike to for reasons that Izzy couldn't quite discern. Levi was handsome and charming, and all the interactions Izzy had had with him had been extremely pleasant.

It made her curious about what exactly Indigo's deal was. Same with Beth for that matter, considering Beth had been relentlessly trying to get past Finn Kelly's reserve for the past week.

The three of them hadn't had much of a chance to talk about other things, what with all the organizing of the store going on, and Izzy decided that she really should rectify that.

"No," Indigo said far too quickly. "I just don't like the smell of testosterone first thing in the morning."

Beth laughed and sent Izzy a sly look. "Well, I don't know about you, but the morning is my favorite time for testosterone. Or even during the day and maybe night too, right, Izzy?"

Izzy, who'd found her gaze lingering on Chase yet again, tried to pretend it hadn't been. "Oh, sure. Testosterone can be quite pleasant sometimes."

The other two glanced at each other, which Izzy did not like at all.

"What?" she asked.

"Nothing." Indigo gave her an owlish look. "Just, if you think you're being sneaky with Chase, you're not."

Izzy could feel the flush begin to creep up her neck. "But I'm—"

"It's okay." Beth gave her a comforting pat on the knee. "You don't have to pretend with us. Also we're not blind. He's one hell of a man and very difficult to ignore."

Damn.

Izzy debated feigning innocence but decided that would

only provoke more questions. "Okay, yes," she said, hoping the wind would calm her blush down. "So I like looking at him. It's no big deal."

"I knew it." Beth's green eyes danced. "And I *know* he feels the same. The tension between you two is insane."

Still blushing, Izzy fussed with the zipper of the fleece jacket she'd thrown on after seeing Cait. "I don't know if he does or not—"

"Oh, he does."

"But I'm not going to do anything about it, okay?" She gave Beth and Indigo a meaningful glance, hoping the minor lie would stop any more questions. "This town is too small and I don't want to make things difficult for him. He's got a child to consider."

Beth opened her mouth, probably to argue, so Izzy said quickly, "Anyway, I'm not the only one staring at attractive men. What about Finn?"

"Oh yes." Indigo, clearly relishing the chance to turn the tables, stared meaningfully at Beth. "Do let's talk about Finn."

Beth rolled her eyes. "I just want to make the wretched man crack a smile. Nothing wrong with that, is there?"

"No." Izzy grinned. "You're sure taking it very seriously though."

Beth stared at her for a second, then glanced away. "Well, making someone smile is a serious business."

And for the first time, Izzy heard a note that wasn't bright or cheery in Beth's voice. It caught at her. She frowned in sudden concern, noting that Indigo was also looking at Beth, a worried expression on her face.

"You okay, Beth?" Izzy asked.

Beth glanced back, her cheerful grin returning. "Yeah, of

course. Just thinking that if anyone needs to smile more it's Finn Kelly."

Yet Izzy couldn't shake the feeling that it hadn't been Finn Kelly who Beth had been thinking about. Still, now wasn't the time to push her on it, not while they were surrounded by tourists and preparing to go on a nature walk.

So Izzy let it go, the three of them chatting happily, good-naturedly teasing each other and laughing as the boat made its way across the lake to where a small jetty stuck out into the water, the end of it disappearing into the bush.

With the casual expertise of long experience, Chase brought the boat up to the jetty and Gus leapt out to tie the mooring. Then he began to gather everyone, helping them off the boat. Indigo, Beth, and Izzy were the last ones off, the two women giving Izzy sneaking glances as Chase helped them up and then turned to her. She didn't want to take his hand, but he was insistent, his gaze flashing silver the moment his fingers closed around hers.

He didn't say anything though, only handed her onto the jetty without a word just as Gus came careering down it, her arms full of people's life jackets.

Izzy ignored her frantically beating heart and the burn of Chase's fingers against her skin and handed her life jacket to Gus before joining Beth and Indigo and the other tourists down at the start of the track.

It was fine. She hadn't expected him to say anything to her and he hadn't. And that was absolutely A-okay with her. She didn't care, not at all.

Somehow, in the time it had taken them to traverse the lake, some clouds had appeared and the sun had gone behind them. The breeze had strengthened and it felt a little cool.

Zipping up her fleece, Izzy looked around at the others and realized that some people were starting to get out rain jackets and waterproof parkas, including Beth and Indigo.

Great. She hadn't thought to grab her parka, not when it had been sunny when they'd left.

Deciding there wasn't much she could do about it and at least she had some decent boots and a warm fleece, Izzy waited with the rest while Chase finished stowing the life jackets in the boat before leaping out and striding down the jetty, a small day pack thrown over one shoulder.

At the start of the track, he gathered everyone around and began a spiel about the falls and the landscape around them, the things they might see and any flora and fauna they might encounter.

Izzy didn't think it was possible for him to get any more attractive than he already was, but apparently she was wrong.

It was clear he was knowledgeable, his passion for the subject obvious in the way he talked and in his expression, in the glitter of silver in his eyes.

She was fascinated and so were the tourists, crowding around him and asking all kinds of questions which he answered with great patience and unexpected humor. Then with a firm admonishment not to feed any of the keas, a native parrot with a reputation for being cheeky, he got Gus to lead them up the track to the falls.

Izzy made a concerted effort to focus on the natural scenery and not the male kind and found herself entranced. The track itself was wide and well maintained, the bush around them astoundingly beautiful. Lots of beech trees and ferns and mossy logs, the air cool and spiced with an earthy, damp scent.

She could hear a familiar liquid call that Cait had told her a few days earlier was a tūī, and as she walked, she noticed a tiny brown-and-white bird with a wide tail keeping step with her, flying from tree to tree and watching her as she moved.

"That's a fantail," Gus said, arriving beside her. "Pīwakawaka in Māori."

"It's cute." Izzy was charmed. "It's following me."

"It's your movement. You stir up insects and they like to eat them."

"Oh, that's—"

"My dad really likes you."

Izzy nearly tripped. "Sorry, what?"

"Dad." Gus jerked her head behind them, where Chase was bringing up the rear. "He likes you."

Izzy desperately tried to think of something to say that wouldn't give either her or Chase away. "Well…" she managed, "I like him too. You know, as a friend."

Gus's gray eyes were guileless as she stared at Izzy. "How long are you staying here?"

Where was the kid going with this?

"Three months." She gave Gus a smile. "So if you've got any more questions about cowboy hats and guns, there's plenty of time to ask them."

Gus looked like she might say something, but then Chase gave her a call to lead the party and she suddenly bounded up the track without a word.

Then the first drops of rain began to fall.

———

Chase cast an assessing glance up the track as the tourists began the upward climb that led to the falls. It wasn't a difficult hike—the track was decent, unlike some of the backcountry trails—but it did require a certain level of fitness to make it comfortably in an hour.

He often got tourists who weren't prepared for the conditions or who weren't wearing the right gear, mainly because it wasn't a very long hike and there were some people who thought an hour's walk meant an amble along a perfectly straight and level concrete path. Sometimes they even turned up wearing high heels or designer sneakers.

Luckily this lot of tourists had come prepared and had brought their own rain jackets. Well, all except one apparently.

Izzy had fallen behind the rest of the pack, currently trudging up the trail with her head bent, absolutely no wet-weather gear about her person. She had on jeans and a pretty dark blue T-shirt that he'd already noted earlier fitted her to perfection, and she had a light fleece jacket over the top.

But no parka. No rain jacket. Nothing waterproof at all.

The irritation that had been grumbling inside of him since the moment he'd caught sight of her getting on the boat along with everyone else wound tighter.

He'd thought his body would have gotten the message that the afternoon they'd had in Queenstown was enough and that it didn't require anything more, and yet his body—or rather certain parts of it—seemed hell-bent on arguing with him.

So he'd thrown himself into working like a dog for the past week, attempting to distract himself and one particularly unruly body part from thoughts of her.

Izzy, naked in his arms, flushed and gorgeous from the pleasure he'd given her. Izzy, looking at him as if he was the most amazing thing she'd ever seen.

Izzy, giving him a cool look and then refusing his offer of help with those stupid shelves.

That's a good thing.

Probably. The last thing he needed was to be in her vicinity, getting all hot and bothered, and that was the reason he hadn't pushed.

But she was still a problem. A beautiful, sexy problem and he didn't know what to do about it.

He hadn't been expecting her to come on this expedition, but Gus had taken it into her head to invite "those ladies" along, and since he couldn't think of one good reason to forbid it, he'd let her.

A mistake.

He'd never found dealing with the tourists annoying—if anything he really enjoyed showing people around, introducing them to new skills and new sights, showing them the beauty of the land around them.

But today it was different. Today he was annoyed because Izzy was here and he literally couldn't concentrate on anything else.

The forecast was for showers, so she should have brought that parka with her. Why hadn't she?

Automatically, he did another head count of the tourists, making sure they were all there and that no one was behind him, then he strode up beside Izzy.

"Where's your parka?" It came out sounding like a demand, which he hadn't intended and did not help his mood.

Izzy gave him a surprised glance, then flushed. The beech forest shielded them, the rain turning into a fine mist that drifted down through the canopy, settling in glittering drops on her black hair. A sheepish expression crossed her face. "Oh…I didn't bring one." She zipped her fleece up higher, hunching her shoulders as a bigger drop of water splashed on her forehead, making her blink. "It was fine when we left."

Chase gritted his teeth. She'd been a last-minute addition to the trip, so of course she hadn't been there for the usual talk he gave people. Still, he had spoken to her before of the dangers of being underprepared.

"The weather here can change in an instant. You should have brought something waterproof with you." Olivia had never listened to him when he'd given her those lectures either.

A glint of temper sparked in Izzy's dark eyes. Clearly, she'd picked up on his mood. "Believe me, I'm well aware of that."

"Then you should know to always come prepared," he said, unable to stop himself. "If you get wet, you'll get cold and there's no shelter here."

"Thank you." She did not sound thankful in the slightest. "I'll be sure to remember that next time."

Anger coiled inside him like a bad-tempered snake and he knew very well that he wasn't pissed at her for not bringing a parka. He was pissed about the constant hum of desire he felt whenever he was around her, about how he could tell himself till he was blue in the face that once was enough but the fact remained that once wasn't enough. Not nearly enough.

Also he didn't want her getting wet. He didn't want her getting cold. He didn't want her first trip into the bush to be miserable, because Olivia's had been and she'd hated it. Oh, she'd said it was fine, that it was lovely and she'd enjoyed it, but he knew she hadn't. She'd made passive-aggressive remarks the whole time about how wet it was and how chilly she felt and how uncomfortable it was, and nothing he did made it better. She'd never come with him again.

"You should go wait in the boat," he said curtly. "You'll stay dry there at least."

Izzy had a grimly determined look on her face that did not bode well. "Gus asked me to come and see the falls, and that's what I want to do. A bit of rain won't hurt me. You don't need to fuss."

Chase ignored her, stopping in the middle of the track and forcing her to stop with him. Then he dug into his backpack, bringing out the lightweight parka he'd packed for himself. "Here," he said, thrusting it at her. "Wear that."

She glanced at the parka in his hand. "But what about you?"

"I'm ex-SAS. I'll be fine." Besides, although the jacket he was wearing had no hood, it kept his torso dry.

She frowned, rain misting her face and sparkling in her dark hair. "Sure, but you're still human. You can die of exposure just as easily as I can."

He nearly growled. "Put it on."

"What if someone else needs it? You don't need to make an exception for me."

But he was in no mood to stand around arguing with her. Already he could hear the sounds of the tourists fading as they went on up the track, and he didn't want to let them get too far ahead.

"I've got other people to manage," he said flatly. "And no time to be standing here bloody arguing with you. Either put on the damn parka or go back to the boat and I'll get Levi to come over and get you."

"But I—"

"I'm already having to make an exception for you because you're being bloody difficult. Now just do as you're told for once in your damn life."

Color flooded her face, real anger glowing in her eyes. "Fine." Temper vibrated in her voice. "Far be it from me to be difficult. I'll wait in the boat."

He'd struck a nerve, that was clear, but he didn't have time to figure out which particular nerve it was and he was too angry himself to bother.

Digging out the two-way radio, he called back to HQ and organized Levi to bring the jet boat to pick Izzy up.

"You could have just put the parka on," he said as he packed the radio away.

Izzy had already turned back down the track. "No, thank you. I wouldn't want to put you out any further with my extreme difficultness."

Way to go for letting your dick do your talking for you, asshole.

"Izzy," he said, a thread of guilt winding through him.

But she ignored him, tramping back down the trail through the rain, her shoulders hunched.

The need to go after her and make sure she was okay tugged at him, but Levi was coming, and besides, Chase had a load of tourists, not to mention his kid, to look after.

Forcing both his temper and his guilt away, he turned in the direction of the falls and continued on up the track.

Despite the rain, the expedition turned out great, the tourists loving the majesty of the falls, spending a good hour taking pictures and asking him questions. Gus, Beth, and Indigo also asked him questions, but theirs were about where Izzy was, and so he had to tell them she'd decided to turn back.

He did not mention that he'd probably put her off from coming the rest of the way by being a bad-tempered dick.

Levi radioed him to let him know that he'd picked Izzy up and then, after Chase had told him to, radioed again when they'd arrived back at HQ. Izzy was apparently fine and no worse for wear.

Given that Levi didn't make any snide remarks, it was obvious that Izzy's bad temper was something she reserved only for him, and he wasn't sure whether that was a back-handed compliment or not.

Whatever, he had to be very strict with himself and not take his bad mood out on the tourists, making an effort to be as pleasant as possible as he guided them back down the track to the boat again.

By the time he'd gotten them back over the lake, made sure hot cocoa at HQ was provided—a complimentary service when the weather was bad that he'd found tourists appreciated—then dealt with the equipment cleanup and inventory that was usual after an expedition, he was feeling a lot less grumpy, but a lot more guilty about his behavior with Izzy.

Sure, he could be a hard-ass about certain things, especially the weather, but he knew that most of his temper was coming from the fact that he still wanted her. Which was stupid. He needed to pull himself together and start being an adult, not acting like a sulky little boy denied a sweet.

She was obviously finding this as difficult as he was, and since they were going to be in close proximity to each other by dint of living in the same tiny town, they were going to have to clear the air.

After he'd finished up at HQ, he took Gus over to the

Rose, found out where Izzy was from Beth and Indigo, who were in the pub having a quiet shandy, left Gus with them, then went next door to the "art-orientated space."

Apparently some tradesman hadn't turned up and Izzy was annoyed about it. Knowing what he did about the local tradespeople and how very few of them came out to Brightwater, he wasn't surprised, but she'd told him in no uncertain terms that she was going to handle it. So he'd let her.

He wasn't quite prepared for the sight that greeted him when he stepped into the gallery though.

Izzy was crouched in the dust on the floor, measuring out things with a tape measure and then pausing to scribble notes down on the piece of paper beside her. She'd changed into some dry clothes, which was something, her hair caught in a loose ponytail at her nape. It had a curl to it that he hadn't noticed before and was disturbed to find he wanted to wind one of those silky strands around his finger, remember what it felt like against his skin.

He shoved away the feeling. "What are you doing?" he asked, stepping into the dusty, empty space. "It's going to get dark soon and there's no electricity here."

She didn't look up. "Can you please stop telling me things I already know?"

Huh. Fair enough.

Chase came to stand next to her, watching her for a moment. Then he said, "You're pissed at me. I get it. I wasn't very nice at the falls."

"You were only trying to make sure I was okay." Her voice sounded stiff. "I shouldn't have walked away like that."

Well, he hadn't expected that. Olivia had never done much conceding.

He crouched down beside her. "I keep on touching that nerve, don't I?"

She sighed, then turned her head, her eyes very dark in the gathering twilight. "You were right. I was…being difficult."

He'd come over here to apologize to her, not to have her apologize to him, and for some reason it bothered him.

"You weren't being difficult," he said. "You were only responding to me ordering you around and being a general asshole. I shouldn't have snapped at you and I'm sorry."

She shook her head. "I shouldn't have argued."

"To be fair, I've already told you that I *like* you arguing with me."

Something shifted in her eyes. "Arguing doesn't help, Chase."

That was true. Not when they both knew what the problem really was.

That problem was crackling in the air between them now, the tension drawing tight, the memory of that afternoon standing between them.

But he'd said once and once only, and he'd meant it. And no matter that every part of him was urging him to take her chin in his hand and kiss her, taste her, he wasn't going to.

That wouldn't help either.

So instead, he cleared his throat and asked, "What are you doing now?"

If she was disappointed in his change of subject, she didn't show it. Her lashes lowered. "The stupid tradesman didn't turn up. And I need to get these shelves made, so…"

"So, what? You're going to do it yourself?"

She frowned. "Nothing wrong with that, is there?"

"Don't tell me," he said, amused despite himself. "You've

built many shelves before and know your way around a hammer."

"I might." Izzy turned away to measure out another length.

"Izzy," he said gently, "I can help you. I did offer, remember?"

"Sure. After you gave me a big lecture on how some people found living here too difficult and too hard, etcetera, etcetera."

Shit. So he had.

He sighed. "Okay, yeah, I did say that. But that doesn't mean people here leave each other to sink or swim. We support each other and help one another, that's how it works." He held out his hand. "Come on, give me the tape measure."

She gave him a look. "This is hardly me handling it, is it?"

"It's you being intelligent and knowing when to ask for help." He gave her the same look in return. "You think I can run a business full-time and bring Gus up without help? Sure, I could, but it's a damn sight easier for both me and Gus to have Finn and Levi and Cait and the rest of the town's support."

Izzy stared at him for a long moment, her expression unreadable. Then abruptly she let out a breath. "I suppose so," she said, then handed him the tape measure.

Chapter 11

A COUPLE OF DAYS LATER, IZZY FINISHED PUTTING THE last touches of whitewash on the newly built shelves Chase and Finn had constructed against the back wall of the new gallery, then stepped back to survey her handiwork.

Beth had gone into Queenstown again to investigate suppliers for jewelry materials, while Indigo had gone up the valley with Finn, who was going to introduce her to someone who had a sheep farm and who could possibly provide her with some local wool for her planned dye works. So Izzy had decided to finish painting the shelves on her own.

She had to admit they looked beautiful. The bare stone walls were to be left as they were, providing a lovely rustic backdrop, the perfect showcase for all the new products they'd soon be stocking.

Turned out Chase had been right. No matter that she'd charged into the gallery with a tape measure, angry with herself and how she'd let Chase's bad temper rile her into behaving like an idiot and wanting to somehow make up for it by building the shelves herself, she probably couldn't. Not when she'd never wielded a hammer in her life.

Accepting his help had been the most logical step, but she'd found it difficult. She was used to getting on and doing things herself, and it felt weird and almost wrong to let someone else do something for her.

Especially him. Especially when in the middle of hammering wood he'd stripped off his shirt because it had been hot. She'd had to leave at that point, making up some excuse to go to the Rose for something.

Stupid man.

She hadn't expected him to come and find her after the aborted trek, and certainly not armed with an apology for his own shortness.

Really, though, the main problem was that she shouldn't have let him get to her. But he *had* hit a nerve. When he'd told her to stop being so difficult, she'd felt exactly the way she so often had as a teenager after Zeke had left and her father's patience had run thin.

"You're always so damn difficult, Isabella," he'd said curtly, after she'd tried to argue with him about something. "Always complaining, always arguing. Well, if you want anything from me, shut the hell up and do as you're told."

So she had shut the hell up. And she'd done what she was told. Because after Zeke had gone, she'd had no one else. No one but a shady father and a social-climbing mother, neither of whom were particularly concerned for her.

However, they were her only family and life had gotten a whole lot easier when she started to play the good-daughter role.

Apparently, though, difficult was all she could be anywhere near Chase Kelly. Especially with him swanning around being all competent and gorgeous and unspeakably sexy.

He continues to be a problem.

He was, damn him.

The sound of the door opening made Izzy turn, and Cait came in with Gus trailing along unexpectedly behind her.

Izzy hadn't seen the girl hanging around lately and had

wondered why and whether it had anything to do with her sudden revelation about her father while they were on the walk.

Putting down her paintbrush, she smiled. "Hey, you two."

"Hey," Cait said, while Gus glanced around the store curiously. "Can you do me a favor? Chase has been off up the river with some tourists, but he's run into some trouble with the boat engine. Levi and a few others have gone to help him, but it's looking like he won't be back for a while, and I have to go to the vineyard to see Clive and Teddy about a few things."

"Oh, sure. What do you want me to do?"

Cait nodded at Gus, who'd gone over to the shelves and was now inspecting them. "Can you keep an eye on her? I don't know how long Chase will be, but it might be a few hours."

Well, it wasn't as if Izzy had a packed schedule or anything. And twelve-year-old girls surely didn't require much in the way of input.

"Sure," she said. "No problem at all."

Cait grinned. "Great. Stick with Izzy this afternoon, Gus. Just until your dad gets home, okay?"

"Okay." Gus sounded not at all bothered, still staring intently at the shelves.

Cait left and Izzy began tidying up the painting gear.

"I'll just clean these brushes," she said to Gus.

The kid nodded.

Izzy waited for her to say something, but she didn't. Huh. The last few times she'd seen Gus, the kid had been very chatty, so what was up? Was she annoyed at being dumped on Izzy? Or was this pretty much par for the course? Maybe it was. Gus must be used to being passed around to different people when Chase was busy.

"*It didn't matter that she had a kid who needed her, she decided she'd had enough and she left. And she never came back.*" Chase's voice from their conversation in the car a week earlier echoed in her head and she could still hear the suppressed fury in it, talking about his ex-wife.

The memory made a tight feeling gather behind Izzy's breastbone.

Poor Gus. Her mother just…gone. Chase was a good man, a good father, she'd already learned that over the past couple of weeks, but with a business to contend with and the little town he saw as his responsibility to save, he couldn't be everywhere at once. No matter that he'd said the town helped out, did this kid have anyone else apart from him to talk to?

Izzy couldn't help thinking about her parents again and her own rather painfully lonely teenage years after her brother had left. Being the good girl, the perfect daughter. Getting a job in the family oil company, going with her mother to the country club and smiling politely for her mother's friends. But her mother hadn't really been interested in *her*, only in what she could do for her.

The tight feeling in Izzy's chest twisted, but she shoved it away. She wasn't thinking of her parents now. She had a kid to look after.

Picking up the brushes and pots, Izzy carried them down to the very basic little bathroom that lay through a door at the back of the store, dumping the lot in the sink. She began to wash out the plastic tub she'd been using for the whitewash, conscious all of a sudden that Gus had appeared in the doorway.

The kid didn't say anything, only watched her.

Izzy kept washing. "You okay with spending the afternoon with me?"

"Oh, yeah," Gus said casually. "Dad's away a lot sometimes. I usually hang out with Uncle Finn or Levi, but they're doing stuff."

"You wouldn't rather hang out with someone you know?"

"Nah. I asked Cait if you could look after me this afternoon."

Izzy paused scrubbing the plastic tub and looked up in surprise. "You did?"

Gus looked back, gray gaze very open. "How come you don't wear those skirts anymore?"

Izzy blinked at the sudden change of topic. "What?"

"Those skirts. You know, the really tight ones. And the shirts with the bows."

Izzy blinked again, nonplussed. Were all twelve-year-old girls this direct? Or was it simply that having been brought up by her dad and uncle she'd adopted their manner?

Whatever it was, it was disconcerting.

"Is that why you wanted to hang out with me?" Izzy asked, deciding that she'd be direct back. "So you could ask me about the skirts?"

Gus leaned against the doorframe, kicking one sneakered foot against it. "Yeah. And other things." She didn't seem to find Izzy's own directness disconcerting.

Okay then. Maybe that's how all conversations with Gus went. She'd certainly been direct on the walk to the falls.

"I don't wear those skirts and blouses anymore." Izzy went back to washing out the tub. "They're for an office. And I'm not in an office here."

"They were pretty though." Gus narrowed her gaze at the fitted pink T-shirt Izzy was wearing, the only thing she had that she didn't mind getting paint on. "I like that T-shirt too."

There was something quite determined in the girl's tone, something purposeful. As if Gus had made a decision and was hell-bent on carrying it through.

Remind you of anyone?

Oh yes. It did.

Izzy rinsed out the tub, filled it with water and put the paint brushes into it to soak, then met the girl's gaze.

Gus's long, dark hair was in an untidy ponytail down her back, and she wore her usual uniform of loose T-shirt and jeans with holes in them, nothing out of the ordinary for a kid. Except Gus was on the cusp of not being a kid anymore. She was approaching young womanhood…

A young woman whose mother had left and had never come back.

That Gus was happy and healthy there was no doubt, but Izzy was abruptly sure that there was a reason the girl had been hanging around her and Beth and Indigo.

"What's this all about, Gus?" She kept her tone as direct as Gus had been, since clearly the girl didn't have a problem with it.

Gus pulled a face and glanced away, her cheeks pinking.

Izzy didn't say anything, letting the girl come to whatever decision she was going to make in her own time.

Finally, Gus's mouth firmed and she looked back at Izzy. "Okay, so it's like this. There's a boy I like in my class, but he's never going to notice me if I keep wearing these." She made an annoyed gesture at her own jeans and tee. "So I want to get some new stuff. Some…girl stuff. But I need someone to take me and someone who can...you know, tell me if it looks nice."

The tight feeling in Izzy's chest was back, tugging harder. "Your dad can't take you?"

Gus rolled her eyes in the time-honored teenage way. "Dad? Seriously? He doesn't want to go into clothes shops, and he'd just tell me I'd look good in anything. Then he'd wonder why I need more than jeans and T-shirts, since a skirt isn't practical for going fishing or whatever." She paused, giving Izzy a very serious look. "And I'm *not* telling Dad about this, okay? He can't know."

Maybe that was for the best. Chase was a protector and she could see him getting quite bothered about his daughter liking a boy.

Izzy folded her arms and leaned against the sink. "Don't worry, your secret's safe with me." She hesitated, then added, "It is kind of uncomfortable though, to know something about you that your dad doesn't."

The girl frowned. "Okay but, like, I'm not doing drugs or anything. Or drinking beer."

Izzy tried not to smile at that. "Sure. But if it gets serious, I can't promise I won't tell him."

Gus rolled her eyes yet again. "Fine."

"Are you really sure he wouldn't want to go shopping with you? He helped me find some great boots."

"He won't." Gus's chin took on a stubborn tilt. "He'd just suggest I get some more T-shirts or something. Because they're 'practical.'" She said the word with so much disgust Izzy had to suppress another grin. "You see these clothes?" Once again she gestured at her outfit. "They're Dad and Uncle Finn's old clothes."

Izzy stared at her. "Chase dresses you in his old clothes?"

Gus flushed. "Oh, it's not too bad. I mean, I like them for mucking around in. And it's good because it means if I get them dirty or rip them, it doesn't matter."

"But you're still wearing your dad's old clothes."

Gus nodded. "I don't want to be mean. Dad's great and I know he cares about me a lot, but…"

"But you're still wearing your dad's old clothes," Izzy repeated, appalled.

A small smile curved Gus's mouth. "Yeah."

Already Izzy could see where this was going. "Don't tell me, you want to ask me if I can take you to get some new ones."

Gus's eyes got very big. "Would you? Those skirts were really pretty and I liked the bows on those shirts. And you had those high heels and—"

"They're really for adults," she interrupted gently, because she could imagine Chase's face if his daughter suddenly turned up in a pencil skirt, a blouse with a bow, and high heels, and it would not be pretty.

"I still want something like that," Gus insisted. "I want something pretty so Jamie will notice me."

This was not exactly how Izzy had imagined her afternoon would go. But Gus had clearly come here with a mission and she'd chosen Izzy specifically, which made Izzy's heart ache. That this girl should come to her, a stranger, with a request that was important to her.

And it wasn't something that Izzy could refuse; she knew that already.

"It's not clothes that make people notice you, you know that, right?" Because it had to be said. "It's who you are that matters."

Gus rolled her eyes yet again, clearly weary of such adult observations. "Oh, I know *that*. Jamie knows me already. He's my friend. But I don't want him to see me as just a friend."

"That's a problem," Izzy replied, trying to think back to when she'd been twelve and in the throes of her first crush, though she wasn't sure if she'd had any crushes at that stage. Boys hadn't been on her radar at all, not until high school. She'd been too busy trying to be her mother's perfect girl. "Have you tried telling him how you feel?"

Gus gave her an exasperated look. "Well, that's what I want to do. But I want to do it wearing something pretty. I want him to know that I'm serious about him."

Izzy was rather impressed. The girl was self-possessed and knew her own mind and obviously had no problems with expressing it, and that was a testament to Chase's parenting. Because that kind of confidence only came from growing up knowing that you were loved. That you were accepted. And having your views and your opinions treated with the respect they deserved.

"I agree," Izzy said after a moment. "If you want to go out and get something, you have to be serious about it. And if that means dressing the part, then yes, you should absolutely wear something pretty. You have to let him know that you mean business, right?"

Gus nodded emphatically. "Right."

Well, there was nothing much else she could say. Gus had chosen her to come to with this request and she couldn't say no.

"Okay, well, since you're straight with me, I'll be straight with you." She pushed herself away from the sink, her decision made. "I don't want to step on your dad's toes or anyone else's here, so you need to ask him if it's okay if I take you out for a shopping trip first. But if he's okay with it, then I am too." She smiled. "In fact, I'd love to take you out if you'd like that."

Chase was tired and grumpy by the time he managed to get home.

It was after seven at night and he'd spent all afternoon with a group of increasingly frustrated tourists whom he'd tried to keep happy, all the while attempting to fix an extremely temperamental boat engine.

None of it had gone particularly well, though he'd managed to cheer up the tourists by having Finn bring some horses down from Clint's stables so they could ride back to Brightwater township, and then gave them a round of free drinks at the Rose before they all got on their buses to go home.

The boat needed to be put on a trailer and taken back to HQ, where hopefully Levi could work his magic with its engine since Levi could make just about anything go when he set his mind to it, and that had taken up a good couple of hours.

Then he'd had to unsnarl another booking stuff-up as well as helping Finn get the horses back to Clint's, and now he was tired and bad-tempered because what he'd wanted to do at the end of the day was sit on the deck of his house, play a couple of games of backgammon with Gus—she was getting quite good at it—and then maybe watch a movie with her.

His time with her was precious, and he was very conscious

that in a couple of years, hanging out with her father was the last thing she'd want to be doing.

Chase's house was a ten-minute drive from the township and up a winding gravel drive. It had been built by his grandfather on the side of one of the hills above Brightwater Lake, and over the years Chase had added little improvements to it here and there. A wide deck at the front of the house to take advantage of the magnificent views over the lake and the mountains. A remodeling of the bathroom that Olivia had demanded. A big cast-iron wood burner in the living area that heated the house and the water. A kitchen update that he had to do in order to install another coffee machine like the one in HQ.

He loved his house. It was warm, comfortable, and surrounded by bush and had a history to it that was important to him—normally the best part of his day was finally getting home and being able to relax.

Yet he knew as soon as he walked in the door that something about it was different. He could hear voices in the kitchen. His daughter's and...

Shit. Izzy's. What the hell was she doing here?

His whole body tightened and his heart gave an unexpected and hard kick.

He'd had to get Cait to look after Gus today since he had a group to take up the river, and he knew that if Cait couldn't manage it, someone else could always be found to keep an eye on the kid. The town had always been good like that, mainly because there weren't many kids around and so the ones they did have were even more precious.

But he hadn't thought that Izzy or any of the other Deep River girls would be roped into looking after Gus.

The sound of Izzy's laughter drifted into the hallway. He'd never heard it before. It was low and husky and sweet, and set off something humming inside him.

He should be annoyed to find her here, irritated that she was in his territory having fun with his daughter, but for some reason he wasn't. No, it was the opposite. There was something...good about the sound of her voice and her presence here. Something that almost felt like rightness.

Which was crazy. Nothing had changed between them. He still wanted her far too much for his own good, and building those shelves for her hadn't helped. He shouldn't have taken his shirt off, that had been unnecessary; but she'd been in the store at the time and he could feel her watching him, and so the wicked part of him had decided, well, why not give her something to look at?

Yeah, she brought out the rebel, the bad boy he'd never allowed himself to be, not even when he'd been young. Because he'd had a younger brother to be a role model for since their father hadn't apparently wanted the job.

It wouldn't have been an issue if he'd had that part of himself under control, but he didn't. Not when she was around.

And now she was here, in his house...

Another part of him, the possessive part, had no problem with this whatsoever. That part wanted her here, could see no difficulty with it, and in fact, now that she was here, perhaps she could stay the night—

No. That was *not* happening. Chrissake, he needed to get himself together.

Shoving aside his persistent dick thoughts, Chase strode into the kitchen.

It was a cheerful, rustic space, with large windows that

looked out into the bush and gave glimpses of the lake, furnished with wooden cupboards and long counters that he'd built, sanded, and varnished himself.

Standing at one of the counters, surrounded by packets of flour, containers of sugar, vanilla essence, baking soda, and lots of other baking detritus, were Izzy and Gus.

Izzy was currently stirring something in a mixing bowl, assisted by Gus who emptied something else into it before tossing the spoon she'd used into the sink, which was full of other dirty mixing bowls.

Flour dusted his counter, his kitchen floor, his daughter's hair, and Izzy's pink T-shirt. And when his boots crunched on the floor, he realized it wasn't just flour everywhere either, but possibly sugar and maybe a few other unidentifiable things.

He stood there for a second, staring around at his previously clean and tidy kitchen, now a mess of flour, discarded measuring spoons, pantry ingredients, and dirty dishes. Then Izzy looked up briefly from her mixing bowl, dark eyes glowing and flour on her cheek. She was so lovely it hurt. "Hey," she said. "Don't worry, we're going to clean up."

Gus beamed at him from the other side of the counter that doubled as a breakfast bar. "We're making cupcakes!"

Chase opened his mouth to say something—he had no idea what—but Gus continued before he could. "We made dinner too."

"Dinner?" he echoed blankly.

His daughter went over to the fridge. "Yes, and there's some for you." She pulled open the fridge door, grabbed one of his favorite cans of beer, and took it over to him. "Here. Go and sit on the deck. I'll bring a plate out for you."

Chase stared at her. If he was late home, Cait would sometimes give Gus something at the Rose, or Finn, who lived in his own house farther up the driveway, would. Levi could put ramen in the microwave and had been known to fry an egg on occasion, but none of them ever thought about feeding his child and him as well. Normally he'd have to get his own dinner.

"Go on." Gus made shooing gestures at him, clearly very pleased at the prospect of bringing him something. "Go and sit down."

Izzy was too busy pouring out cupcake mixture into some ancient cupcake pans he hadn't even realized he had.

It seemed stupid to argue, not that he even had a clue what he'd be arguing about, so he took the beer without a word, went into the living room, and opened the doors that led onto the big, wide deck out the front.

A few old wooden chairs were grouped together, but he sat down on his favorite, a long wooden bench with a back and a thick seat cushion to make it comfortable. In front of it was a low wooden coffee table that he liked to kick his boots up on whenever he sat down, and he did so now, relaxing back into the seat.

Normally he liked to sit there and enjoy the quiet and perhaps to contemplate the beauty of the intense mineral-blue of the lake against the deep dark-green of the bush.

But the view was the last thing on his mind as he picked up his beer and cracked it open, still thinking about his daughter's bright face and Izzy in his kitchen, making bloody cupcakes of all things.

He hadn't ever done any baking with Gus, mainly because he hadn't ever thought about it—baking wasn't his thing.

He hadn't thought it was Gus's thing either, but she'd sure looked pretty happy.

In fact, he couldn't remember the last time he'd seen her looking so excited.

Something in his gut clenched, but before he could identify what it was, Gus came clattering out the french doors from the living room, carrying a plate and a knife and fork. On it was a fresh-looking salad, a perfectly cooked steak, and a big pile of mashed potatoes.

He stared at it as Gus put the food down on the coffee table.

"There," she said grandly. "Dinner."

Chase took his boots off the table and looked at the plate, conscious that Gus was staring at him, obviously waiting for his reaction.

"This looks delicious," he said honestly. "Did Izzy make this?"

"Yes. She thought you might be hungry."

Izzy had made him dinner. Izzy had thought about him.

No one thought about him, not in that way. No one ever worried about him. No one ever cared if he was tired after a long day. No one was ever there to give him a beer, make him a meal, let him have a few minutes to himself.

Not even Olivia had done that for him.

The tight feeling inside him clenched tighter, but he didn't want to think about it, not when there was this delicious dinner right in front of him.

So he leaned forward and picked up the plate, grabbing the knife and fork with it. "I thought Cait was looking after you today?"

Gus stuck her hands in her pockets and rocked on her

feet. "She was. But then she had to go to the Granges', so I asked if Izzy could look after me instead."

Chase stared at her in surprise, momentarily distracted from his food. "What?"

Gus ignored this. "Dad, can I ask you something?"

He started to ask her whether it could wait until he'd had a least a bite of his steak when she went on in a rush: "I want to go out shopping with Izzy. Can I?"

"Shopping," he repeated blankly. "With Izzy."

"Yes. I want some new clothes and I want to go to town and Izzy said she'd take me but I had to ask you first, so can I? Please?"

Chase was very conscious that the word no was automatically forming in his mouth, driven by his usual protective impulses when it came to his daughter. But there was something in Gus's face that made him say "I'll need to talk to Izzy about that" instead.

"Shall I go and get her?" Gus asked excitedly.

He gave her a firm look. "Let me eat my dinner first."

"Okay. I'll go and tell her to come out when you're finished." She gave him a brief but tight hug. "Thanks, Dad," she said, as if Chase had already given her permission, then vanished into the house, no doubt to tell Izzy the good news.

Damn.

He was tempted to go straight after her and sort the whole thing out now, but he needed to process how he felt about it because he still wasn't sure.

And anyway, he was hungry.

So he sat out on the deck and ate the food that Izzy had cooked, which was very good indeed, and then sat back and sipped on his beer, taking a few moments to enjoy the unfamiliar sensation of someone looking after him.

Then, finishing the beer, Chase rose to his feet, picked up his plate and his cutlery, and went back inside.

In the kitchen, Izzy was putting the cupcakes into the oven, while Gus stood at the sink washing some bowls. The counters were a lot cleaner and the floor had been swept, and if it wasn't quite up to his usual pristine standards, it wasn't far off.

Gus put the bowl she'd been cleaning on the plate rack to drain, glanced at Chase, then announced loudly, "There's something I need to do in my room. Can I wash the rest of these later?"

Izzy straightened up, also giving Chase a glance, though hers was much more enigmatic than his daughter's. "Sure," she said.

Gus dashed out, giving Chase a meaningful look as she did so.

He put his dirty dishes down next to the sink, then turned and leaned back against the counter, folding his arms.

Izzy was fiddling with the timer on the stove. The color of her flour-dusted pink T-shirt made her skin glow and her hair look glossy, and his ever-present desire tightened its grip. Did she feel any of this too? Or was it all him?

Not that they should be discussing that.

"So," he said at last. "Want to tell me why my daughter has a sudden burning desire to go shopping with you?"

Chapter 12

Izzy gave Chase an assessing glance. He'd looked tired when he'd walked in and if it had taken him this long to deal with a broken-down boat motor and ferrying disappointed tourists around, no wonder.

She'd been wary of making him feel as if she was muscling in on his territory, so she hadn't wanted to spring the shopping discussion on him immediately, thinking he'd probably be more receptive after a beer, some food, and a sit down.

As she'd already thought numerous times, he was a single dad with a busy company and a town to look after, not to mention an overdeveloped sense of responsibility, and even though he might have Finn and Levi and a few others to help, he had no one to look after *him*.

Did he have anyone to make sure he had dinner? To give him five minutes at the end of the day to destress? Who could, for an hour or so, take some of those heavy responsibilities from his broad shoulders?

No, he didn't. So she would.

He'd been so nice to her after that little hissy fit she'd thrown on the track, and then had helped her build some shelves, so returning the favor had seemed only fair. Plus she liked looking after people. Especially people who needed it, and she sensed that he needed it.

"Okay," she said calmly. "It all started because Cait had some things to do, so Gus asked if I could look after her this afternoon. I was free and of course I said yes. We hung out at the Rose for a while and then Cait came back to say you'd be longer than anticipated, so Gus decided we should come back here. Jim gave us a ride and I—"

"Yeah, Gus told me." Chase was frowning.

He was in full outdoors mode again today, those forest-green utility pants that hugged his lean hips and thighs in ways that should be illegal, his usual black Pure Adventure NZ T-shirt, and battered hiking boots.

He looked every inch the dangerous SAS paratrooper he'd once been and she wanted him even more than she had in that hotel room in Queenstown.

So much for casual.

She folded her arms across her thundering heart and tried to keep her tone calm. "That's not a problem, is it?"

"What? Her wanting you to look after her? No. But I'd kind of like to know why."

Here was the tricky bit. And she knew it was going to be tricky, because over the past few hours, Gus had artlessly shared quite a bit about her father. That she loved him was without question. That she worried about him in the way kids worried about their parents was obvious too.

He tried to do everything for her, tried to give her everything, or so Gus had said, but there were some things he couldn't. And although she hadn't fully said what those things were, Izzy could read between the lines.

Gus missed her mother quite desperately, and she didn't want her father to know because she didn't want him to be upset. And he'd be upset because a mother was the one thing he couldn't give her.

"She wants to go shopping," Izzy said carefully. "For girl clothes. And she wants a woman's opinion on them."

A muscle flicked in Chase's strong jaw. "Why does she need that? She's got plenty of good, practical clothing that she can wear."

This was going to be even more tricky. She didn't want to betray Gus's secret crush, but she also didn't want to upset Chase.

And he would be upset. Chase was a man who went above and beyond for the people who mattered to him, and he'd probably be angry. Not with her, but with himself for not being able to be all things to his daughter.

Izzy dropped her arms and took a couple of steps toward him. "Gus is nearly thirteen," she said. "She's just starting to figure out what being a woman means. She's been hanging around me, Beth, and Indigo because…well. She wants some female guidance."

Chase's dark brows lowered. "She's got Cait."

"I know. But she didn't want to stay with Cait today. And she didn't ask Cait to take her shopping. She asked me."

"Why you?"

"She liked my skirts and my blouses. I did tell her that a pretty dress wouldn't make her a woman, but she wants to try on some anyway." Izzy gave him a small smile. "She's stubborn. No idea where she got that from."

He didn't smile back. Really, a frown suited him far too well.

Eventually, she said, "This isn't a failing on your part, you know that, don't you?"

He let out a breath and abruptly ran one hand over his face. "Yeah, I know."

Oh, he was tired. And despite what he'd said, she did wonder if he really knew that he wasn't failing Gus, not on any level.

Her heart felt a little tight, so she took another step forward and before she could think better of it, she'd laid a hand on one of the strong forearms folded across his chest, and looked him in the eye. "Do you know? Really?"

Chase was silent, but his gaze was full of thunderclouds.

"She's a wonderful kid," Izzy went on, suddenly very much wanting to ease his worry. "She's direct and open and honest. And she seems really happy and secure. That's a testament to you, for being such a great father." His skin felt very warm beneath her fingertips, and even though she knew that touching him was a very bad idea, she didn't take her hand away. "And you *are* a great dad, Chase. I'm not looking to muscle in on your territory here or do anything you might not want, so if you think that her taking a shopping trip with me is a bad idea, then we won't go. But I really like her. And if you're okay with it, I'd love to take her out if she wants to."

Chase had gone very still, that muscle leaping in the side of his jaw, a subtle tension radiating off of him. He stared at her from beneath his straight, dark brows, his beautifully carved mouth in a hard line.

She couldn't tell what was going through his head.

"You should probably not touch me right now," he said at last, his voice rough, something hot glimmering in the depths of his eyes.

Oh, right. It was *that*.

Izzy took her hand off him, flushing.

At that point the timer on the oven went off and Gus came dashing back into the kitchen. "Are they ready?"

Izzy turned away from him, opening the oven and checking on the cupcakes. Her heart was beating far too fast and she couldn't get the glint of heat she'd seen in Chase's eyes out of her head.

Oh boy, the sexual tension between them was still strong and, yes, still a problem.

Izzy forced that thought away and concentrated instead on the cupcakes, which were indeed ready.

"So can I go?" Gus was asking Chase, her voice full of hope. "Please, Dad?"

There was a pause and then Chase said, "I suppose so."

"Yay! Thanks, Dad!"

"But you're not wearing a brand-new dress when you're coming fishing with me."

"Of course I'm not going to wear a dress when I come fishing with you." Gus sounded scornful. "I'm not *that* stupid."

Izzy allowed herself a smile as she took the cupcake pan over to the counter and tipped the cupcakes out onto a wire cooling rack, the tight feeling in her chest beginning to ease.

She'd hoped Chase would allow it and she'd thought he probably would. His daughter's happiness was very important to him, she'd gotten that loud and clear. More important than his own fears too, judging from his granting of her request.

He's a good man.

The thought came out of nowhere, lingering in her head.

Yes. Yes, he was. A very good man.

Better than Josh.

A small thread of pain wound through her, no matter that she tried to ignore it. He *was* better than Josh. Protective and giving while Josh had been nothing but selfish, and how she hadn't seen that in her ex-fiancé she didn't know. But she saw it now.

She had to stop thinking about it though. She wasn't romantically involved with Chase. She'd had sex with him once and that was it. And the sex they'd had was casual. Very, *very* casual.

Yes, Chase had made her feel special and desirable and important, but that didn't mean it mattered.

What she should be thinking about was the new business she and Beth and Indigo were in the process of starting up, and speaking of which, she probably needed to get back to the Rose and check with in with them, leave Chase and Gus to have some time to themselves.

"Well," she said, turning around to face the other two, "since that's settled, I should head back to the Rose."

Gus's happy smile vanished. "What? But you can't leave yet. We need to ice the cupcakes and then you need to have one."

"I know, but I think your dad might want some time with you. And you're probably sick of me by—"

"Stay."

The word was rough, bitten out, filling the kitchen with a sudden weight.

She met Chase's gaze. It was still dark, still stormy, but lightning glittered in it.

She swallowed, her mouth dry. "I don't want to intrude."

"You're not intruding." Gus dug an elbow into Chase's side. "Dad, tell her."

He didn't smile, his expression fierce. "Stay," he repeated. "Please." The hard line of his mouth relaxed a fraction. "Gus will never forgive me if you don't get a cupcake."

"No," his daughter replied, agreeing. "I definitely wouldn't."

It was a bad idea, but how could she refuse with the kid staring at her like that? After Chase had said "please"?

You can't and you don't want to.

That fluttering feeling in her stomach was back, a fizzing kind of lightness that she couldn't ignore.

She smiled, unable to help herself. "In that case, of course I'll stay."

It ended up being one of the nicest evenings she'd had in years.

Once the cupcakes had cooled, she and Gus iced them. Gus ceremonially presented one to Chase, who took a bite and pronounced them excellent. Then they all watched a movie together in the living room—chosen from a vast DVD collection stacked neatly onto wooden shelves that took up all of one wall—while eating the rest of the cupcakes. Gus paired hers with a hot chocolate, Chase with another beer, and Izzy with a glass of astonishingly good red wine he'd somehow unearthed from a cupboard in the kitchen.

And as she sat there watching the movie—some action film that Gus was particularly enamored of and clearly knew by heart since she and Chase narrated the entire thing—she realized that she loved Chase's place.

The old wooden house had a bit of a "cabin in the woods" vibe, but in a good way. There was nothing fancy about it, nothing particularly stylish, but it felt lived in. The decks that surrounded it were amazing, and the living room had the most comfortable old leather couches she'd ever sat on. There were a few pillows here and there, and a wall of shelves that contained books and DVDs and photos and other interesting-looking things.

It was nothing like her apartment in Houston, which was

clean and white and full of carefully chosen, stylish, and lux-
urious items that had taken her fancy.

It wasn't a showcase like her parents' house either, stuffed
full of expensive items and art as a declaration of success.

No, this was simple, down-to-earth, and comfortable.

A home.

It was late by the time the movie ended, and Gus was
vocal in her reluctance to go to bed but Chase was firm. It
was a school night, and besides, he was tired and he needed
to make sure Izzy got back to the Rose.

Gus reluctantly acquiesced, surprising Izzy with a firm
good-night hug before heading to her bedroom, Chase going
with her to tuck her in.

Five minutes later, he was back, and Izzy was conscious
suddenly that they were alone in the house and the sexual
tension that had been put on hold while they watched the
movie had sprung back to life again.

She pushed herself up from the couch, trying to hide her
attack of nerves. "I'd better get going, I guess."

Chase gave her an enigmatic look, then glanced down at
her glass that stood on the coffee table near the couch. "You
haven't finished your wine."

"No, but I—"

"Let's go sit outside." Without waiting for her to respond,
he moved across the room to the french doors that led out
onto the deck and opened them. "Bring your glass."

Left with no other option, Izzy picked up her wine and
followed him.

The sun had set, the darkness absolute. The air was cool,
raising goose bumps on Izzy's skin, and it was full of the
damp, spicy smell of the surrounding bush.

"Sit." Chase indicated the big wooden bench seat, piled with a thick seat cushion on the bottom and lots of pillows.

She did, while he disappeared back inside, coming out again a few minutes later with the beer he'd been drinking, plus a thick, cozy-looking patchwork quilt that he laid around her shoulders before sitting down next to her on the bench.

She shivered, though that had more to do with Chase than it did with the cool air. With the pressure of his hands as he arranged the quilt and then the heat of his body as he sat next to her. Not too close, but close enough to make her stomach swoop and dive.

There was a moment's silence, the night still and quiet around them.

The silence here was like a thick blanket, and she still hadn't gotten used to it, but the sky above more than made up for that. Stars glittered, a scattering of jewels on black velvet, and there were so many of them, and they were so bright. It was beautiful. A reminder of the greater universe of which they were one tiny part.

She wasn't sure why that comforted her, but it did.

"This area is a dark sky reserve," Chase said into the silence. "No light pollution allowed. Means you can actually see the stars."

"They're beautiful." She stared out into the darkness, the stars glowing like tiny pinpricks in a sheet of black paper with the light shining through. "This whole place is beautiful."

"Yeah, it is. We're lucky."

From some distance away came a rather bloodcurdling screech. It wasn't human, obviously a bird of some kind, but it made Izzy jump.

"What's that noise?" she asked.

"It's a kiwi. They do a lot of screeching sometimes."

"Sounds like someone being murdered."

"You are not the first person to have noted that." His voice was deep and dark as the night itself, the rough note in it oddly pronounced.

Her mouth went dry, her heartbeat accelerating. "Chase," she began.

"Izzy, you're a problem," he said in the same moment.

Surprise rippled through her and she turned to look at him.

There was enough light coming through the windows of the living room to illuminate some of his features, the high forehead and straight nose, carved cheekbones and black brows. The rest was lost in the darkness.

He wasn't looking at her but out over the bush toward the lake, his posture seemingly relaxed against the back of the seat. But he wasn't relaxed, not in any way.

"I see." Her heartbeat thudded loudly in her ears.

"No. I don't think you do." He paused. "I hope I wasn't too bad-tempered tonight."

"No, you weren't at all. You were being protective of Gus, anyway, and it sounds like you had a hell of a day."

"Yeah, I did." He took a sip of his beer. "But that's not the issue."

She clutched her wineglass tightly. "Oh?"

"I think you know what I'm talking about."

She swallowed. "Perhaps you'd better say it so we're both on the same page."

"Fair enough." He leaned forward and put his beer back on the coffee table in front of them. Then he turned and looked at her, the gray of his eyes lost in the darkness of the night. "I want you. All the time. I thought what we did in Queenstown would solve the problem, but it didn't. It hasn't. Every time you're in my vicinity, all I can think about is taking you to bed, and it's turning me into an asshole. I'm tired of it."

———

Chase was conscious of exactly how far away from him Izzy was sitting. He could have said to the millimeter. She sat there with her legs curled up under her, the quilt around her shoulders, the light coming through the windows glossing her hair. She was looking down at the wineglass in her hand, her lashes veiling her gaze, her expression impossible to read.

He wasn't sure whether he should have been so direct, but direct was all he had when it came to her.

Her staying had been a bad idea, but the moment Gus protested her leaving, he'd realized he didn't want her to leave either. His daughter clearly enjoyed her company, and after she'd looked after Gus, cooked dinner, and then been so understanding with him despite him being reluctant about the shopping trip, he couldn't then kick her out without even a thank-you.

He hadn't wanted to, either. His house had felt full of a warm, bright energy it had never had before and he wanted to keep it. He wanted Gus chattering happily and Izzy's warm hand on his arm, her dark eyes full of understanding as she looked up at him. Seeing into him, realizing he was tired and that he worried for his daughter, and acknowledging it.

Olivia had never been that perceptive. Everything was a

personal attack and her feelings were always the most important. She hadn't made any effort to understand, even though
he'd tried his best to understand her, and in the end the only
person she'd been interested in living with was herself.

Like his father in so many ways. The old bastard had
always been more about his own misery than about caring
for his two sons.

Izzy hadn't turned his off mood into an attack the way
Olivia might have, nor turned the whole thing into a fight.
She'd put her hand on his arm and told him that he was a
great dad. That he didn't need to feel as if Gus wanting some
female company was a failing.

How she'd seen that when he'd only been half-aware of
it himself, he had no idea. But he appreciated it. And something inside of him told him he'd needed it too. Just someone
to tell him that Gus was okay, that he hadn't totally screwed
up somehow.

The rest of the evening had been…well, pretty great. Just
sitting on the couch watching a movie with Gus and Izzy,
drinking their preferred drinks and eating cupcakes. She'd
pretended not to know what was going on in the movie so
Gus could tell her about it in great detail, something that
Gus absolutely loved doing, another thing that Izzy had
somehow guessed without anyone needing to tell her.

He appreciated it. And he appreciated her, smiling and
laughing with them, looking so pretty sitting on the end of
his couch in her pink T-shirt and jeans. He'd realized early on
that it wasn't flour on her tee or her cheek but paint, and he'd
decided he wouldn't tell her about it because she looked so
adorable. All kind of ruffled and less put-together than she
normally was. It suited her.

Like sitting out here in the dark with the quilt around her shoulders suited her.

"Ah," she said, her tone very neutral.

He was very conscious of her nearness, of the warmth of her body mere inches away. Reminding him of what it had felt like to have her beneath him, all soft and silky, her panting breaths in his ears.

"I'm not telling you this because I want you to do something about it, okay?" He stared at her still profile. "This is my problem to deal with. I only wanted to give you some context, in case you were wondering why I seemed bad-tempered."

Slowly, she lifted her head, looked out into the blackness of the bush around them, then turned and met his gaze. Her eyes were as dark as the night sky above their heads and just as deep, just as soft.

"Okay, well, since you mentioned it…" Her voice was very quiet. "I…can't stop thinking about you either. I want to do what we did in that hotel room again. I want…well, I guess what I'm trying to say is that I'd really like to have some more casual sex with you."

Electricity pulsed down his spine and into the space between them, making tension hum in the air like high-tension wires.

He didn't move. Couldn't. Not when he was sure that if he did he wouldn't be able to stop himself from reaching for her and dragging her into his lap.

She didn't look away. "So I suppose the next question is do you want to do something about it?"

Oh yes, he did. It would just be a really stupid idea. Once, he'd told himself. Once, and that would be enough. But it wasn't enough, and now he couldn't think of anything else but having more.

"One night," he bit out. "I want one whole night with you."

Her eyes darkened even further. "When?"

Something tight in him relaxed, while something else got tighter.

"Saturday night," he said. "Gus has a sleepover with a friend up the valley. Finn will be away, taking a group on a three-day weekend expedition, and Levi's going into town that night. I was going to go with him, but I can think up some excuse to stay here. You could come over, spend the night with me."

"Here? At your house?" Surprise flickered over her face. "Are you sure?"

It wasn't ideal, but quite frankly he didn't want to wait for the time it would take to organize something else.

"Yeah. It's easier than trying to think of excuses to spend a night in Queenstown." He paused. "What about Beth and Indigo? Can you get away without them suspecting anything?"

"I can do that." She gave him a searching look. "It's really that important to you that no one knows?"

She wouldn't understand. She hadn't been here long enough to know how small towns worked, how everyone was all up in everyone else's business and nothing ever stayed a secret for long. She didn't know either that people always had an opinion on whatever you were doing and weren't shy about telling you exactly what that opinion was.

He could only imagine what people would think about him and Izzy, and while he didn't care for himself, he didn't want any of that getting back to Gus. He didn't want his daughter to get too attached to someone who wouldn't be around for the long term.

"You and I are casual," he said. "But small towns don't really do casual—or at least this small town doesn't. The whole place is a hive of gossip too, and I don't want Gus getting caught in the middle of that."

"No, it's okay, I get it." Her hand reached out to him again in an instinctive gesture, her fingers resting lightly on his forearm, sending shocks through him. "You want to protect your daughter."

God, it was such a relief not to have to justify himself or explain his logic in exhaustive detail the way he'd had to do with Olivia.

He didn't have to do that with Izzy. She took him at face value. She understood.

The touch of her hand filled him with heat and he had to resist the urge to put it somewhere that would appreciate it even more than his arm did.

"Yes," he said, the word sounding rough. "I don't want her thinking that this is something it isn't. I don't want her hurt."

"I know. I understand." Izzy smiled. "You know, it's almost a bit like being a teenager and sneaking around so your parents don't find out. Not that I was ever that teenager, but... hey, it'll be fun for me."

He took a deep, slow breath, trying to force down his physical reaction, concentrating instead on what she was saying instead to distract himself. "What kind of teenager were you, then?"

She gave him a rueful look. "The boring kind. Got good grades, obeyed my curfew, never went to parties, did whatever I was told."

"Sounds like the perfect teenager to me."

"Yes, I suppose so. Every parent's dream."

There was a slight acid tinge to the words that caught his attention. "Not your parents' dream, I take it?"

She flushed, as if she'd let something slip she hadn't meant to. "It's nothing. Too much wine. Forget it." Her fingertips brushed along his skin as she began to pull away.

But he reached out, his hand coming down on top of hers, pressing her fingers lightly down.

"That's the second time you've told me that," he murmured, his curiosity now fully engaged. "And I still haven't forgotten."

Even in the dark, he could see the flush that spread out over her pale skin. She glanced down at his hand covering hers. "Chase."

"Izzy."

Her gaze lifted back to his, and for a second he was lost there. Then before he could stop himself, he moved, taking her wineglass from her fingers and putting it down on the coffee table. Then he slid one hand behind her head, gripping her ponytail gently, pulling her toward him until her mouth was almost but not quite touching his.

She didn't resist, her dark brown eyes glowing with sudden hunger.

Which of course meant he had no choice but to close that last inch between them and kiss her. A light kiss that would mean nothing. A taste of what was to come. A reminder...

Except her mouth opened beneath his, hot and sweet from the wine she'd been drinking, and before he knew what he was doing, he'd hauled her into his lap, his fingers buried in her hair as he devoured her.

Her hands pressed hard to his chest, not pushing him away but as if she was testing the firmness of him, her fingers spread out, hungry for the feel of him, kissing him every bit as desperately as he was kissing her.

Madness. What the hell was he doing? Gus's room was close and she probably wasn't even asleep yet...

He tore his mouth from Izzy's before he lost it, pressing his forehead to hers while her hair, now loose from its ponytail, fell like warm satin over the backs of his hands. The weight of her in his lap, pressing against his groin, was the most delicious agony.

"You're a terror," he said roughly, breathing hard. "What the hell am I going to do with you?"

"I have a few ideas." She sounded as breathless as he did.

"I'm sure you do. But Gus is in the house."

She let out a shaky breath. "That's true. Sorry."

"No, don't apologize. That was my fault."

"I shouldn't have touched you."

"You're fine to touch me." He brushed his mouth over hers. "In fact on Saturday night I'm going to insist on it."

"Good." She sighed against his lips, her fingers pressing lightly on his chest. "I should go."

He didn't want her to. He wanted to keep her right there with him for a little longer, but since that would be a big mistake, he released her with some reluctance.

She slipped away, leaving his lap feeling empty and cold, and he almost reached for her again, wanting to keep her close against him, but that would be an even worse idea than what he'd done already, so he controlled himself and let her go.

There wasn't much more to be said.

It was late, but Finn would be up, since the guy wasn't big

on sleeping, so Chase called him, telling him he had to run something urgently to the Rose and would it be okay if Finn came down the drive and stayed in the house for an hour or so, to make sure Gus was okay.

Finn, of course, didn't have a problem with it, though he certainly had more than a few questions.

Chase ignored them. He'd handle the third degree in the morning about late-night urgent delivery requests to the Rose, but for now he had all night to come up with an excuse that didn't involve Izzy staying far too late at his house, long after Gus had gone to bed.

That done, he got Izzy into his truck and drove the ten minutes down the dark road to the Rose.

Just before the township, he pulled the truck over to the side of the road and killed the engine.

It was very dark—there were two streetlights in Brightwater and they were near the Rose—and there was a fair amount of bush at the side of the road.

He glanced at her. "Meet me here, Saturday night, around ten. I'll bring you back to my place."

She nodded, then leaned forward suddenly and brushed her mouth over his. "Can't wait," she whispered.

A moment later, she'd slipped from the truck without another word, leaving him to watch her walk all the way back to the Rose and disappear inside it.

Chapter 13

Saturday evening, Izzy stepped into Bill's general store and headed automatically toward the aisle that contained all the bathroom products.

Bill's sold a lot of different stuff, from cigarettes to candy to a whole slew of grocery items, plus bait and tackle and some very basic outdoor gear. There were magazines too, and books, and, strangely, a cabinet of baked goods that Bill himself made fresh every morning. His scones, sausage rolls, and meat pies were his specialty, and Izzy had only found out about them after Finn had told Beth to try them and she had and they were indeed very good.

Bill's scones in particular were the best Izzy had ever eaten.

"Gidday," Bill said from his place behind the counter, his faded blue eyes watching her beadily. "What can I do for you today?"

Bill wasn't being friendly. He was being nosy. And since the welcome barbecue and a few visits to his store to get necessities like toothpaste and a few other things, he still hadn't thawed much toward her, Beth, and Indigo.

But Izzy had figured out that since the locals here were fairly direct, they appreciated directness in return, so that's what she'd tried to be. Plus politeness. Everyone always appreciated a bit of politeness. Except it wasn't until she'd stepped inside the store that she suddenly realized that she had a major problem.

Being in an isolated small town for the past couple of weeks had involved some minor irritations. Yes, the internet thing was a pain, but not as bad as she'd first envisaged. Yes, the lack of coffee was a problem also, but Chase and his coffee machine had made it bearable. Getting new clothes hadn't turned out to be a drama because Queenstown wasn't *that* far, and since the rest of her time had been spent at the Rose, where all the meals were provided and the rooms cleaned, she'd kind of felt like she was on vacation.

But not now. Because even when on vacation, she could still have gone into the nearest drugstore and bought herself some condoms without it being an issue. Not that she ever had, since Josh had been good about providing them initially and then she'd gone on the pill.

She wasn't on the pill now, though. And while Chase was bound to have some—he was the very definition of the Boy Scouts' "be prepared" motto—she felt a certain responsibility to get some herself.

An impulse she was now regretting with Bill gazing intently at her.

Chase had said small towns were hives of gossip, and while she'd thought she'd understood his need to keep their liaison secret to protect Gus, the why of it hadn't sunken in until now.

She could prevaricate and pretend she wasn't after condoms, but she'd still have to take a box up to the counter, and she could only imagine the look on Bill's face as she presented it to him and all the gossip that would set off…

So much for her nod toward responsibility. Chase would have to do it.

"Oh, it's okay." Izzy pretended to scan the shelves before

picking up a packet of dental floss and waving it triumphantly. "I've found it."

She came up to the counter and put down the floss she didn't want, glancing at the cabinet just to check there were no scones there. And there weren't. Dammit.

Bill took the floss and rang it up on the till, giving her a narrow glance as he did so. He had to have been in his early seventies, was short and round, with a lot of wispy white hair and a craggy face that seemed set in permanent lines of skepticism. Unlike Jim in the pub, who was laconic in the extreme, Bill was very talkative.

"You weren't looking for floss, were you?" he said. "Because if you were, you would have grabbed it since it was right in front of you. Did you want something else?" He paused and coughed. "Ladies' products?"

"Uh, no." She gave him a smile that he did not return. "I was hoping for a scone, but I see you're out."

"Yep. I only make 'em in the mornings. Once they're gone, they're gone." He eyed her. "Or better yet, get Kelly to bring you one along with the coffee he delivers to the Rose every morning."

Izzy's cheeks abruptly heated. "Excuse me?"

"He brings a coffee over to the Rose every morning bang on seven. Just you. No one else."

Her cheeks got even hotter. "Beth doesn't like coffee." She hoped she sounded very level and cool. "And Indigo only drinks tea."

Bill snorted. "Are you sure there isn't anything else you want to get? Something other than dental floss?"

Izzy kept her expression determinedly neutral. "No, thank you." She pushed the money over the counter at him.

He took it and ostentatiously put the floss in a paper bag. "His wife left him. Just up and left, didn't even take her little girl. He was cut up, the poor bloke, had to raise that kid on his own."

Izzy wasn't sure what to say or why Bill was telling her this. "I see," she said. "That must have been very hard."

"Yeah, it was." Bill handed over the bag, his blue gaze very direct. "He's as close as we get to a mayor around here and a good man. Born and bred in this town, looks out for its interests and the people here, and we need him. What we don't need is fly-by-nighters coming here and tempting him away."

Okay, so now it was clear. This was a warning.

Izzy decided that any protests regarding the tempting of Chase would not be well received, so she only nodded, gave Bill a blank smile, took her floss, and hurried back to the Rose to get ready.

She had no idea what to wear. Her hair dryer still wouldn't work, not even with the adapter she'd bought for it in Queenstown, and the sexy skirt and blouse combo she'd considered wearing were all crumpled and she didn't have an iron.

She didn't have any of the pretty dresses and cute little heels she normally put on when she went out with Josh because he liked her to look pretty, and since she'd abandoned most of her makeup, leaving even the eyeshadow behind, she only had one lipstick to choose from.

The only things she had were jeans yet again and one of the practical T-shirts she'd bought on her shopping trip to Queenstown and had been so proud of, and yet now seemed...boring. And not sexy.

Wow, nervous much?

Izzy grimly contemplated the contents of the drawer where she'd put her clothes. Yes, she *was* nervous. Though she wasn't sure why. She'd already slept with Chase once, so it wasn't as if he was an unknown quantity. And would he really care if she didn't get all dolled up for him? Actually, more to the point, why did she care?

Because he matters.

The thought felt far too weighty to have before a night of casual sex, so she tried not to think about it.

Tonight *was* casual. It was only sex and nothing else. And that moment when he'd pulled her into his arms on the deck and kissed her, then pressed his forehead to hers, was only casual too.

It didn't mean anything. It didn't make her feel good to know that he wanted her as badly as she wanted him. It didn't warm her that he'd asked her what kind of teenager she'd been and had wanted to know the answer.

An answer she might have gone into detail over, except she didn't want to talk about herself. About the end of her boring career and her boring breakup. Those things were in the past and they didn't matter now, and anyway, if she told him, it might jeopardize what was happening between them and she didn't want that.

A sudden knock came on the door of her room.

Izzy made a face, shut her drawer, and went over to the door and pulled it open.

Beth stood in the hallway. "Hey, Levi's offered to take us all into Queenstown for a night on the town. Do you want to come?"

Well, that was handy.

Izzy raised a hand and rubbed at her temple. "Um, no thanks. Got a bit of a headache."

"Awww, well, that's a shame. Are you sure?"

"Yeah, it's fine. Go and have some fun."

"I'm not sure that's possible," Beth muttered darkly. "Not since Indigo seems hell-bent on not having any."

Izzy gave her a grin. "No, but you might get some watching Levi try to get a rise out of her."

Beth perked up at that. "True. Good point. Ah, well, hope you feel better. We'll have to stay in Queenstown, so I'll see you tomorrow morning."

This really couldn't have worked out better if she'd tried.

After Beth had gone, Izzy reached for her phone, thinking to text Chase to tell him she could even come earlier since she wasn't going to have to worry about Beth and Indigo, but then remembered the lack of service.

Maybe she should just walk there and surprise him instead?

The idea took hold, and since it was better than sitting in her room for the next few hours, getting more and more nervous about what to wear, she left on the jeans and white T-shirt she had on already and slipped out of the Rose.

It was a beautiful evening, the sounds of the cicadas rising from the bush, the lake glittering. The warm, earthy spice of the bush hung heavy in the air, the silence broken only by the sounds of a nearby tūī.

She glanced toward Pure Adventure HQ, but it was closed for the night, the tourists gone, which meant Chase would be at home. Great.

As she started down the road toward Chase's place, a by now familiar shape slunk out from underneath the Rose's deck and came trotting up to her.

Mystery, the mystery dog.

"Hello, boy," she murmured, pausing as the animal sat down at her feet and gave her a doggy grin, his tongue lolling out.

She grinned back and held out her hand for a sniff, which he accepted, this time sniffing without a sneeze. He accepted a stroke on the head too, his fur softer than she'd expected and silky too.

"Do you think this is a good idea?" She gave him a scratch behind the ears. "Or am I making a big mistake?"

Mystery's nose went up abruptly, clearly catching a whiff of something interesting on the air, then he shot off into the bush behind Bill's.

Obviously he didn't care whether she was making a mistake or not.

Izzy sighed then set off down the road, her boots crunching on the gravel.

Even though the sun was going down, it was still hot, and she belatedly realized she should have put on some sunblock since the sun in New Zealand was very strong. But it was too late now, so she walked along holding her hand up to shade her face.

Sweat trickled down her back, her feet in her boots feeling uncomfortably hot.

From the town came the rhythmic sound of helicopter rotors and she glanced behind her to see Levi's machine lift off from behind HQ, soar into the air, and take a couple of circles around the lake before heading off to Queenstown.

She envied them, out of the sun and cool in the helicopter, being flown straight to their destination with no sweat, no sunburn, and no potential blisters.

She could go back to the Rose, but that seemed too much like giving up the way she had on the track to Glitter Falls, and hell, if she couldn't handle a walk along a flat gravel road for half an hour, then she had no business being here at all.

Izzy pushed on, trying to remember where Chase's house actually was from her visit a couple of days ago, wishing she could text him to double check.

Eventually she came to the driveway that she thought was his, resolutely trudging up it and cursing its steepness.

She arrived at the top sweaty and hot, her heels painful from no doubt growing blisters, but relieved to see that yes, indeed, it was Chase's house with its familiar decks.

She went up the wooden stairs to the front door and stood there for a moment, irritated with herself for her decision because she probably looked a fright, which wasn't ideal when it came to a sex date. She wondered if she should turn around and go back to the Rose, have a shower, and wait until ten—and felt a little like a failure for not managing even a half-hour walk without it being a drama.

Maybe she should. Maybe this was a bad idea.

She was on the point of turning around and heading straight back to the Rose when the door opened and Chase was standing on the threshold.

Tall, broad, gorgeous Chase. Looking all kinds of hot in jeans and a dark blue T-shirt that made his gray eyes look like storm clouds. He was barefoot and delicious, while she was sweating and gross, with her hair sticking to her forehead. She felt suddenly so self-conscious that all she wanted was to be back in Houston, in her own apartment with all her things around her, where everything was familiar.

But then something caught fire in Chase's gaze and before she could get out the awkward greeting hovering on her lips, he reached out and grabbed her, hauling her into his arms.

Chase had never been so impatient for a day to end. He'd woken up impatient. Impatient to have Izzy in his arms and in his bed.

Impatient to be inside her.

Actually, just impatient to be with her, which he'd never felt about another woman, not even Olivia. Which might have been a worry if he'd let himself think about it, but he didn't let himself think about it.

He certainly hadn't thought about it when he'd heard someone on the steps outside and had pulled open the door to find Izzy on his threshold, looking flushed and mussed and irritated and so completely sexy he hadn't been able to think at all.

Days he'd been waiting for this. Bloody days. And now she was finally here and she was early and he was damn near ecstatic.

She pushed lightly against his chest. "Hey, wait. I'm all sweaty and horrible and—"

"I don't care," he growled, his gaze roaming all over her, taking in her pink face and damp forehead. She looked hot, it was true, but in more ways than one. He'd never minded a woman who looked like she'd just engaged in some kind of hot and sweaty activity. "You look beautiful. What are you doing here so early? And make no mistake, I am not in any way disappointed that you are."

She pushed a little harder at him, so he let her go, though with some reluctance. "Beth and Indigo left for Queenstown with Levi, so I thought I'd walk to your place. Which was a mistake since now I'm all damp and yuck, and I need a shower."

"You might feel damp and yuck, but you look like you've gone several rounds in my bed already." He gave her an intense, hungry look. "And I think you should know that I find that incredibly sexy."

She went the most delightful shade of pink—at least he thought she had, though it was difficult to tell since her face was so flushed already. "I'm glad someone does. It doesn't make me feel very sexy, however."

He smiled. She was adorable when she was cross and she did seem very cross. Not that he could blame her. The sun was still hot even though it was evening and it could be pretty savage in these latitudes. She wouldn't be used to it. Come to think of it, that pink tinge to her skin looked like it was more than just heat. She might have caught a touch of sunburn too.

"Well," he said firmly, "we can't have that. Come with me. I'll show you where the shower is."

He turned and went down the hallway that Gus had lined with her drawings and favorite photos, leading Izzy down to the back of the house where the bathroom was.

He'd gutted the old bathroom after his father had finally left Brightwater and had it redone very simply, plain white tiled walls and a wooden floor. He'd kept the big windows because he had no neighbors for miles and because he enjoyed lying in the bath looking out at the bush outside. The shower was separate and had its own window, making it feel like you were standing in the middle of a rain forest.

Izzy looked surprised as she stepped into the bathroom, which pleased him. He did like setting her off balance a little.

"Here's a towel." He pulled open the set of wooden cupboards beside the vanity and got out a thick white towel, handing it to her. "And there's soap in the shower." He gave her a critical once-over. "Looks like you've caught some sun too, so when you're done, I've got a gel you might like to use for that."

Something in her eyes, a hint of uncertainty that he hadn't realized had been there until now, faded. "Thanks, Chase. That would be great."

Ah, shit. Had she been nervous? He needed to remember that while they might have slept together once, she still wasn't a woman who did casual, so this was a big deal for her.

It shouldn't be.

No, but he suspected it was, and even though it shouldn't, a part of him liked that very much. He hadn't been a big deal to someone, not in that way, for a very long time and it felt good. Maybe too good. Still, he wasn't going to be second-guessing his decision to have this night, not now she was here, no bloody way.

He smiled to reassure her. "Don't be nervous, beautiful. I've been waiting for you all day and there's basically nothing you could do that would make me change my mind or want you less, okay?"

"Oh." More pink stole through her cheeks. "Am I that easy to read?"

He reached out and cupped her jaw in one palm, bending to brush a kiss across her soft mouth. "Only because I feel the same way." He resisted the urge to deepen the kiss, because he knew if he did, that shower wasn't going to be happening. "Go on, have your shower." He held her gaze, letting her see the hunger in his. "I'm getting impatient."

Her expression relaxed and she threw him a smoldering glance from underneath her lashes. "They do say good things come to those who wait."

"In that case, I'm going to get some very good things indeed." He gave her cheek one last brush with his fingertip, then he left her to it.

He headed straight to the kitchen, because that uncertain look in her eyes had made him want to do something about it, ease whatever nervousness she had, so he quickly pulled open the fridge and got out the bottle of wine that he'd put in there to chill. Pouring her a glass, he then got some ice out and paired the wine with a nice cold glass of water.

Then he got together the platter he'd planned and bought food for the day before, with crackers, locally made cheeses, olive spread and pesto, and a few other little snacks someone who was maybe missing the city would appreciate.

He didn't think why preparing her a special platter was important or why he wanted to put her at ease. Only that he wanted to take care of her, because she'd come early and had walked all the way here, got sunburn and blisters and all because she'd wanted to see him.

Sure, they were here for sex only, but he'd thought they could relax afterward with some food. Didn't mean they had to have it then though. They could have it first. No need to rush, not when they had all night, and particularly not if she wasn't feeling it yet.

He wanted it to be good for her. He wanted this to be good for both of them, because that was all they'd ever have.

Didn't you do this dance with Olivia? And your father too?

Yeah, he had. He'd done a lot of things for Olivia because he'd believed himself in love and he'd wanted her to stay. And even before that with his father, making sure the house was clean and his dad's favorite beer was in the fridge. Not bugging his father about the fact that he'd neglected to buy food again, so he and Finn had nothing to eat.

What? You think all of this will make her stay? When it didn't stop Olivia or your dad from leaving?

Chase ignored the turn of his thoughts. It was just a bloody food platter, for chrissakes, not a wedding ring and an offer of marriage.

It didn't mean anything other than being a friendly gesture.

He finished preparing the platter and took it out to the deck off the living room, setting it down on the coffee table, before going back inside and bringing out the wine. It was another Brightwater Valley vintage from the Granges, since she'd seemed to like the other one so much.

He was in the process of arranging everything when he heard a soft footstep behind him.

Electricity shot through him. He straightened and turned to find Izzy standing behind him. Her hair was damp and hanging down her back, beginning to curl in the warm air the way it did sometimes. Though why he was obsessed with her hair when all she wore was a towel, he had no idea.

Her skin glowed in the setting sun, pretty and pink, making her eyes look even darker, like his very favorite espresso.

Desire was a low hum inside him, his fingers itching to grab her towel and pull it away. But he controlled himself. She'd been uncertain when she'd arrived here, and the last thing he wanted was her being uncertain.

"What's all this?" She stared at the platter and wine on the coffee table behind him.

"Refreshments." He shoved his hands into his pockets.

"That was a long walk you just had, and I thought you might like to sit and have a glass of wine and something to eat first."

She stared at him for a long moment, her delicate features unreadable. "That's very thoughtful, Chase. Thank you."

He lifted a shoulder, uncomfortable with the way her simple thank you made something warm glow just behind his breastbone. Because that was ridiculous. He didn't need thanks for providing the basic necessities of life, surely?

"How was your shower?"

Her mouth curved. "Lovely, actually. Just what I needed." She lifted a hand and he saw that she was carrying a small tube of green gel. "Is this what you were talking about? For sunburn?"

"Yeah, that's the one." He nodded at the bench seat they'd sat on a couple of nights earlier. "Sit down over there and I'll put some on for you."

She moved over to the bench, sitting down with a certain primness, all tucked up in her towel, that made him smile.

There was something so particular about her. Something a little refined that he shouldn't like as much as he did because refined wasn't a quality that went well with Brightwater Valley.

It was a hard-scrabble life out here, with no room for soft-ness or daintiness; nevertheless, he liked that she was just a bit soft and dainty regardless.

He had no idea why.

Chase sat on the bench behind her and grabbed the tube of gel she handed him. He flipped the top open and squirted some into his hand, discarding the tube before putting his fingers on her bare shoulders.

She shivered, goose bumps rising as he rubbed the cooling gel into her skin.

She felt so soft and she smelled of his soap.

He'd never been a particularly possessive man, but he liked that she smelled of him.

"Ooooh," Izzy sighed. "That feels really nice."

Her melted-honey accent had become even more syrupy, the slight husk in her voice making parts south of his belt tighten and ache.

Hell, she was tempting. Did she have any idea of how much?

She gave another of those sexy little sighs and then her head bent.

And her towel abruptly fell away.

Everything in Chase went still.

Slowly, she turned around, sitting naked on the bench, her pale skin glowing in the setting sun, her black hair curling all around her face and down over her shoulders. Her cheeks were flushed, her dark eyes glowing like stars.

"Lie back," she said with a certain amount of firmness. "I want to give you something."

He ached to touch her, literally ached. He hadn't realized how badly until right in this moment.

"Oh, beautiful," he murmured, tracing every line of her body with his gaze, unable to stop. "Are you sure you don't want to relax with a glass of wine first?"

"No." One hand reached out, delicate fingers brushing their way down his chest, sending bright sparks scattering along his nerve endings. "I have a favor to return."

"Izzy, you should—"

"Lie back." She gave him a firm stare. "Don't make me say it again."

Hell. Who was he to argue?

His pulse was going haywire, the pressure of his fly against his abruptly hard and aching flesh maddening. But he pushed himself back on the bench cushions, his breath catching as Izzy climbed on top of him.

"Holy shit, woman," he growled, his hand lifting to grip her hips. "You're going to be the death of me."

She gave him the sexiest, wickedest smile, as if she was enjoying herself very much indeed. "I'm afraid you're not allowed to die. I will be very disappointed if that happens." She leaned down, the heat of her body seeping through his T-shirt and jeans, the soft curves of her breasts pressing against his chest, and she brushed her mouth over his.

He groaned, lifting his hands to slide his fingers into her hair to hold her there, and deepened the kiss.

But she pulled away before he could, her eyes glittering. "No, don't," she whispered. "I want to do something for you, Chase. Will you let me?"

"Beautiful, I'll let you do anything you want, as long as I get to kiss you again."

The sensual promise in her smile made the ache in his groin even worse. "All in good time." She hesitated a moment. "No one can see us, right?"

"No." Silently, he thanked God that he had the good sense to build decks right where the bush was thickest. "And the nearest neighbor is Finn up the hill and he's not here anyway."

"Good."

She kissed him again, hungry and hot, like lightning, fusing him to the bench he was lying on, making every thought in his head blow away like smoke.

Then she ran a hand down his chest again, to his stomach,

finding the hard outline of him behind the zipper of his jeans and stroking.

The lightning crackled in his veins, his breath catching hard.

"Izzy." Her name came out harsh and raw.

"Do you want me to stop?" she murmured against his mouth.

Little tease. He could hear that wicked note in her voice, taunting him. God, he loved it.

"Absolutely goddamn not." He flexed his hips, pushing up into her hand, wanting more pressure. "Is this what you want?"

"Maybe." Her hand stroked him with a firmer pressure, pleasure like a thousand tiny sparks glittering along all his nerve endings. "Or maybe I just want to enjoy having you at my mercy for a bit."

He cursed and kissed her back, nipping at her bottom lip, pushing his tongue inside her mouth, tasting her the way he'd been dying to for the past few days.

She gave the sweetest moan, then her fingers were tugging at his zipper, pulling open his jeans, and when she pulled him free from his underwear, he couldn't help the growl that escaped him. Her fingers were deliciously cool on his hot, hard flesh and he wanted more.

Izzy pulled her mouth from his, then wriggled down his body, all bare skin and warmth, until she was right where he wanted her to be.

Her grip on him tightened and then her mouth lowered, taking him in, enclosing him in heat and delicate pressure, making him groan aloud.

He shut his eyes, because looking at the picture she made

crouched over him, with him in her mouth, was too damn erotic and he wanted this to last as long as possible. Instead he reached for her, burying his fingers in the softness of her hair, letting the pleasure come for him.

He'd had plenty of women go down on him, but there was something about Izzy. She paid attention to him, real *close* attention. As if making him feel good was important, and that mattered because Olivia had seemed to view sex as something she was expected to do rather than something she wanted to do, or as a payment in return for something else.

No, this was for him. And exactly the way he liked it. On his deck, at his house, with nothing but the bush all around him. A hot mouth on him and the most delicate licks and nips and a slight yet intense suction.

His fingers tightened in her hair as she intensified the pressure, and he couldn't stop himself from moving, thrusting up into her mouth as the slick, wet heat of it drove him on toward insanity.

God. He'd died and gone to heaven, hadn't he?

She was bloody heaven. Lightning in a jar and somehow he'd captured her.

The orgasm coiled at the base of his spine, ready to explode, and he growled her name, wanting to pull her off him. But she didn't move, only increasing the pull of her mouth until the orgasm uncoiled, shooting up his spine and exploding out the top of his head.

And all he could do was roar her name as it hit, annihilating him utterly.

Chapter 14

Izzy lay on Chase's recumbent figure, her cheek pressed to the smooth, hot skin of his bare stomach, and grinned, feeling exceptionally pleased with herself. His broad chest was heaving, his breathing harsh in the air, his fingers still wound tightly in her hair, and she felt like she'd been given a medal.

She'd made the uptight, controlled Chase Kelly lose it and that made her very happy indeed.

It hadn't been the first thing she'd thought of to do as she'd stepped out of the shower, but when she'd wrapped the towel around her, not wanting to dress in her sweaty, hot clothes, and ventured into the house in search of Chase, finding him on the deck preparing a platter of delicious food, she hadn't been able to help herself.

As much as she enjoyed how much he wanted her, she really liked that he'd made sure she had a shower before setting out some food and wine, thinking she might enjoy something to eat after her long walk—simply thinking about her and her needs in a way Josh never had.

Thinking about her in a way her parents never had, either.

He was a kind man, generous and caring, and she wanted him very, very much. Wanted to show him that she appreciated him in return as much as he appreciated her.

And wow. She'd enjoyed every bit of that appreciation and then some.

His fingers loosened and suddenly she found herself

being gripped and hauled up his body. His eyes had gone that fascinating electric silver color and the intensity in them made her heartbeat very fast.

"You," he said, his voice full of rough heat, "are downright bloody amazing, and I think it's time I give you a taste of what I've been fantasizing about for the past three days."

Before she could move, he'd gathered her up in his arms, slipped off the bench, and began to head for the door to the living room.

"But the food," she protested, part of her secretly thrilled at the possessive way he held her and the impatience that was clear in every line of him.

"It'll keep," he said shortly, striding into the living room and through it into the hallway.

Down at the end of the hall was another set of narrow stairs. Chase strode up them, taking them two at a time with seemingly zero effort.

He was so strong. She could feel it in the iron-hard muscle of his chest and arms, in the way he held her firmly against him.

As if he never wants to let you go...

No, that was stupid. He had to let her go and she was more than okay with that. This was just sex and that was fine. She was allowed to enjoy his physical strength though, nothing wrong with that.

At the top of the stairs was a big open attic room, with large windows that gave the same views over the lake as the deck. The evening sun was streaming through the glass and over the huge wooden bed that had been pushed beneath it, made up with white sheets and a plain navy quilt cover.

The room was very neat, personal items lined up with

military precision on the dresser. Boots lined up at the wall beside it. Some clothes were folded perfectly on a wooden chair that stood against one wall, and there was not one speck of dust anywhere.

Chase's bedroom…

But she wasn't given much time to inspect more of it, because then Chase had tossed her on the bed, getting rid of his own clothes in record time before coming down onto the mattress beside her.

She reached for him, wanting to touch him, but he very firmly rolled her onto her front and then pinned her there with his big, muscular body.

"Just lie there," he murmured, his breath on the back of her neck. "And don't move a muscle."

Izzy closed her eyes, the breath going out of her in a soft rush as his fingertips brushed down the length of her spine, stroking her in a leisurely way, as if he had all the time in the world and had no plans to rush.

Then he did it again, gently, his mouth following along, trailing kisses down her back.

She shivered, her skin prickling deliciously, heat spreading out through her body. But not the sweaty uncomfortable kind—that was gone, banished by the cool shower and the gel he'd spread on her sunburn, and the rough sound of her name as he'd come apart from the orgasm she'd given him.

Now there was only the good kind of heat, the one that built on itself, making her skin get sensitive and the ache down between her thighs become needy.

His kisses went lower, his hands stroking over the curve of her butt, squeezing lightly but gently. Treating every part of her as if she was some rare and precious thing, more than just the good girl who never stepped out of line or caused a fuss, who never made things difficult. Not just the supportive fiancée who gave whenever it was required and never demanded anything in return, who was always happy with whatever Josh had wanted to give her. Which wasn't much, as she was beginning to realize.

He'd never made her feel special the way Chase made her feel special.

Izzy pressed her face into the warm sheets, the sun falling over her bare skin, every sense she possessed concentrated on Chase's touch, on his hands stroking down the backs of her thighs, on the rain of kisses that followed after them, trying not to focus on the sharp ache that had settled just behind her breastbone.

But then he flipped her over onto her back and proceeded to give her front the same attention, his hands roaming, stroking the curves of her breasts, his thumbs circling her nipples. Then those soft, maddening kisses were there, his lips brushing the tip of her breast and drawing her nipple into his mouth, the light suction driving her mad.

And he kept stroking, her hips, her thighs, her stomach. Then he nudged her thighs apart, trailing kisses down over her stomach before going lower, nuzzling against her, exploring her.

"Chase." She shifted against him, the flick of his tongue making her gasp. "Please…"

But he continued on with his leisurely exploration of strokes and licks and nips, moving even lower, soft kisses falling on the sensitive skin of the inside of her knee and around her ankle bone.

And only when she was trembling with desire did he

finally move and settle himself between her thighs. He paused to grab a condom and protect them both, then his arms slid beneath her, lifting her and holding her close. His gaze was on hers as he pushed inside her, slow and easy and deep.

Izzy gasped in delight, the press of him inside her the most perfect thing she'd ever felt in her life.

Chase paused, looking down into her eyes, and he smiled, so warm and full of heat and something else that made her ache.

"You okay?" His voice was rough and full of heat.

"Yes," she managed to get out. "Yes, oh my God, so okay."

His smile deepened and then slowly, so achingly slowly, he began to move. And oh, it felt so good. A gentle rocking like the sea, making sensation ripple out, those layers of pleasure building higher and higher.

He held her gaze the whole time, and there was an intimacy to it that should have disturbed her, but she didn't feel disturbed. She felt close to him, as if they were sharing something wonderful between them, sharing pleasure and closeness, a wordless connection that was more than simply physical.

Josh had never looked at her when they'd had sex. He'd never touched her the way Chase had, never looked down into her eyes as if this was some amazing secret and he wanted to share it with her.

He'd kept his eyes closed the whole time and sometimes she'd wondered if it was someone else he saw behind his closed lids. If it was someone else he was fantasizing about instead of her.

Chase wasn't though, and that was clear. The only person he was looking at, thinking about, was her.

The pleasure was wondrous, magical, spreading out inside her, filling her up, and she could see it doing the same for him too.

She'd never had that before. She'd never looked at another person and knew they were feeling the exact same thing as she was at the exact same time. No one had ever known how she felt, not really. No one had ever understood the loneliness she'd felt after her brother had left or her anger at her parents for refusing to understand him and driving him away. Her anger at Josh for throwing the two years they'd spent together and her own feelings for him away, as if they didn't matter.

No one understood, but now, in this moment, Chase did. Maybe not all the negative emotions, but he could see her passion. He could feel it. And he liked it, accepted it.

Sensation built and built, and she began to move with him, her hands stroking down his back, wanting to get closer to him, to fill herself up not only with pleasure, but with him as well.

It wasn't enough.

"Chase," she said thickly. "Oh…Chase…"

His eyes were glittering with hunger, his smile still warm but a little sharper now. His movements became more insistent, his rhythm faster, and she clung to him, digging her nails into his shoulders.

She could feel the climax approaching and she knew it was going to be overwhelming, and part of her was scared by how intensely this was going to affect her, by how much it might strip away from her, leaving her vulnerable and exposed. Yet Chase's gaze held her anchored, his arms around her keeping her safe, and when he did some kind of subtle twist of his hips, hitting the most sensitive part of her in just the right way, and she felt everything inside her begin to shatter, it wasn't exposure or vulnerability that she felt, not with him.

As the pleasure overwhelmed her, the glitter in his gaze turning to fire letting her know that he was being overwhelmed too, all she felt was strong. And complete. And right. As if this was where she'd always been meant to be.

Right here, in his arms.

Afterward, she just lay there, pinned to the mattress by his large, hard body and more than okay with that, since she felt so light, she was worried she might float away if he hadn't been there to hold her down.

He had his face buried in the side of her neck, his breath ghosting over her skin. She stroked him, up and down his wide, strong back, feeling the same tremors that shook her shaking him also.

They lay quietly like that for long minutes, the silence deepening around them into something peaceful and intimate and just for them. At last, Chase shifted, putting his hands on either side of her head and looking down at her.

The electricity had faded from his gaze, the gray deepening into dark charcoal, embers of heat still glowing in it.

"Beautiful, that was something else," he murmured. "And so are you."

Izzy lifted a hand and touched his face, her fingers tracing the carved line of one cheekbone. "Back at you." It was a lame response, but right now, she couldn't seem to find the words to encompass how he'd made her feel.

He smiled again, the smile that turned him from the uptight drill sergeant into literally the hottest, most mesmerizing man she'd ever seen. "I think we need to do that again. In fact, I'm probably going to insist on it. But since we have all night, right now I think you need a tall glass of water, some food, and a nice glass of wine more."

Izzy grinned, the prospect of an evening with delicious food, good wine, lots of sex, and Chase making her feel better than she'd ever felt in her life. "I don't mind if we don't eat now," she said, stroking her fingers over his chest, loving the hard contours of it and the feel of his hot skin, the light prickle of hair.

"No," Chase said firmly. "Sustenance first." He gave her one of his deliciously wicked smiles. "You're going to need some energy for what I have in store tonight."

Another shiver of anticipation went through her. "Well," she murmured, "I guess if you insist…"

A few minutes later, wearing one of Chase's Pure Adventure NZ T-shirts and nothing else, Izzy was comfortably ensconced on the cushioned wooden bench on the deck. Chase made her drink the whole glass of ice water— for rehydration purposes, or so he said—then he handed her a glass of white wine before piling up a little plate with crackers, cheese, and some spreads, plus a few other treats, placing that on the table in front of her.

He sat down beside her, bare-chested, wearing only his jeans, which was quite frankly unfair when he was so distractingly gorgeous, holding his own glass of wine.

"So," he said, his silver gaze resting on her, "I think it's time you told me what secret it is that you're hiding, beautiful. Don't you?"

Izzy tensed, the warm smile on her face fading.

He knew it would happen; asking her about her secret—whatever it was—wasn't going to make her comfortable. But he'd had to ask. Twice now he'd sensed something painful inside her, like a splinter hurting her, and he'd broached the topic only to have her brush him off.

He'd let her, not wanting to push because he didn't have a right to her secrets. But after what had happened between them upstairs, after he'd held her in his arms, looked down into her beautiful dark eyes and seen her uncovered soul staring back, he knew he couldn't let her brush him off again.

She seemed so cool and so put-together, so in command of herself, yet when she was with him, naked and in his bed, he felt like he'd unwrapped the very best present, finding her warm and passionate and sensual, so generous with her emotions, displaying a trust in him that had reached inside his chest and squeezed him tight.

He wanted to know about her. He wanted to know *everything* about her, including who'd hurt her. Someone had made her hide herself beneath that cool, smooth shell she wore every day. And he was betting it was some guy who didn't know what he had in her and made Chase tempted to fly all the way to Houston and punch him.

Izzy glanced down at the little plate of food he'd gotten together for her, black hair falling over her shoulders and veiling her face, and said nothing.

He didn't move. "Your hair is gorgeous," he said after moment.

"Thanks. I normally straighten it." Her voice was quiet.

"Why?"

She let out a breath and then raised her head, turning to

look at him, her dark eyes guarded. "Because my mother preferred it straight. She thought curly hair looked unkempt."

Was that part of the story? Chase was certain of it; he could hear the tension in her voice. But he didn't push; he wanted her to give that story to him. He didn't want to force it out of her.

"I think it's gorgeous," he said easily. "And if that's unkempt, then unkempt's sexy as hell."

The tense look on her face eased. "You are far too good for my ego, you know that?"

"If all it takes is a couple of compliments about your hair to be good for your ego, then it's clear your ego could do with a lot more stroking."

She smiled, giving her head a little shake.

He wanted to reach out and touch her, run those soft black curls through his fingers, but he didn't. Distance was probably what was needed now.

Izzy took a sip of her wine, then said, "It's not a particular secret. Or at least, I didn't mean it to be. And it's not that interesting either. But…that bad breakup I told you about? He was my fiancé and he broke up with me a couple of weeks before our wedding."

He was right. It had been a guy.

Chase went very still, anger and possessiveness pulsing through him, neither of which he should have felt and yet he felt all the same.

Because seriously? Some asshole had left her? Broken their engagement just weeks before they were to get married? How? Why? What fool would do that when they had this lovely, lovely woman ready to be their wife?

He very much wanted to punch something but got ahold

of himself, gripping his wineglass tightly and focusing on her instead.

"Right," he said, his voice bordering on a growl. "Do you want to tell me what happened?"

She sighed. "Oh, it's a boring story. He…met someone else. He didn't cheat, at least not physically. He did the decent thing and told me." Her voice sounded very level, very neutral. "Calling off the wedding was the only thing to do, so that's what we did."

Chase's jaw ached and he had to take a sip of wine to unclench it. "He sounds like a tool."

"He wasn't when I first met him," Izzy said quietly. "He seemed like a decent guy. Career-oriented and successful, partner in a law firm, which was what I was looking for at the time… Anyway, canceling the wedding was a logistical nightmare and I was having a few…career difficulties as well, and I just couldn't bear to be in Houston anymore. My brother had told me about Brightwater Valley needing entrepreneurs to start up new businesses and it seemed perfect. I couldn't wait to get away." She took another sip of her wine. "So I jumped on the first plane out of Houston and here I am."

Chase stared at the calm expression on her pretty face. A mask, he could see that so obviously now. Just as he could hear the hurt in her voice despite how level she sounded.

What exactly had happened in Houston? She'd said other things before, giving him hints of difficulties that had caused her pain, and he wanted to know more. He wanted to know everything.

Putting down his wine, Chase held out his arms. "Come here."

She stared at him a long moment, her expression still guarded, and he thought she might not take up his invitation. So he lifted a brow, both a question and a challenge.

Izzy snorted, knowing exactly what he was doing. Then, much to his delight, she scooted along the bench and settled herself in his arms, her back to his chest, her hair silky and warm across his bare skin.

"That's better." He nuzzled against the top of her head, inhaling her delicious scent. "Now, why don't you tell me what's going on, hmm?" He settled her more firmly against him. "Tell me, and I don't want to hear any 'it's boring' or 'it's not interesting' or any of those kinds of excuses, understand?"

Izzy sighed. "You're so bossy. No wonder they call you the drill sergeant."

"Hey, you can take the boy out of the army, but you can't take the army out of the boy. Besides, you like me being bossy."

Her hand had settled on the forearm he'd wrapped around her, stroking him absently. "I couldn't possibly comment."

Chase smiled, kissed the top of her head, and waited.

"Okay," she said eventually. "It's not very interesting, but—"

"What did I say about the not interesting excuses?"

"Okay, okay. It's fascinating and you'll be riveted to every word."

"Better." He tightened his arm around her, letting her know that he had her, that he wasn't going to let her go. He wasn't sure if that's what she needed, but he wanted her to know that all the same.

"The board of my family's oil company wanted me out,"

Izzy said at last. "I'd made sure Dad put me in charge when he retired, because his business practices were...shady, let us say. I wanted to fix things, so I instituted a culture of change, focusing on green energy instead. It took a lot of hard work and time, and Dad wasn't into it, but eventually the company came around. But...the board felt I was too tied to the old regime, and they wanted some fresh blood. So they asked me to step down."

She sounded so matter-of-fact yet Chase heard the soft note of hurt in her voice all the same. Corporate careers had never appealed to him and he couldn't think of anything worse than working trapped in an office, but her job had obviously meant something to Izzy.

"Green energy, hmm?" He brushed his mouth over her hair. "Sounds like you did great. And their loss might be Brightwater's gain."

She let out a breath. "Maybe. But I worked hard for them. And while I understood their logic, it was...difficult to accept. It didn't help that they asked me to step down the same day as a gala celebrating the new company direction, and the same night Josh told me he'd fallen in love with someone else." She paused. "I guess it felt as if my life was falling down around my ears."

Chase's chest tightened with sympathy. He hadn't had the same professional disappointments, but he could certainly relate to having someone you thought loved you suddenly tell you out of the blue that they didn't.

"I understand," he murmured. "I felt that way when Olivia left."

Izzy shifted in his arms, twisting slightly and turning her head to look up at him. "You did? What happened?"

He didn't much like talking about it, but it felt natural

to tell Izzy. "We argued about something silly, I can't even remember what. Then the next day I walked in on her packing a bag. I asked her what was going on and she said she was leaving, that she felt stifled being here. She couldn't stand the isolation, couldn't stand being trapped here with a young kid, with no one to talk to. She hated that I didn't understand her or appreciate her, and she'd had enough."

Izzy frowned. "She didn't think to talk through this with you first? And what about Gus?"

An old anger simmered in Chase's gut, though he tried not to let it get to him. "She didn't much care about anyone but herself and her own feelings. Though..." He stopped and then made himself go on, made himself voice it. "A marriage is a two-way street. Part of me wonders if she was right. I was young when we married and I thought I knew everything." The anger shifted, turning inward. There was more he could say, but he didn't want to. This wasn't his turn to talk.

A crease appeared between Izzy's brows. "Chase—"

"No, beautiful. This isn't about me. Tell me about the bloody idiot who had the gall not to fall in love with you."

She shook her head. "Not much to say, really. He was the son of one of Dad's friends and my parents liked him. I thought we were well matched, both of us ambitious and looking for success. But...the more I think about it, the more I realize now that it was only his success that was important to him. He didn't really care about mine. He wanted a trophy wife, I think. Someone pretty who made less money and who'd eventually quit her job so she could stay at home with the kids."

Chase's simmering anger found a target. "Then he was an asshole. A total dick."

Her expression softened. "I can't fault him for that. He was up-front and—"

"He didn't even have the decency to let you be properly angry with him from the sounds of it. So yeah, total dick."

Something shimmered in her eyes and his heart caught. "Well, I was angry with him. I just didn't yell at him or anything because that doesn't help."

"You should have." He watched her face, studying the hot glow in her eyes that she tried to hide. "You wanted to marry him and he left you and it wasn't fair. And it doesn't matter that he was up front about it, it still hurts."

She stared at him, not speaking, that glow burning in the depths of her gaze. Then abruptly she looked away. "I was always doing things for him, always smoothing the way and never asking for anything in return." Her voice had a bitter edge to it. "I was like that with my parents and my brother too. Dad had a difficult relationship with Zeke because Zeke was so straight up and honest, and my father was so manipulative. I always ended up being the peacemaker, trying to smooth things over. Zeke left in the end though, joined the army, then went up to Alaska, and that was the best thing for him, but…I was angry with Dad for letting him go and I told him as much." She took a breath. "Dad just said that he was tired of difficult, and that if I wanted anything from him and Mom, I'd better be easy."

Her body had gone tense so he tightened his arms around her, letting her know he had her.

"So I was easy," she went on. "And I didn't get mad that Zeke left me alone. And I didn't get angry at how my parents treated me, as if I were some object they could use to make their lives easier and not their daughter. And even when my career went down in flames and Josh told me he was in love with someone else, I didn't say a damn word." She looked up at Chase all of a sudden, tears shimmering in her eyes. "But I was angry. I was furious. So...*mad*. At the board and my parents and my brother and Josh. No one cared that I'd worked hard for the company. That I was loyal. That perhaps I might need support, even just a hug. No one cared about me at all." She glanced away. "Not being difficult only makes you easier to leave. Easier to forget."

Chase's heart twisted in his chest and he found himself pulling the wine from her hands and turning her in his arms so he could cup her pretty face, look into her beautiful eyes. "I don't know about your parents or Josh—they sound like fools to me—but there's nothing about you that's easy to forget, Isabella Montgomery. And I should know. I've been doing my damnedest to forget you for the past week and a half without success. And you haven't been easy, you've given me hell, and I just want you to know that what I told you before is true. That I like it. No, I bloody love it, understand? So be difficult all you want—get angry with me, disagree with me. You don't have to be calm and you don't have to be easy. Just be you, okay? Because you're the most fascinating woman I've met in my entire life."

Izzy stared at him, not saying a word. But he could see the emotion in her eyes—something deep and intense that reached inside him and gripped him tight.

Then she put her hands on his bare chest, pushing herself up slightly, and kissed him hard.

And after that there was no more talking.

Chapter 15

A WEEK LATER, LEVI PAUSED OUTSIDE THE DOOR TO THE pub and ceremoniously pushed it open. "Ladies," he said grandly, making an ostentatious gesture with one hand to usher them both inside.

Izzy, who'd decided that Levi's easygoing charm and general flirtatiousness hid a serious and caring soul, grinned, took an excited Gus by the arm, and walked with a certain degree of flounce into the pub.

They'd just come back from Gus's shopping day in Queenstown, and a *very* successful day it had been too. Not only had they hit the shops, they'd also gone for a nice lunch on the waterfront, then much later had met up with Levi, who'd taken them to a very hipster burger joint with lines out the door for dinner before the trip home.

He'd blanched at the number of bags Izzy and Gus were carrying, making jokes about having to hang them off the chopper's skids in order to get them home, but he'd somehow managed to fit them all inside, and now they were stacked up at HQ ready to be taken back to Chase's house.

Chase wasn't at HQ himself, and given there were relatively few places he could be, they'd all trooped over to the Rose so Izzy could deliver Gus safely back.

Her stomach fluttered hard as she stepped into the pub, twisting and coiling with an excitement she couldn't pretend she didn't feel—an excitement that had been there ever since they'd spent the night together the previous week.

It had been, quite simply, magic. There was no other word for it.

From the moment he'd ushered her into his shower, to the passionate sex in his bed, to sitting on the deck in his arms, wearing his T-shirt, telling him about Josh, then looking up into his eyes as he'd told her that he didn't want easy, that she could be difficult, that he *liked* her like that…

Yes, it had all been amazing.

They'd made love on the deck, right there in the bush, and afterward, they'd eaten and drank wine and talked. Chase had told her more about his business and what he was trying to do with it, his passion for the environment and this little valley and all the people in it evident in everything he said.

She'd told him about working in the oil company and how she'd tried to change things, and if nothing else she'd been proud of that at least, that she *had* managed to effect some change.

Chase had been very approving and had told her so, and they'd then gotten into a discussion about the environment and green energy and how best to build an ethical business that made money for the local community.

He was such an interesting man, full of ideas and passion, and it was inspiring. *He* was inspiring.

They'd gone up to bed after that and spent a good couple of hours exploring each other and the magic they could create between them. He was a generous, inventive, and rather wicked lover, clearly experienced, and yet she'd managed to surprise him a couple of times, which satisfied her very much.

The next morning, she'd woken up before he did and had

gone downstairs to cook breakfast, eggs and bacon and toast. She'd figured out how to work the coffee machine and had brought him up a coffee. He'd been so pleased he'd dragged her back to bed and the breakfast had nearly gone cold.

It had been wonderful and she hadn't wanted to leave.

But they both knew that this had only ever been a one-off, and since they couldn't leave it too late for him to drop her back at the Rose, not without generating a few questions, eventually she'd dressed in her clothes from the day before and Chase had run her back to the pub.

He'd pulled up just before the township, so they wouldn't be totally on show, and even though she'd wanted very much to kiss him goodbye, she hadn't. Instead, she thanked him for the wonderful night, meaning every word, and had slipped out of the truck the way she had the night she'd looked after Gus—without another word and without looking back.

When she'd heard the rumble of his truck driving away, the day somehow darkened, the sun seeming a whole lot less bright, but she told herself that was just a cloud.

It had nothing to do with him.

Just like the low mood that had dogged her this entire week had nothing to do with him. Or the broken sleep she'd had, dreaming of him and his hands running over her skin, his mouth brushing the back of her neck, his arms holding her tight. Nope, that had nothing to do with him specifically either.

She'd probably dream of any man she'd had sex with like that.

What had been annoying though was that the other two had noticed. Beth kept asking her what was wrong, Indigo wondering aloud if she was coming down with something. But luckily the pair of them had been very involved in getting supplies for their separate businesses, not to mention viewing the house the three of them were going to move into imminently.

Izzy had tried to be enthused about it, just as she'd tried to sort through the inevitable paperwork that came with setting up a business, double-checking finances, and beginning to look at marketing.

It was all stuff that she should enjoy, since she liked doing admin work, but not having internet access for any of it was a pain in the butt, especially when it came to dealing with the finances, and she wished for an office that wasn't one of the tables in the Rose's dining room, where someone stopped to chat—or the library that the old guy used as his bedroom.

Of course, the reality was that her problem didn't have to do with having no internet or an office, but a distinct lack of Chase Kelly.

What was even more difficult was that, unlike a city where she could actively avoid him, a small town was different, and unfortunately he was basically everywhere she turned.

Tall. Broad. Gorgeous. Striding around dealing with tourists or talking with various members of the town. Leaning against the counter chatting to Bill in the general store or greeting Gus at the school bus. Somehow always in the hallway of the Rose when she was going past or sitting with Finn and Levi whenever she was in the pub enjoying a shandy with Indigo and Beth.

What was worse was that he didn't seem to find the constant proximity a problem. He seemed to have no issue meeting her gaze or being in her presence. He treated her the same as he always did, like a business associate or a new acquaintance.

She tried to do the same, but it was difficult. Too difficult.

She should have understood when he'd told her that getting involved with someone in a small town was hard, but she hadn't. And now that she did understand, it was too late.

Taking Gus out had been a bright spot and Izzy had loved spending time with her. The kid was a delight. She had her father's passion and seriousness, leavened with his slightly wicked sense of humor. She was open too, and somehow she'd decided that Izzy was someone she trusted and had talked candidly to her about her mother, who sometimes sent her letters since Gus couldn't get emails, but whom she basically never saw.

Gus seemed remarkably sanguine and mature about it— she told Izzy she didn't remember much about her mother anyway—but Izzy knew that Gus wasn't as okay with it as she made out, and Izzy thought that might have something to do with Chase and his daughter's fierce loyalty to him.

They were quite the pair, both incredibly protective of each other, which she admired, but it was also tough, since although Chase had his brother and Levi to talk to, Gus didn't have anyone. Or at least no one female. Hence Gus's abrupt embrace of her.

It was a responsibility, and one Izzy took seriously.

She glanced now at Gus as they walked through into the pub, the girl's gray eyes shining, a grin just about splitting her face.

Instantly she spotted her father and shouted, "Dad!" dragging Izzy up to the bar where Chase was standing with Finn.

Izzy tensed instinctively as she and Gus neared the pair. A bright flash of lightning showed in Chase's eyes, but then it was gone, and his gaze shifted to his daughter instead.

He smiled, the guarded look dropping, his expression softening in that way that made Izzy's heart ache whenever he looked at Gus.

"Hey, Gussie," he said. "How was your day?"

"It was fantastic!" Gus let Izzy go and gave her father a massive hug. "You should see what I got." She looked up at him, her expression turning serious. "Fashion show, okay?"

"Fashion show," Chase repeated blankly. "What?"

Despite the fluttering in her gut, Izzy couldn't help smiling at his bemused look.

"Yes," Gus said. "I want you to see what everything I got looks like on."

Chase blinked a couple of times, then glanced at Izzy as if for some explanation. "I'm sure everything will look great on."

"Wrong answer," Finn muttered.

"Why don't you go tell Beth and Indigo about what you bought," Izzy said to Gus, "while I instruct your father about the importance of fashion shows?"

Gus grinned and raced off.

"It went well, then?" Chase's gaze came to hers and stayed there, the warmth in his eyes and the humor in his tone making that fluttering sensation inside her intensify.

"Yeah, it was great." She couldn't help smiling at him. "Gus is really the most fantastic kid."

"We like her." Chase smiled back, little sparks in his eyes. "I mean, she is my daughter after all."

Izzy's heart gave a sudden hard beat, a flood of happiness washing through her.

She'd missed his company the entire week and it felt so good to be near him.

You're a lost cause, you do realize that, don't you?

Finn coughed ostentatiously, making Izzy nearly jump. "I have…a thing," he said vaguely. "Going to see…someone about…something." Without another word, Finn headed off through the crowded pub.

Chase's smile faded, his gaze following his brother's tall figure. "Damn," he muttered.

"What?" Izzy asked, still lost in a happy glow.

Chase glanced back at her. "I think he's picked up on you and me."

Well, you were just standing there staring at Chase like a lunatic.

So she had. Great.

"Sorry," she said automatically. "I didn't mean—"

"This isn't a good idea." Chase's voice got abruptly low and urgent, the gunmetal gray of his eyes flickering silver. "You and I together in public like this."

Her stomach twisted, the happy feeling beginning to fade. He'd always been clear he hadn't wanted anyone to know about them, so his reaction wasn't entirely unexpected. Then again, it wasn't as if they were doing anything incriminating. And it was only Finn who'd picked up on it.

"We were just talking, Chase." She tried to sound cool. "Not having sex on the bar or anything."

His eyes darkened. "I know but…" He stopped abruptly and glanced around as if checking for eavesdroppers. "We can't talk about this here. HQ. Meet me there. Five minutes." Without another word, he pushed himself away from the bar, moving quickly over to where Finn had gone to sit with Indigo and Beth, pausing for a brief chat, then striding out the pub door.

Izzy blinked, then took a breath, her pulse ramping up. Okay, so no doubt she'd get a lecture on why keeping their distance in public was important and how he didn't want Gus to find out. Great.

Part of her was tempted not to meet him because she was tired of lectures. Tired of being told what was permitted and what wasn't. And she was very tired of battling her feelings for him.

She'd told herself that getting involved with someone was the last thing she wanted after Josh, but a bit less than four weeks ago, Chase had arrived on the scene and had blown all her good intentions sky high.

Just physical, he'd told her. But it had never felt just physical to her. Sure, maybe she was reading into it something that wasn't there, but she couldn't deny that fluttering, desperate, excited thing that lived inside her, that flew dizzily around whenever he was in her vicinity.

That wasn't just physical. That was something deeper and she wanted more of it. She wanted more of him.

So no, she wouldn't leave him to stew. And perhaps meeting him now was a stupid idea, but she didn't care. She wasn't going to pass up the chance to see him in private and maybe...tell him that she didn't want to keep her distance any longer. That twice wasn't enough.

You're falling for him.

Was she? Was that what the feeling was? The swoop and dive of her stomach and the rush of happiness whenever he was around?

She hadn't felt that with Josh though, and she'd loved him.

Did you, though? Or did you only tell yourself you did?

Izzy stood there for a long moment, staring at the door of the pub Chase had disappeared through, the buzz of the conversation around her fading as the beat of her own heart became more insistent.

No, she'd never felt this with Josh. She'd never wanted to be with him the way she wanted to be with Chase. Never had the day darken when he wasn't around and never had a flood of fizzing happiness wash through her whenever he appeared.

He'd told her, with what she could now see was casual cruelty, that he hadn't known what love was until he'd met the woman he'd fallen for, and Izzy hadn't understood. She'd always thought that they'd had love between them already.

She understood now though that they hadn't. They'd never had it.

But she did with Chase.

And maybe it was time he knew that.

———

Chase paced back and forth upstairs in the living area of HQ, trying to force away the roiling sense of possessiveness that had gripped him the moment Izzy had come into the pub with Gus.

It had been dogging him the whole week since the night they'd spent together, and he knew it was tempting fate, but he found himself lingering in the places where he knew she was going to be and then watching her as he pretended to talk to someone else, hungry for the sight of her.

It was ridiculous. He wasn't a teenage boy, mooning after

a girl. He was a thirty-five-year-old man with a twelve-year-old daughter. He was above that shit.

Yet here you are, desperate to get her alone.

Yes, but that was only to tell her to keep her distance. That they had to watch themselves out in public, otherwise people were going to guess what was going on and that would be a mistake.

Finn was okay. His brother wasn't a gossip. But it couldn't go further.

Not after he'd seen Gus's shining face as she'd come into the pub with Izzy. It was clear she'd had a wonderful day and the way she'd clutched Izzy's arm as they'd come in together, looking at her as if she adored her…

He couldn't have his daughter getting attached. Not to a woman who'd only committed to staying here for three months. A woman on the run from the life she'd left behind in Houston. He couldn't blame Izzy for that though, not after that night on the deck when she'd told him what had happened.

She'd quite categorically been rejected by everyone in her life, and God knew he understood what that felt like. It made him ache for her. But still…

What if the company she'd left behind saw the mistake they'd made in getting rid of her and asked her to return? What if the asshole who'd broken off their engagement decided he wanted her back?

She was a woman in a million and no idiot in their right mind would let her get away, so it could happen. And if she'd left Houston for New Zealand, she could certainly leave New Zealand for Houston.

There wasn't anything keeping her here. She liked Gus

and Indigo and Beth. And she liked everyone in town. They liked her too, if what he'd heard from people was true.

But what else would keep her here once the store was up and running? She wasn't providing stock for it the way Indigo and Beth were. She was doing the admin, and while that was important, it could also be done by someone else. It didn't have to be her.

She could leave this all behind quite easily.

She could leave you.

No, this didn't have anything to do with him. What was between them was casual, and anyway, that was over now.

The itch had been well and truly scratched.

Keep telling yourself that.

Chase ignored the thought as he heard the door downstairs close. He stopped pacing, turning toward the top of the stairs, his pulse beating loudly and insistently in his head.

A moment later Izzy appeared, a determined look on her lovely face. She wore a little denim skirt with a plain white T-shirt that molded to the curves of her breasts in the most distracting manner. Her hair was in a loose ponytail and he couldn't help but notice that it wasn't as poker straight as it had been when she'd first arrived here, but curling prettily over her shoulder. Framing her face were loose tendrils the same sooty black as her long lashes. Her eyes were that dark, rich espresso and they were glowing the way they always did when she was aroused…

Hell.

Electricity pulsed through him and he moved without thought, as natural as breathing, striding toward her, his hands landing on her hips, propelling her up against the wall near the kitchen area. He bent his head to take her mouth as she wrapped her arms around his neck and rose up to meet him, her kiss as hungry and desperate as his.

Heat ignited inside him, the taste of her making the hunger that had been simmering all week rise up to choke him, and it was all he could do not to shove her skirt up and bury himself inside her right then and there.

She felt soft and hot and perfect in his arms. As perfect as she had the night they'd spent together...

God, would it be so wrong to have another night? Just one more. That would surely put an end to this need.

He tore his mouth from hers and lifted his head. They were both breathing hard and her face was flushed, her body pressed to his in the most distracting way.

"Izzy," he began roughly.

But she got in first. "Chase, I want to keep seeing you," she said before he could continue. "I've been trying all week to treat you like everyone else, and it's not working." Her eyes were very dark, very wide. "I know you have good reasons for not wanting us to get involved, but...can't we try it? Can't we see what happens?"

Her scent wound around him, sweet and musky, and he didn't want to talk about this. Didn't want to think about it either, because thinking involved logic and logic dictated that trying anything with Izzy would be a bad move.

He couldn't risk anything on "try." *Try* implied failure and that wasn't an option when Gus was part of the equation.

Gus, tonight, looking at Izzy adoringly...

Gus, who'd cried after Olivia had left. Who'd looked at him with her big gray eyes, expecting him to do something— the way Finn used to look at him, expecting him to do something, every night after their father had left to go to the pub, leaving two little boys at home on their own.

He was the leader; he was the one in charge. It was up to him to do the right thing, the responsible thing, no one else. After all, that's what his mother had told him just before she died, that he had to take care of the family, that it was up to him...

"It's a bad idea." He knew he should push himself away, but he couldn't seem to do it. "If things between us go south, it won't be just us affected. Any kind of difficulties people have with each other only get worse in a town this small, and that's not even going into how that would affect Gus."

A small line deepened between her brows. "I know, believe me. I understand and I don't want to hurt Gus. But we're adults, aren't we?" Her hands rested against his chest, her touch doing nothing but making the heat inside him burn hotter. "If we start something together and it doesn't work out, we can stay friends, right? We don't have to let it affect anything or anyone else."

The softness of her body was a temptation he didn't need, and parts south of his belt were being enthusiastically encouraging, telling him that she was right, that of course they were adults. They could have an affair and it would be fine.

But his head kept insisting that it was wrong.

Now was not the time for selfishness, not when he had Gus to consider. And anyway, it was only sex, wasn't it? He could get that from anyone; it didn't have to be her.

It does have to be her. Only her.

He nearly growled at the thought, trying to disengage his unruly nether regions and think with his head.

"I can't have anyone knowing," he insisted. "If you want an affair, then fine, I'm up for it. But we have to keep it on the down low."

"So more sneaking around? Is that what you're saying?"

"Yeah, that's exactly what I'm saying." The more he thought about it, the more excellent an idea it seemed. The sex was fantastic, and they enjoyed each other's company, so why not? He could still have her. He didn't have to stop...

But a telltale spark of temper was glittering in her eyes. "No," she said slowly. "No, I don't think I want that."

This time it was his turn to frown. "What? Why not? You said before you liked the idea of sneaking around."

"I did. But I don't want to now."

"Why? What difference does it make now?"

Izzy said nothing for a long moment, staring up at him. Then abruptly she shoved at his chest. Hard.

Chase got the hint and reluctantly stepped back, his body very unhappy with this development. "What?" he demanded. "What's going on?"

She was breathing very fast, the currents of her emotions shifting and changing as he watched. Hurt and anger and something else he couldn't name rippled over her delicate features.

"Izzy." He tried to moderate his tone. "Izzy, I—"

"Tell me," she interrupted flatly. "Tell me why you can't be with me openly."

He blinked, not understanding. "Be with you? But we're not together. This is only casual sex and—"

"It's not just casual sex." There was something bright in her eyes, something fierce. "At least it was never just casual sex to me. And I don't think it's casual for you either."

Something lurched inside him, like he'd been climbing some stairs and had missed a step.

Come on, did you really think she wouldn't feel something for you?

Oh, he'd hoped she wouldn't. Or rather he hadn't considered it, thinking that it wouldn't happen.

"Izzy," he began, "I told you casual is all I do."

She pushed herself away from the wall, anger glowing bright in her eyes. "Why?" she demanded. "Why is that all you do? I made an exception for you in Queenstown. Why can't you make an exception for me?"

His own temper sparked. "I did," he snapped. "And I told you what I could and couldn't give you. You can't turn around and change the rules on me now."

Izzy shut her mouth, storms in her eyes. Storms he didn't understand. She looked so distressed he couldn't bear it.

Chase took a step forward. "Beautiful…"

"No. Stay where you are."

He stopped, a tight feeling in his chest. A tight feeling that was getting tighter and tighter.

"I know what you told me," she went on, her voice calm, the look on her face the opposite. "And I know this is changing the rules. But…I'm falling for you. I didn't want to, Chase. Honestly, it was the last thing on earth that I wanted. But…you're so…" She made a vague gesture with her hand. "So much of everything that I admire. You're honest and passionate and caring. Responsible. You've got this wicked side that I just can't resist and you make me feel…so happy." The fierce light in her eyes glittered, and it wasn't anger this time. "I couldn't help it."

His heart twisted, like a towel being wrung out, squeezing

all the breath out of him. "I...can't," he said, struggling to find the words.

"I should be quiet," she said, her gaze very level. "I shouldn't say a damn word. I should take whatever you give me and be grateful, shouldn't I? I shouldn't make this difficult, I shouldn't make this hard." A tear sparkled in the corner of her eye. "But you know what? Screw that. I've been doing that all my life and I'm not going to do it anymore. You wanted me difficult, Chase, so here's difficult for you." She took a step toward him, the look in her eyes suddenly blazing again. "I don't want any more casual sex with you. And I don't want an affair. I want more than that. I want to be with you. I want a relationship with you. I want to try and see where it goes because I think what we could have together could be...magical."

She was trembling, and that squeezing sensation in his chest wouldn't go away. He wanted to reach out and drag her to him, tell her that he wanted to try too. But...it wasn't possible.

He shoved his hands into his pockets, his fingers itching to reach for her. "I'm sorry." He had to force out the words. "My position hasn't changed. Casual sex is all I can give you. And I told you why."

"No, you didn't. All you gave me were excuses." Her chin lifted. "And don't tell me it's about Gus again. Stop hiding behind your daughter, Chase, and give me the real reason."

She's right. You're using Gus as an excuse.

No. Shit. She was *not* right.

Anger shot through him. "Leave Gus out of this."

"Gus is a wonderful, mature, and perceptive young woman," Izzy snapped. "And if you think she'd be devastated by us getting together and wouldn't be able to handle our breakup, then you're fooling yourself and underestimating her."

She's right again.

Something inside of Chase shifted, his anger simmering and red-hot. But it wasn't at Izzy, and it wasn't at Gus. It wasn't even at Olivia.

"When I was eight, my mother died," he said roughly, the words coming out before he could stop them. "My dad was left alone to bring up Finn and me. But do you think he actually brought us up? No, he bloody didn't. He spent every night at the pub, drinking away his money. Drinking away his grief. And drinking away his goddamn responsibilities." An anger he'd thought he'd left behind years ago was coursing through him and he had to grip hard onto himself to stop it from overflowing. "He *abandoned* us. He left us alone. He gave us *nothing*." His voice was shaking, vibrating with the force of his fury. "I was the one who had to take care of everything. I was the one who had to make sure there was food on the table. I had to go to Bill and beg for food because Dad was always too fucking busy to check we even had the basic necessities." His jaw ached—everything ached. "He *left* us, Izzy. Maybe not physically but in every other way that mattered, he was gone. Just like Olivia was gone. Just like my mother was gone." His heart felt as if there had been fractures in it that he hadn't known were there, and they were suddenly coming apart. "I can't do it again. I won't. I won't trust someone, feel something for someone, *care* for someone only to have them leave. Not again. *Never* again."

Tears collected in Izzy's dark eyes, the light from outside shining on them. The anger had faded from her face and all that was left was a terrible sympathy.

"Oh, Chase." Her voice was soft. "I'm so sorry. I had no idea."

"No, because I didn't tell you." He took a breath, fighting to get his anger at his father, at Olivia, at everyone who'd ever left him to deal with everything on his own under control.

Anger at yourself, come on.

He ignored the thought.

"What can I do?" Izzy took a step toward him then stopped. "Tell me. I'm not like your dad, you should know that by now. And I'm not your ex-wife. I told you I was here for three months and—"

"You left Houston when things were tough," Chase interrupted, knowing it was a low blow yet saying it anyway because he was angry. Because this was all coming apart and he hated it. It made him feel as if he was losing something precious and he didn't know how he could stop it. "You just up and left without a word to anyone."

Shock rippled over her face—and a dawning hurt. "That's not fair. The situation here is entirely different—"

"It's not," he cut her off. "What's to say if things went wrong between us you wouldn't do the same thing? Get back on that plane to Houston and never see us again."

She opened her mouth, then shut it, pain shining in her eyes. "Is that what you truly believe? That I'd up and leave you at the first sign of trouble?"

"Everyone else did." It sounded pathetic, but he couldn't stop himself. "Why wouldn't you?"

Izzy stared at him. She looked small and delicate and pale, and he wanted to sweep her up in his arms. But he couldn't let himself do it. He couldn't. He wasn't going down that path again.

"What about love?" Her voice was very quiet. "What if I said I loved you?"

The fractures in his heart widened, deepened. He could barely breathe.

"If you think love makes any difference, then you're deluding yourself," he forced out. "Love was the reason everything went wrong. It's either too much or not enough, that's the problem with love."

Another expression crossed her face like a shadow, pain or shock or something else, he didn't know what.

She lifted a hand and wiped away the tears, and he felt like the biggest asshole on the planet. Like he'd deliberately smashed something beautiful and delicate and very important.

You have.

Yeah, maybe he had. But at least the feeling wouldn't last long. The pain would stop. It always did.

"Okay," she said, her voice thick. "Okay. If that's the way you want it, I won't force you." She turned and headed toward the stairs before pausing and turning to look at him. "But if you think I'm leaving on the next plane out of here, you're mistaken."

And before he could say another word, she vanished down the stairs, the door slamming behind her as she went out.

Chapter 16

IZZY STOOD BEHIND THE COUNTER OF THE GALLERY A week later, looking at the items spread on top of it. Beth and Indigo stood opposite her, the three of them examining the potential new stock.

There were some exquisite soaps and skin care handmade by Cait—Beth had discovered she made her own and had demanded some samples since Cait's skin was amazing— plus some photos of beautiful patchwork quilts made by Shirley, who worked at Bill's on occasion and whom Indigo had befriended. Izzy had contacted the Granges after that delicious platter Chase had put together and had discovered that Teddy Grange had diversified into making cheeses and preserves and was more than happy to provide some stock for sale.

Beth had volunteered to make friends with Evan McCahon, the eccentric artist, and to try and coax him into maybe providing a couple of smaller works if not for sale then at least as some local art on the walls. So far she'd had no luck, but Izzy was feeling optimistic.

It was an optimism that she had to drag kicking and screaming from the depths of her soul, of course, but she dragged it nevertheless.

Since the confrontation with Chase in HQ a week ago, she'd been drifting around in a fog of misery. She had known he wouldn't come after her, and he hadn't.

In fact, she'd barely seen him all week, which she was

extremely grateful for. Especially when seeing him made her broken heart jostle around in her chest, the sharp edges rubbing against one another and causing her pain.

After that night, after she'd spent most of it up in her room, soaking her pillow with hot tears, she'd been very tempted to pack up her stuff and do exactly what he'd thought she would: take the first plane back to Houston.

But even in the depths of her anguish, she knew she wasn't going to. There were too many people here depending on her, too many people she didn't want to disappoint. And apart from anything else, she was starting to like it here. The people, the landscape, the little business the three of them were setting up... It felt like something worthwhile, something good, something that she had a part in that didn't have the shadow of her family hanging over it.

A new start that was hers and hers alone.

Besides, she also just couldn't bring herself to give Chase that satisfaction.

He didn't feel the same way about her and she knew that, but he should have known that she'd never be the kind of person who'd give up at the first hurdle.

Then again, she had her suspicions about why he felt that way. It wasn't about her, not really. It was about him and about fear. About the raw anger she'd seen in his face as he'd told her about his father.

Everyone he'd trusted had left him. His mother. His father. Olivia. Everyone he loved had gone. They'd abandoned him, and she knew that feeling all too well. She'd been left too. Zeke. Her parents. The company. Josh. They'd all gotten rid of her and those feelings of abandonment and loss were hard ones to overcome.

Being here and being with Chase had helped her over-come her own doubts about herself. But she clearly hadn't helped him. She wasn't even sure if he *could* overcome his.

But even as she'd walked away from him that night, she knew one thing: she couldn't leave it at that. She couldn't be just one more person who left him.

She was here for the long haul, and she wanted to prove that to him.

It was hard because she had no idea if he'd change his mind—*ever*. But she had to try. She couldn't give up when it got hard, and even though his accusation that she'd left when things had gotten difficult in Houston had hurt, she also knew he wasn't wrong.

She *had* left when things had gotten difficult. And things were difficult now.

But she wasn't going to give up this time. She had a point to prove.

She loved Chase Kelly and even though he might not feel anything for her, nothing on earth was going to drag her away from him.

And one day he'd realize that.

"These are fabulous," Beth said, picking up a picture of one of Shirley's quilts. "Good spotting."

Indigo grinned. "Aren't they great? Her house is full of them. She told me she'd be fine with stocking as many quilts here as possible because she's running out of room."

"Excellent. We'll take as many as she wants to give us." Izzy nudged a jar of one of Teddy's offerings, the olive pesto. "What do we think of these?"

"We love," Beth said firmly. "Or rather, *I* certainly love."

"Me too," Indigo replied. "No reason we can't sell food

as well." She gave Izzy a look over the top of her glasses. "Do you think we can get Bill to do a special batch of those scones of his?"

Izzy, who'd broached the topic with Bill, shook her head. "No. He said he only baked them for his store and wasn't about to sell to the competition."

"Fair enough," Indigo said. "I probably wouldn't want to either."

Izzy realized Beth was studying her with a rather sharp look in her green eyes. "Hey, I tried," she said. "But he wasn't—"

"Are you okay, Izzy?" Beth asked abruptly.

Izzy's stomach sank. Oh God, had they noticed? "Uh, what do you mean?"

"You've been very quiet all week, and yesterday...well, yesterday your eyes were all red."

Her throat closed. She looked down at the things on the counter, her vision blurring slightly. Damn, she didn't want to cry. Not now. Not in front of Beth and Indigo. They'd think she was ridiculous. Who fell in love with one stupid man four weeks after her wedding to another had been canceled?

An idiot, that's who.

Beth put a hand over hers. "It's Chase, isn't it?"

She swallowed. "It's nothing."

"It doesn't look like nothing." Indigo's gaze had narrowed. "What did he do?"

Izzy looked up. The other two were both looking at her, both with obvious concern and sympathy, and it came to Izzy that these two women, whom she hadn't known well at the beginning of all of this, had become her friends. And they were clearly worried for her.

"We had a thing going," she heard herself say. "He didn't

want anyone to know because of Gus, and that was fair enough. It was supposed to be casual but…" She swallowed. "I fell for him. And he…"

"Please tell me he wasn't a dick to you." Indigo looked suddenly very fierce. "Because if he was, I will hurt him."

A tear rolled down Izzy's cheek, but she smiled. "He wasn't a dick. He was just…afraid, I think. Lots of people have abandoned him in his life and I suspect he has difficulties with trust. It's especially hard with Gus."

"Yeah, it would be." Beth patted Izzy's hand comfortingly. "He's still a dick, though. And clearly needs to get over himself."

"It's okay." The more she said it, the more true it would become. "I'm hoping that if I stay here, let him know that I'm not going anywhere, he might change his mind."

Beth frowned. "Are you sure he's worth it?"

Izzy thought about him. About the way he'd cared for her, helping her with the shelves, arranging a little platter of treats, putting gel on her sunburn, giving her a lecture on boots because she had blisters.

Chase stroking her. Chase smiling at her and calling her beautiful.

Chase, who'd been abandoned by everyone who'd mattered to him…

"Yes," she said thickly. "He's worth it."

"Okay then." Beth had the air of someone who'd made a decision. "In that case, we need to rub his face in the fact that you're here every opportunity we get."

"Damn straight," Indigo said.

Izzy wiped her eyes. "You guys don't owe me anything, you know that, right?"

"Bullshit to that," Beth said. "You're our friend. And besides, we have to stick together. Especially with all these stubborn-ass Kiwi blokes around."

Izzy opened her mouth to tell them how much she appreciated them, but the familiar growl of a truck engine rumbled outside and she stopped, glancing out the window in time to see Chase's truck pull up.

"Speak of the devil," Beth murmured.

The truck door slammed shut and then the door of the gallery slammed open and Chase stood on the threshold.

At the sight of him, Izzy's heart fluttered around madly, like a bird trapped in a room, the pieces of her broken heart grinding together.

The last time she'd seen him was from afar a couple of days earlier, but now he was here, closer, and in the flesh, and all she wanted was to throw herself into his arms.

The other two women had somehow put themselves between him and Izzy, staring at him with obvious hostility.

"Yes?" Beth asked with some haughtiness. "Can we help you?"

Indigo glared fiercely at him.

Chase gave no sign that he'd noticed, his handsome features set in hard, rigid lines, his gray eyes gone that dark charcoal color that usually indicated he was in a temper.

"Izzy," he said, ignoring the other two. "I need you for something."

Well, whatever it was, it wasn't for a declaration of love, that was for sure.

Izzy's heart felt sore and bruised, and she wanted to tell him to go away, that whatever something he wanted she didn't have it in her to give, but then he added, "It's Gus."

Her stomach dropped away, all her anger vanishing in an instant. "What's wrong?"

"She's okay," Chase said. "But she's got a problem and won't talk to me." An expression that looked like frustration crossed his face. "She wants you."

Izzy didn't even have to think about it. "Of course." She glanced at the other two.

"Go," Beth said before Izzy even had a chance to ask. "Indigo and I will make some important decisions and then inform you of them much later when you can't do anything about them."

She gave them both a grateful smile. "I'd expect nothing less."

Once she and Chase were outside, she turned and looked up at him. "What's going on?"

"If I knew, I'd tell you." Chase's tone was flat as he headed for the truck. "But since Gus won't talk to me, I don't know what the hell happened."

Worry wound through her. "Is she okay?"

"Yeah. But she's upset about something. Get in the truck."

Izzy didn't waste time arguing and climbed inside.

Chase gunned the engine, spun the truck around, and took it down the road toward his place.

"It's okay," she said, trying to reassure him. "It won't be—"

"You don't know that," Chase interrupted shortly. "You don't know anything until you've talked to her. And good luck with that because she was adamant I couldn't help her."

Worry for Gus was pouring off him, along with the frustrated anguish of a man used to fixing things and yet who couldn't fix this. She wanted to put her hand on his thigh, reassure him, but she knew he wouldn't welcome it. Plus it wasn't her place to do that, so she kept her hands to herself.

A few minutes later, they were pulling up the drive to Chase's house.

"She's in her bedroom," Chase said as they got out of the truck and went up the stairs to the front door. "I told her I'd bring you back so you could talk to her."

Izzy nodded, then stepped inside as he held the front door open for her.

Gus's room was at the back of the house, opposite the narrow stairs that led to Chase's bedroom, and the door was firmly closed.

Izzy stopped outside it and gave it a tentative knock. "Hey," she called softly. "It's me, Gus. What's wrong?"

"Dad's not there, is he?" Gus's voice sounded muffled.

"No. He's in the kitchen. He's…worried about you."

The door opened and Gus appeared. Her face was pink and streaked with tears, and she was wearing one of the outfits Izzy had gotten her in Queenstown. A little denim skirt that went to her knees and a pretty pink T-shirt.

Izzy's heart contracted painfully. "Oh, Gussie," she murmured. "What happened?"

Gus stood back to let her come into the room, then slammed the door after her. She turned, wiping her face. "I went to see that boy I liked. I wore this skirt and everything, but he told me I was just a friend. He didn't want to go out with me."

Well, that explained things. It also explained why she hadn't wanted to talk to Chase. Poor kid. First love was the worst. Izzy knew how that felt. She knew it intimately.

"Oh, honey, I'm so sorry. Do you want a hug?"

For an answer, Gus simply flung herself into Izzy's arms and wept.

Izzy held her tight, pulling her over to the bed and sitting down on the edge with her. "I know," she murmured into Gus's dark hair. "It's really hard when you feel something for someone and they don't feel the same way about you."

"How do you know?" Gus said thickly. "Has that happened to you?"

She couldn't tell Gus about Chase, but she could about Josh.

"Yes." Izzy took a little breath. "Just before I came out to New Zealand, I was engaged to this guy. And he decided he liked someone else more."

Gus lifted her head, looking horrified. "He called off your wedding?"

Izzy nodded solemnly, rather surprised to find what had seemed so painful not a few weeks ago felt much less so now. In fact it felt distant, her feelings for Josh...muted.

And no wonder. She'd never been in love with him at all—now she knew what the real thing felt like.

"How could he like someone else?" Gus asked in genuine puzzlement. "You're an absolute icon."

"Aw, thank you." Izzy gave the girl a squeeze. "But you know, if he hadn't called off that wedding, I'd still be in Houston. And I wouldn't have come out to New Zealand and I wouldn't have met you."

Gus wiped her eyes. "I knew you'd tell me something mature and adult."

"I'm not wrong though."

"And you wouldn't have met Dad either."

"No," Izzy said, her voice gone husky despite herself. "That's true. I wouldn't have."

"We love you," Gus said generously. "We think you're amazing."

Gus might. But Chase? He was a different story.

Izzy smiled, her eyes prickling. "I'm the one who's supposed to be comforting you, not the other way around."

The kid sniffed. "I wore the outfit and everything."

"I know. But if he doesn't see what an amazing girl you are, then forget him. There's someone for you out there, Gus. Someone who will appreciate you for who you are, I know it. And you won't have to wear a fantastic outfit for them. You won't have to be pretty or be a great conversationalist or good at drawing or whatever. You just have to be you."

Gus's eyes narrowed in that sharp way she had just before she made some kind of observant comment. "Like Dad does with you?"

Izzy blinked. "I…"

"Because that's what I want," Gus said, as if what she'd said hadn't shocked Izzy into silence. "I want someone to look at me the way Dad looks at you." She wiped her eyes. "Because you know what? I'm awesome. And if Jamie doesn't see that then he's…he's just a bloody dick."

Izzy's heart pressed painfully against her breastbone. Chase had taught his daughter well, had brought her up believing in herself and her own value, not to mention giving her some resilience, and really…

If you didn't love him now, that alone would make you fall.

Izzy took a little breath. "Yes, my sentiments exactly. Now, you're probably going to have to tell your dad, you know that, right?"

Gus pulled a face. "I don't want him to worry. Plus…" She sent Izzy a meaningful look. "I also don't want him going to Jamie's place and getting angry. You know how he is."

"He won't do that." Izzy thought about it, then amended, "Well, he might if Jamie were older, but not now."

Gus sighed. "He won't understand."

"Give him a chance, Gus. He gets worried about you."

"I know. But I don't want him to."

Izzy looked at the girl a moment, then said, "You know the best way to handle a worried dad? Let him do something practical for you."

"Like what?"

"Like…take you out fishing? Or…find something that's broken that needs repairing." She grinned. "That works for men in general, so save that for later, okay? For when your friend Jamie finally sees a cool girl has been right under his nose all this time."

"Okay." Gus gave her a glum look. "But he won't."

"Hey, you never know." Izzy gave her another squeeze, then tried to pull away.

But Gus wouldn't let go.

"You're not going to leave, are you?" Gus sounded suddenly small. "I don't want you to."

Izzy's heart tightened and something shifted into place inside her, like a key fitting perfectly into a lock.

"No," she said, holding on to the girl. "I'm not going anywhere."

———

Chase found himself pacing around the deck for the second time in as many weeks, his mind revolving around his daughter's tearstained face and the way she'd shaken her head as he'd picked her up from school and asked her what was wrong.

She hadn't wanted to talk to him. Izzy, she'd said. She'd wanted Izzy.

Izzy was the answer to seemingly every question that Gus had, and he was starting to think she might be the answer to every question he had too, and even though he knew that couldn't happen, he just couldn't shake it.

This week without her had been a bloody nightmare. He'd actively avoided her this time around, trying not to be anywhere near her, because every time he was, the urge to take her in his arms was almost overwhelming. He couldn't even look at her.

He was an idiot. A damn fool.

She'd told him she loved him and he'd said…well, he'd told her that love didn't make a difference, and it didn't.

Love hadn't stopped people leaving him, so why on earth would it?

But she hasn't left.

He couldn't understand why. By rights she should have been on the first plane out and he expected her to, yet she hadn't gone. She'd stayed instead.

Stubbornly around whenever he was, with her laughter and her smile and her long, glossy hair. Her sweet scent. The memory of her hands on him and her mouth and the way she looked at him. The way she saw him…

"Chase?"

He turned sharply toward the french doors to see Izzy come out onto the deck, looking casual and gorgeous in jeans and a dark- blue T-shirt. She gave him a tentative smile, which was obviously a good sign about Gus but it was going to make it immeasurably harder for him.

"What happened?" he demanded.

She stopped not far away from him, but he swore he could have told to the millimeter just how far. "Gus is fine. She said it was okay to tell you. But the issue she had was with a boy."

"A boy?" he echoed, the words not making sense.

"Yes. A boy she likes."

Tension rippled through him, his brain struggling to comprehend what Izzy was telling him. "But no. That's not it. She's too young. She's—"

"She's twelve," Izzy interrupted gently. "And she'll be thirteen soon."

Chase took a breath and then another, grappling with this new change in his daughter. And then another, more primitive reaction hit. "What happened? Did he hurt her? If he hurt her, by God—"

"No, it wasn't like that. Gus liked him, but he doesn't see her that way, and that's what she was upset about. That's why she wanted to go out shopping in Queenstown to get some different clothes—she wanted something feminine to wear."

Things were shifting around inside him. Painful things.

His daughter was growing up. She'd never again be that happy little girl who only wanted to do whatever he did. She was going to turn into a young woman, with her own thoughts and dreams and, God help him, her own desires. And she'd start getting interested in boys and…

Shit.

She didn't want to talk to him about any of this. She'd wanted to talk to Izzy.

Chase abruptly stepped back, turned, and strode to the edge of the deck, looking out over the glittering lake and the bush, the silence of the place settling deep inside him. But there was no comfort there.

You can't give her everything she needs.

The shifting things inside him were painful and jagged, and he didn't know what to do. He'd tried all his life to give the people that mattered to him what they needed, but sometimes it wasn't enough.

It's never enough, though. You're not enough for your daughter and you'll never be enough for Izzy either.

There was warmth at his back, but he didn't turn around. He didn't want to. He didn't want to see what would be in Izzy's eyes, because he had a horrible feeling it would be understanding. And sympathy. And the fierce, bright thing that had been there the night at HQ when she'd told him she loved him.

That's why this is hard. You love her. You want to give her everything, but you can't. You can never be enough, not for her. Not for anyone.

He closed his eyes, every part of him acknowledging the painful truth of it. His father hadn't cared enough about him to be a proper father. Olivia hadn't cared enough about him to stay.

Izzy said she cared about him, but how long would that last? Eventually she'd want more, and he wouldn't have it to give her. And he couldn't bear that.

"She asked me if I was going to leave," Izzy said very quietly. "And I told her I wasn't. So basically, now I can't. I'm stuck here."

"You should go." His voice didn't sound like his, harsh and rough. "There's nothing for you here."

"Yes, there is." Warmth bloomed against his back as he felt her palm rest there like a bright patch of sunlight. "There's you, Chase Kelly."

His heart felt raw, battered, and bruised. "You think you'll find any kind of happiness with me? That I'll be able to give you what you want? I won't. Ask Olivia."

Slender arms wound around his waist, a gentle heat against his back. Delicate yet he could feel the strength in them. Steel threaded through with a caring that found the cracks in his soul and shone through them, bathing him in light.

"You don't have to give me anything," Izzy said. "And you don't have to be anything. You're already everything I want just the way you are."

He was wound so tight it felt as if the slightest movement would break him. "No," he said roughly. "That's not what—"

"I love you, Chase." She said it like it was easy, the simplest thing in the world to say. "That's what love is about. It's acceptance. It doesn't require you to do anything or be anything. It just requires that you be yourself."

For a second he stood there, with her warm arms around him, staring out at the bush. "Then why did my dad…do what he did? Why did Olivia leave? Why did—"

"Because they were idiots," Izzy said, as if it was obvious. "Because the problem was them, not you."

Her warmth had sunk into him, finding the little piece of ice in the center of his heart that he hadn't even known was there. Melting it right through.

She hadn't gone. She'd stayed.

Chase felt the jagged pieces of his heart grinding together, then locking tightly, firmly.

He turned around.

Izzy didn't let him go, still standing there with her arms around him, her dark eyes looking up into his, something fierce and strong and enduring glowing there.

Something he felt inside his own heart.

"I couldn't give them what they wanted," he said hoarsely. "Not Dad. Not Olivia. Not—"

"I told you a week ago what an amazing man you are." Her hand touched his face. "It's not your fault they couldn't see it. It was never your fault. You go above and beyond for the people you care about, you always have. And if they didn't understand that, if they didn't value it, then that's their loss." Her dark eyes were full of warmth and understanding. "Too bad for them. I get to have you instead."

"Izzy…"

"You don't have to give me anything, Chase, and I mean it. I would never demand anything you didn't want to give, and I'm not going to now." Then, much to his shock, she let him go and stepped back. "I hope one day you'll change your mind. That you can trust me. Because like I said, I can't leave. I made a promise to Gus and that means I'm here to stay."

He stood there for a moment staring at her, conscious of the distance between them. And that she was going to go. That she actually meant what she said, that she wasn't going to make demands, she was just going to turn around and leave.

And conscious of the fact that he would be standing there like an idiot, watching the woman he loved walk away.

For the second time.

You asshole. You know what you feel. She might not be leaving Brightwater, but are you really going to let her go thinking she means nothing to you? Stop being a selfish dick and man the hell up.

She was already turning away, already leaving.

"Izzy." Her name was hoarse and scratchy, vibrating in the air around them.

She stopped.

He was afraid, he could see that now. Afraid of trusting her. Afraid that love was the sham he'd always thought. But…Izzy wasn't his dad. And she wasn't Olivia. And if his twelve-year-old daughter could put aside her fear and trust, then…maybe he could too.

"Don't go," he said roughly.

She turned, her face pale.

He loved her. He'd loved her from the moment he'd first seen her. That's why she'd gotten under his skin so badly. That's why he'd been afraid all this time.

But she wasn't afraid. No, she'd told him she loved him without hesitation. How could he do any less?

"Stay with me." His voice was hoarse.

Her gaze met his, bright with what he thought were tears. "Chase, are you sure? I don't—"

"I love you, Isabella Montgomery."

She blinked, her mouth opening, color rushing into her cheeks.

And he couldn't stand the distance anymore, so he closed it, coming for her. But by then her arms were already opening, and as he swept her up in his, hers came around him and her mouth found his. And then they were kissing each other hungrily, desperately, giving not one single thought to the fact that Gus had come out of the living room behind them and was now watching them with interest.

"Ew," she said.

Chase jerked his head up while Izzy buried her face against his chest. Her shoulders shook with muffled laughter.

"Do you mind?" He glared at his daughter. "We were having a moment."

Gus wrinkled her nose. "Does that mean Izzy's coming to live with us, then?"

"Yes," Chase said, every part of him suddenly bursting with happiness. "Is that okay?"

"Absolutely." Gus grinned. "Can we make cupcakes? I'm starving."

"Is your stomach all you ever think about?" Chase asked, half laughing. "Go inside."

Gus pulled a face but did as she was told.

Izzy looked up at him. She'd gone the most delightful shade of pink. "I guess cupcakes are very important."

They were, but not as important as what he had to say to her. Chase took her face between his hands and looked down into her eyes. "I don't want casual," he said fiercely. "I want to try. I want you in my life and in Gus's life too. I want you here in my house, living with me. Baking cupcakes in my kitchen and taking my daughter out shopping. Drinking wine on my deck." Her skin was warm against his palms, her eyes glowing in the way he knew so well. "I want you sleeping in my bed. And also not sleeping, also in my bed. I want you loving me the way I love you."

"Chase—"

"I want a home, Izzy. I want a home and a family with you."

The sheen of tears was in her eyes. "Do you remember when you told me that sometimes you have to go away from a place in order to find out where your home was?"

He smiled. "I do."

"Well, I don't think my home was ever in Houston."

"No." He tightened his arms around her. "Your home is here, in Brightwater Valley." He kissed her. "With me."

And it was.

All this time he'd been trying to build a home and a family, a life that he could be proud of, and he'd never realized that there was a reason it hadn't worked before. Because he was missing a piece of it.

And that piece he was missing was her.

Epilogue

IT WAS FRIDAY NIGHT AT THE ROSE AND THERE WAS A party in the pub. A little celebration for Izzy and Chase, who had fallen in love and were now engaged.

The two of them had been seeing each other in secret, or rather they thought they'd been seeing each other in secret. The truth was that most of the town knew already, because it had been obvious from the get-go that the two of them were hot for each other.

Certainly Beth had known right from the moment Chase had opened their car door that Izzy was meant for him and he for her.

She'd always been able to tell if people were soul mates. It wasn't like she could read minds or anything; she could just...tell. Being sensitive to other people's emotions helped, though quite honestly, it could also be a drag.

The vibe in the pub was good tonight though. No bad feelings at all, just everyone in town being happy.

Well, not quite everyone.

Beth picked up the two bottles of Finn Kelly's favorite beer—one for him, one for her—gave Jim a smile, then headed determinedly over to the table where Finn was sitting by himself.

He'd shown no inclination to join the crowd around Chase, Izzy, and Gus, merely watching them, the expression on his drop-dead gorgeous face inscrutable.

There was a dark cloud around that man. Beth had sensed it

the instant she'd met him, and she'd decided in that same instant that she was going to be his friend, dispel that dark cloud.

She couldn't help herself. It was just what she did. And she'd been trying to do it for the past four weeks since arriving in Brightwater, except Finn Kelly had rebuffed every advance she'd made.

Beth had never met anyone she couldn't determinedly cheer up, so this was starting to feel a little personal now.

Anyway, a couple of days earlier, she'd promised to buy him a beer in return for his help in getting Evan McCahon to lend them one of his paintings for the gallery. So here she was, with the promised beer.

She approached the table and put the beer bottle down in front of him. "Here," she said, smiling. "I owe you, remember?"

Finn's dark gaze met hers, guarded, wary. Always *so* wary.

He didn't speak or offer an invitation, but she sat opposite anyway. The gallery was opening next week, so they had to sort out this stuff with Evan now.

"I thought you might want something to toast the happy couple with," she said when he remained silent. "It's your favorite, Jim said."

Finn glanced down at the beer, then looked back at her. "Thank you." His voice was as deep and dark as the color of his eyes.

Beth leaned her elbows on the table. "You mentioned helping me with Evan…"

His gaze flickered, and then much to her shock, he suddenly shoved back his chair and rose to his considerable height, making her feel very small and delicate and a touch too feminine, which she did not like. At all.

Her smile faltered. "What's wrong?"

"We'll do this later," he said shortly.

Seriously? He was bailing on her again?

"But what about your beer?"

Finn stared at her. Then he reached for the bottle, picked it up, and downed the beer in one swallow.

Then he gave her a nod, turned on his heel, and walked toward the exit.

"Hey, wait!" Beth called in some annoyance. "What about Evan?"

He didn't respond, vanishing through the door.

Okay, no. Just no. He was *not* walking out on her again.

She lifted her own bottle and swallowed the beer in one go. For luck.

Then she went after him.

Keep reading for a sneak peek at the next book
in Jackie Ashenden's Small Town Dreams series:

All Roads Lead to You

Available November 2022
From Sourcebooks Casablanca

Chapter 1

OH, THANK HEAVENS. THERE WAS ONE LEFT.

Bethany Grant slid back the glass door of the food cabinet and reached for the delicacy sitting in splendid isolation on the top shelf, just as a large and definitely male hand reached for it at the same time.

Beth, who'd never been faster than when it came to getting food she loved, quickly whipped the sausage roll off the shelf before her rival could get a good grip on it and slid it triumphantly into the paper bag she was holding in readiness.

Getting the last of Bill Preston's sausage rolls in Brightwater Valley's General Store was a feat equivalent to being the last gladiator standing in the Colosseum, and she was going to enjoy the hell out of it.

Ready to be magnanimous in victory and maybe offer him half, or at the very least be sympathetic, Beth glanced at her opponent, her gaze settling on a broad, muscular chest covered in a black cotton T-shirt with a familiar logo.

Her stomach dipped.

Really? Did it have to be?

She glanced further up.

Her stomach dipped further.

Eyes the color of espresso coffee, check. Black hair worn just a little too long, check. High forehead, sharp cheekbones and straight nose, check. Beautifully sculpted mouth, the kind that made you think of kissing, also check.

Brooding as hell and radiating I-have-a-secret-dark-past-that-I-don't-like-to-talk-about vibes, double check.

It was Finn Kelly, all right.

Dammit.

The man was so reserved he made a stone seem garrulous and outgoing, and had resisted all her efforts to make friends with him since she'd gotten here.

Quite frankly, she was getting a little tired of it.

Beth had come to Brightwater Valley in New Zealand's South Island six weeks ago, along with Izzy Montgomery and Indigo Jameson, and in that time she'd successfully befriended just about everyone in the tiny town.

Everyone except Finn.

He was the younger brother of Chase Kelly, whom Izzy had fallen for and was now living with, and part owner of Pure Adventure NZ, an outdoor adventure company based in Brightwater. The business was also owned by Chase and a third, their friend Levi King, and basically offered any outdoor experience you'd care to name: hiking, hunting, kayaking, fishing, heli-skiing, horse riding…all of the above.

Over the past few weeks, Beth had come to know the other two guys well. Chase was officious and bossy—he was ex-SAS and that kind of went with the territory—yet he was also a caring, kind-hearted man, with a delightful, funny teenage daughter called Gus, and Beth liked them both very much.

Levi, by contrast, was pure playboy. Ridiculously good-looking, charming and just a touch wicked, Beth would have considered him a nice distraction—if she'd been in New Zealand for men.

But she wasn't in New Zealand for men.

She was in New Zealand ostensibly to find new markets for the jewelry she designed and made herself. But she also had a deeper, more private goal that she'd told no one else about. She was here for escape and to find the happiness she'd lost back in her hometown of Deep River, Alaska.

Brightwater Valley was similar to Deep River, yet different enough that Beth had found arriving here like a balm to an aching wound. It had the same snow-capped mountains, dark green bush-clad hills, and a large body of water—in the shape of a lake instead of a river. But what Brightwater Valley had that Deep River didn't were total strangers. People who didn't look at her with that awful combination of sympathy and uncertainty, as if they didn't know what to do or what to say. As if she was some fragile thing made of glass that might break at any moment.

She'd gotten tired of that. Tired of the weight of their concern for her. What she wanted were people who didn't know her or the past she was trying to leave behind.

Here was her new beginning, where she could be whoever she wanted to be and what she wanted to be was strong, fearless, and definitely *not* fragile. And happy. Just...happy.

Even if Finn Kelly was the one dark cloud on her blindingly bright horizon.

He was guarded bordering on unfriendly, and had barely

said more than a couple of words to her the whole time she, Izzy and Indigo had been here.

Beth was starting to find that something of a personal challenge.

There had been some resistance from the locals of Brightwater to her attempts at friendship—they were a crusty lot, full of mutterings about a "bunch of Americans" coming in and "changing things." But Beth had been relentlessly friendly and cheerful, and soon their chilly Antipodean reserve had thawed.

Except for Finn. The chill around him remained and she was desperately curious to know why.

Beth gave him her extra-friendly and extra-wide smile. "Hey Finn. Sorry, did you want the last sausage roll?"

He did not smile back, his almost black eyes impenetrable as usual, his reserve fathoms deep. "No, thanks." His voice held a kind of darkness and grit that set something very female inside her vibrating.

It was annoying. In fact, her physical reaction to him as a whole was annoying. She didn't want to find him as ridiculously attractive as she did, because that was a complication she *so* didn't need right now.

Friends. That's all she wanted. Just friends.

She and Indigo and Izzy were on the point of opening Brightwater Dreams, the little gallery they'd spent the past month setting up, selling local arts and crafts, as well as locally produced artisan delicacies. It was a commercial enterprise that was supposed to help revitalize Brightwater—the town was tiny and on the verge of becoming a ghost town—by bringing in new blood in the form of the three Deep River ladies and potentially more tourist dollars.

Brightwater Valley had sister-city links to Deep River going back to the forties, when American GIs had been stationed here during the Second World War, so when Brightwater had called for help to save their dying town, Deep River had answered.

The three of them loved it here. But while Izzy had found love and a new future with Chase Kelly, Beth had more important things to do.

Things such as making sure she had enough stock of her jewelry. She was also trying to secure the last thing Izzy had wanted in the store before it opened—paintings by a well-known New Zealand artist that would hopefully draw in more people.

Except the well-known New Zealand artist was a recluse who lived in Brightwater and had so far refused to speak to Beth.

Okay, maybe Finn Kelly wasn't the only holdout in her friendship drive.

Evan McCahon was too.

"Are you sure?" Beth lifted the paper bag containing the sausage roll and waved it at Finn. "I can halve it with you?"

Bill baked many delicacies that he kept in a cabinet on the counter, and his sausage rolls, meat pies, and scones were the best Beth had ever tasted. Particularly the sausage rolls, which were rolls of delicious flaky puff pastry stuffed with fresh sausage, onions and herbs.

She loved them, but sadly so did everyone else in Brightwater Valley, which usually meant they sold out by midday.

Finn stared at her a moment, his handsome face completely unreadable, while Beth fervently wished she didn't feel quite such a strong urge to stare at the fit of his black Pure Adventure NZ T-shirt, the cotton lovingly outlining the broad width of his shoulders and chest.

He was a tall guy, much taller than she was, six two, six three at least, and muscled like a gymnast or a swimmer, with wide shoulders and a lean waist.

Hot. Exceedingly hot.

Beth, much to her annoyance, felt herself blushing under the weight of that dark stare.

"It's fine." Finn shoved his hands into his pockets. "You can have it."

"Oh, I don't have to." Beth waved the paper bag at him again, determined now that he should accept at least something from her. "I can get one tomorrow."

"No thanks." He turned away.

Rude.

Beth watched him stride out of Bill's store with the kind of purposeful grace that made the very female, quivery thing inside her quiver again. She ignored it.

Really, this was starting to feel personal now. Finn was nice to everyone but her and even though she'd been telling herself for the past couple of weeks that she didn't care, she kind of did.

Had she done something to him he hadn't liked? Said something offensive? Because if so, she wanted to know so she could fix it and maybe not do it again.

Bill, a short, round man in his early seventies with a few wisps of white hair still clinging to his head, a craggy face, and bright blue eyes, gave her a knowing look from behind the counter.

"It's me, isn't it, Bill?" Beth put the sausage roll down on the counter. "I mean, is there anyone else he's like that with?"

"Who? Finn?" Bill peered inside the paper bag then rang up the pastry on his till. "Nah, it's just you."

"Why? What did I ever do to him?" Clearly it had been something.

"Well, you're bright, you're pretty, and you're American." Bill held out his hand for the money, which Beth dutifully gave him. "But mainly you're too cheerful and Finn Kelly's not in the market for cheer."

Beth sighed. She was pleased to be called bright and pretty, but there was nothing she could do about that or about the fact that she was American. And as for cheer, if only they knew. Lucky for her they didn't.

"Thanks, Bill. But who isn't in the market for cheer? The man could obviously use some."

The old man counted the change and dumped it into her palm. "He lost his wife five years ago so I'd say that has something to do with it."

Beth's heart gave a sudden, sharp kick.

"Oh," she said, a little shocked. "I didn't know that."

"Why would you? It's not a secret, but obviously no one talks about it on a daily basis."

So, that was the dark past thing she'd sensed about him. Or at least, it must be. He was a widower.

Her heart gave another little kick then clenched hard. She'd always been sensitive to other people's emotions— probably too sensitive—and had a strong sense of empathy. Maybe that's why she'd been drawn to him. Why she'd wanted to be his friend. She'd sensed his grief and wanted to make it better.

"That's awful," she said quietly.

"Lovely woman, Sheri," Bill went on, since there was nothing he loved more than imparting information. "Family lived up the valley. She and Finn grew up together. He was devastated when she passed." He gave Beth a serious look. "Cancer."

Well, that was terrible. No wonder he was so silent and grave all the time.

"I should have let him have that sausage roll," Beth said, feeling guilty. "Poor man."

Bill shook his head. "Oh no, he wouldn't have accepted it anyway. Hates sympathy. And he doesn't like to talk about it, either, so I wouldn't go around mentioning it to him if I were you."

She could relate. She hated sympathy too.

"No, of course I won't," she murmured. "But…is there anything I can do?"

"It's been a few years now, so probably not. I'd just take this friendship thing slow. He's a very reserved, private bloke, is Finn Kelly."

Oh, she knew that already. He was so reserved it was amazing he spoke to anyone at all, let alone her. But this at least was some context.

Still didn't explain why he was nice to everyone except her, though.

What does it matter? Do you really care that much?

Maybe she shouldn't. And maybe if she hadn't known about his wife, she wouldn't. But now she knew…

She wanted to help him, make him feel better. Bring a smile to his fascinating, handsome face, make that hard mouth soften and curl. Relieve the darkness in his eyes.

Which was stupid, because she knew that all the smiles and optimism and positive thinking in the world couldn't help some problems. But it couldn't make it worse, right?

She knew the darkness. She'd been there herself.

"Okay," she said. "Good to know. Thanks, Bill."

She picked up her sausage roll and stepped outside into the brilliant sunshine of a late summer day.

Brightwater Valley was tiny, the "town" consisting of one street and three buildings. The first was a long, low stone building that housed Bill's General Store and Brightwater Dreams, the new gallery. The second was a two storied, ramshackle old wooden building that was The Rose hotel/pub/restaurant. And the third was also wooden and two storied, but a lot newer and housed Pure Adventure NZ, Chase, Finn and Levi's outdoor adventure company.

Opposite the town's buildings was the lake and a small gravel car park where some cars were parked, a few tourists picnicking on the grassy lakeshore. The lake was a deep, turquoise blue, the mountains ringing the entire valley white-capped and sharp, while the foothills were covered in dark green native bush.

The colors in this place constantly astounded Beth, as did the wildness of the landscape. She loved it. Her sketchbook had never been so full of inspiration for new designs.

Except right now she wasn't looking at the scenery. Her gaze was firmly on the Pure Adventure NZ building. Considering.

Finn Kelly was a man in need of a friend, she could sense that loud and clear. But it was also clear that she had to go about this carefully. He had suffered a significant loss, so she couldn't just blunder about trying to get a smile out of him or pushing for something he wasn't ready to give. As Bill had said, she had to take it slowly.

Perhaps needing his help would be a good way in, such as

making contact with the elusive Evan McCahon, for example. Apparently, the painter liked no one else in town but Finn, which meant if she wanted to convince him to show his paintings in the gallery, she was going to need someone to introduce her.

Evan didn't have a landline and since there was no cell phone service in Brightwater Valley, she couldn't either text him or call him on a cell. He didn't have a computer either, so she couldn't email him. In fact, the only way to get in touch with him was to visit him in person, and since he hadn't answered the door the one time she'd made the trek to his house up the valley, she hadn't managed to do that either.

All of which boiled down to a perfect excuse to talk to Finn Kelly.

The door to Pure Adventure NZ opened and Finn stepped out, heading toward the mud-splashed truck that was parked out the front.

"Right," Beth murmured under her breath. "Finn Kelly, I'm sorry, but be prepared to be aggressively friended."

———

"Hey," a sweet, lightly accented female voice called. "Hey, wait up, Finn."

Dammit. It was Bethany Grant. What the hell did she want with him?

Finn debated ignoring her, but in the time it took to decide his options, she was already walking down the street from Bill's toward him, the sun making the cloud of white-blonde hair that had been tied in a loose ponytail at the nape of her neck, look like a collection of thistledown.

She was of average height, though that was short to

him, and had the lushest curves, especially in the jeans that molded nicely to her hips and thighs, and the green T-shirt—the exact color of her eyes—that did the most wonderful things to her chest.

Which he should not be looking at. In fact, he shouldn't be looking at her, period.

It had been five years since Sheri had died and in that time he'd never once been with another woman. Initially grief had put his libido on ice for a couple of years and after that, he'd deliberately chosen to keep it in the deep freeze. His brother and Levi would be appalled if they knew he hadn't had sex for five years—longer considering Sheri had been ill for a while before she'd died.

But he hadn't missed it. Nothing had been the same after Sheri had gone and he hadn't met anyone else since who even made him consider thawing a bit.

And then Bethany Grant had turned up. Bethany, with her delectable figure and the brightest, sunniest smile he'd ever seen. Bethany, with the small dusting of freckles over her nose and green eyes that stunned him every time he looked at them.

Bethany, who'd appeared like a sunbeam in the middle of the darkest pit of hell and had not only turned his frozen libido molten, she'd also blown his previously rock-solid denial to smithereens.

And he was pissed about it. Majorly pissed.

It wasn't fair to blame her. It wasn't her fault that she was pretty and sweet and sunny, and that he was attracted to her. Just as it wasn't her fault that he was a moody bastard who'd lost his wife five years ago and didn't want to be attracted to anyone else.

But he didn't care what was fair or otherwise.

He'd been done with fairness when Sheri had first gotten her diagnosis.

It was too late to pretend he hadn't heard Beth calling his name so now if he ignored her, he was only going to seem rude. And while he was fine with being rude in private, there were enough tourists around that he didn't want to do it in public since it wouldn't exactly be good advertising for the company.

Muttering a curse under his breath, Finn paused opening the door to his truck and turned in Beth's direction. Her sweet, heart-shaped face was pretty in a freshly-scrubbed, girl-next-door fashion, with a turned up nose and a generous, full mouth, currently curved in one of her infectious smiles.

In one hand she carried the paper bag that presumably held the last of Bill's sausage rolls, the sight of which made him annoyed all over again. He'd been looking forward to that and she'd bloody well taken the last one and he was pissed about that too.

"Can I help you?" he asked coolly as she approached, her sandals crunching over the gravel.

She came to a stop by the truck, close enough for him to see that exposure to the harsh southern-hemisphere sun had made the faint little dusting of freckles across the pale skin of her nose darker, and that she had a touch of sunburn to her cheeks and forehead.

She always wore a lot of jewelry too: a quantity of silver bracelets chiming on her wrist, plus the necklace she always wore. A small silver pendant in the familiar, curled spiral of a koru, a fern frond, hung from a delicate silver chain that nestled just in the hollow of her throat.

It was pretty, just like her, as were the small silver hoops in her ears, the surface of the silver etched with intricate swirling designs. Had she made those? She was a jewelry designer, or at least he'd heard she was. Not that he'd been paying attention. At all.

"Funny you should ask," she said. "Because yes. Yes, you can."

Great. This was the last thing he needed. He had to get up to Clint's, the horse farm he'd been helping Clint manage and was in the process of buying. There were a few things he needed to finalize, and he didn't particularly want to get side-tracked into helping Beth with whatever it was she wanted.

He didn't particularly want to get side-tracked by Beth at all, but while he didn't care about a bit of absent rudeness, he couldn't quite bring himself to be an active dick with her, especially when she'd been nothing but nice to him.

And *most* especially when the problem wasn't her.

He dragged his gaze from the necklace and the hollow of her throat to meet her clear green eyes. "Make it quick. I have to get up to Clint's."

"Oh?" Beth looked momentarily concerned. "Is he okay?"

"Yeah, he's fine. Just some horse stuff I have to do."

"That's good." Her smile crept back, like the sun slowly dawning over the sky at the end of night. "You know, I think that's the longest sentence you've ever spoken to me."

Wonderful. Like he needed a reminder of how he'd been avoiding her ever since the day she'd arrived.

Deciding to ignore it, he said, "What kind of help do you need?"

"I hope I haven't offended you or anything."

"What?"

"Oh, it's just that you...well, seem kind of annoyed with me."

She didn't sound the least bit accusing, only curious, which was somehow worse, because he'd thought she wouldn't notice his reserve around her.

Seriously? You really thought she wouldn't?

Okay, maybe not, but he'd hoped.

"I'm not annoyed," he said shortly, wishing she'd leave it at that, because this was not the conversation he wanted to be having in the middle of town with a whole lot of tourists around, not to mention a few locals.

Bill had come to stand in the doorway of the general store, watching them, and he could also see Cait O'Halloran, who owned the Rose along with her father Jim, standing on the veranda of the Rose next door, also watching.

They liked Bethany because everyone liked Bethany. Hell, he'd probably like Bethany too if he hadn't been attracted to her.

But he was attracted to her.

Which apparently means acting like a sulky teenage boy.

Finn didn't like that thought, mainly because he had a suspicion it was true. In which case it was time to draw this little scene to a close.

"Can we talk about this another time?" He turned back to the truck and pulled open the door. "Like I said, I have to get up to Clint's."

"Oh sure." Beth's smile became even sunnier. "I'll come with you if you like. We can chat on the way there."

Finn opened his mouth to tell her that she would not be coming with him anywhere, when she lifted the paper bag containing the sausage roll. "Here's a bribe," she said. "It's yours if you can bear my company for ten whole minutes."

Her green eyes danced, the color accentuated by the slight bit of pink sunburn, which made him even grumpier because she was just so pretty. And he didn't want to spent ten minutes alone with her in his truck, or indeed, anywhere, but he couldn't think of how to refuse her, not without seeming like a total tool. Not a great look considering all the interested bystanders.

Also, he kind of wanted the sausage roll.

"Fine," he said with what he suspected was shockingly bad grace. "But you'll have to wait around until I'm finished if you want a ride back into town."

"Oh, I don't mind. I love horses."

He suspected that she did not, in fact, love horses, since she'd never once to his knowledge shown any interest in going to Clint's before. But all he said was, "Hop in then."

Bethany's grin widened. "Yay. The sausage roll shall be yours."

She stepped toward him and he wondered what she was doing, then she stopped and blinked. "Oops. Keep forgetting. Door's on the other side, isn't it?" She gave a soft laugh. "I'll remember one of these days." Then before he could say anything, she'd gone off around the other side of his truck.

Of course, the passenger door was on the opposite side to what she was used to. He didn't know why he found that endearing, but he did.

Irritated with himself, he tried to ignore the sensation, pulling open the door and climbing inside. Bethany had already seated herself and was putting her seatbelt on, the paper bag containing the sausage roll on the console between the seats.

She pushed it toward him as he got in. "Never let it be said that a Grant doesn't pay their debts."

Finn grunted and started the truck, the realization slowly creeping up on him that he'd made a mistake. That he never should have agreed to have her in such close quarters. Because she was sitting close to him now and the delicate scent of something sweet was filling his cab. Like peaches or apricots, which were fruit he particularly liked.

You bloody idiot. Settle down.

Finn gripped the steering wheel and pulled the truck onto the road that wound around the lake. Clint's farm wasn't far, ten minutes down the road and then another five up a long, winding gravel drive that led up into the hills, rolling green fields on either side.

Not long. He could handle fifteen minutes of Bethany sitting in his truck, filling up the space with her warm, bright presence. He wasn't a teenager. He could deal.

For a minute as they drove there was blessed silence.

Then he felt Bethany's attention turn unerringly on him, making every single muscle he had tighten up in response.

"So," she said brightly. "What were we talking about again? Oh yes. Why don't you like me, Finn Kelly?"

Chapter 2

FINN'S ATTENTION WAS FIXED STOICALLY FORWARD OUT the front windshield, which Beth supposed was a good thing, since he should have his attention on the road ahead. Except, she kind of wished he'd look at her.

His big, muscular body was radiating I-am-not-in-any-way-comfortable-with-this vibes and his handsome face was set in hard lines, his strong jaw sharp enough to cut.

She shouldn't have been so blunt, but her question had just popped out. And why not? She *did* want to know why he didn't like her, because it was clear that he didn't. And while she didn't mind that—he was allowed not to like her—she wanted to know for sure. Just so everyone was clear where they stood and there were no misunderstandings.

Still, tension filled the cab and she felt the urge to put her hand on his shoulder to soothe him, reassure him somehow, but she had the sense that he wouldn't welcome it, so she kept her hands to herself.

Perhaps you shouldn't have this conversation now?

Maybe not. It was clear he hadn't been happy with it as they'd stood beside the truck, his dark eyes wary and guarded, his expression taut.

What was it about her that made him so tense? Did it have something to do with his wife? And if so, what was it? Because if she was hurting him in some way, she'd really like to know so she could stop. Her instinct was to come right out and ask, but since Bill had told her that Finn didn't like talking about it, she didn't want to bring it up and perhaps hurt him even more.

She bit her lip, watching him instead.

When she'd first met him, she'd thought him a very still man, especially in contrast to the much more intense, kinetic energy that his brother radiated. Like a lake on a calm day, the surface smooth, hiding deep, dark depths.

But she realized now she'd been wrong. Because while he might be perfectly still, he radiated tension, almost vibrating with it like a telephone wire in a high wind.

"Sorry," she said into the silence. "I suppose that was kind of blunt."

"Yes." Finn's voice was curt.

Beth waited, but he didn't say anything more, his gaze firmly on the road.

Great, this was going well. Getting conversation out of Finn Kelly was like getting blood out of a stone.

Maybe you could have started with something less contentious straight out of the gate?

She let out a silent breath. Okay, yes, she should have. After all, hadn't she told herself that she had to handle this carefully? Bill had mentioned she should take it slow with Finn so perhaps she should start doing that.

Beth automatically reached for her silver koru pendant, holding it, feeling the silver warm against her palm. It fitted perfectly there, as she'd designed it to, the reassuring warmth of the metal easing her own tension and the little sliver of doubt that had begun to crack the shell of her positivity.

She couldn't afford doubts. Couldn't afford second-guessing. That way lay a path she didn't want to go down, not again. She had to keep looking forward to the future, be confident in the new path she'd chosen for herself. Being here, in Brightwater Valley. Where no one knew her and she could be whoever she wanted to be.

Bright. Happy. Fearless. Strong.

She took a breath. "Okay. So if you don't want to answer that question, how about this one instead? I'd really like to get Evan's paintings for the gallery. They could really draw in the crowds and since he's a local—"

"He won't agree," Finn interrupted. "He hates showing his paintings. He also hates people."

For some reason that amused her and she smiled. "Hates people? No wonder you're friends then."

Finn glanced at her, his gaze a flash of intense darkness in the bright sun coming through the front window of the truck.

For some inexplicable reason it made her breath catch.

"My advice?" he went on, ignoring her comment. "Don't even ask. You're not the first person who's tried to get to his paintings and you probably won't be the last, and you'll only end up disappointed."

Beth's amusement faltered. There was something fierce about Finn she hadn't noticed before, a kind of intensity that she found both compelling and disturbing at the same time.

He had the darkest eyes, almost black, which was strange when his brother's eyes were so light. Yet it was a fascinating darkness. She's always been drawn to the bright and shiny, like a magpie, but there was something deep and dark in Finn Kelly that she couldn't deny was...magnetic.

"Wow." She tried not to sound as breathless as she felt. "I got a whole three sentences this time. I must be doing something right."

Finn's expression smoothed and he glanced back at the road ahead. "Don't say I didn't warn you."

"Okay, message received." She waited a moment. "Actually, though, that's the help I was talking about. You're his friend, right? Perhaps you could—"

"No."

"Seriously? Just flat out no?"

He didn't reply, slowing the truck down and then pulling off into a small, narrow gravel driveway. A rickety wooden farm gate stood across it, and without a word, Finn got out, strode to the gate, and unlatched it.

Beth watched him from the front seat of the truck, thinking.

He really was being quite rude, and if Bill hadn't let slip a piece of Finn's past the way he'd done, then she might have been annoyed. But he had let it slip, and it was pretty awful, and so she didn't feel annoyed. She felt…sorry for him.

Five years, Bill had said, which meant there had been some water under the bridge. But grief didn't have a time limit, she knew that all too well, and sometimes the years were eons and sometimes they were the blink of an eye.

So no, she couldn't be angry. She'd be understanding and empathetic and careful instead.

Finn got the gate open and headed back to the truck, climbing back in and driving it through onto the driveway. Then he got back out again to close the gate behind him, and all without a word.

Beth decided not to push it, so she sat there silently as Finn drove the truck up the winding gravel drive to Clint's horse farm, looking out the window and admiring the view.

It really was in a pretty location, set on the green hillside, with lots of farmland around and some bush creeping up the hills behind the house. The views over the lake and the mountains beyond were spectacular, reminding her a bit of Deep River.

Not that she was homesick. How could you be homesick for a place you couldn't wait to leave?

Finn pulled the truck up into the big gravel turnaround next to a cluster of farm buildings that included the stables, then turned off the engine.

"Evan is difficult," he said unexpectedly.

Beth stared at him, surprised that first he'd actually spoken and second that it was something useful.

"Like you, you mean?" she said, teasing.

His expression was opaque. "I suppose I deserved that."

Beth was about to tease him again by telling him he absolutely deserved it, when old Clint came out of the stables and headed for the truck, a big German shepherd trotting at his heels.

Finn gave her one last enigmatic look, before he turned away, getting out and going over to greet both the old man and the dog.

Beth stayed where she was, uncertain what to do now she was here. She'd said hello a couple of times to Clint, but she didn't know him, and despite what she'd told Finn, she didn't know much about horses either. Her affinity was with sparkly things rather than livestock.

She watched Finn and Clint chat for a moment before both of them headed toward the stables. Then frowned as Finn abruptly stopped and turned around, striding back to the truck.

He pulled open her door. "Come on," he said shortly. "Come and see the horses."

Surprise rippled through her. "Me? But I'm only here to—"

"I'm going to be awhile and I'm sure you don't want to sit by yourself in the truck for the next hour." His eyes gleamed abruptly in a way that made something fizz and spark inside her. "Anyway, didn't you say you loved horses?"

Heat climbed in her cheeks, because of both the way he looked at her and the total lie she'd given him about the damn horses. "Oh, I don't mind sitting—"

"Beth." His voice was softer this time and very low. "Come on."

The way he said her name, the deep timbre of the word, set off a small electric charge inside her.

She didn't know what was happening. Attraction was something she hadn't looked for and didn't want, still less having that attraction for a man as complicated as Finn Kelly. Simple, that's what she wanted. That's why she'd come here. Simple and easy was the path to happiness, not complicated and dark and difficult.

Not a man still grieving.

She needed lightness and charm, which meant if she was that hard up for some uncomplicated sexy fun, she should be looking at Levi. He was a man who was certainly up for that kind of thing, not Heathcliff over there.

Ignoring the fizz and pulse inside her, Beth put on her usual cheerful mask and grinned. "Well, okay. But only if you help me with Evan."

"You just don't give up, do you?"

"Nope. Alternatively…" She drew out the moment for effect. "I'd settle for proof that Finn Kelly knows how to smile."

A muscle flickered at the corner of his mouth. "I know how to smile. I just don't smile at you."

It was nearly a win. Nearly.

"Ouch," she said with feeling. "You really know how to win a girl over."

Something in his face eased slightly. "Come and see the horses or don't, it's up to you."

Beth debated teasing him some more since she found it oddly exhilarating, but since that only seemed to make the fizz and crackle she felt around him worse, she settled for sliding out of the truck instead.

Clint's dog came over to give her a sniff then wagged his tail and she grinned. "And who is this lovely boy?"

"That's Karl," Finn said.

"Hey Karl." Beth dropped her hand to give the dog a scratch behind the ears. Karl wagged his tail ecstatically. "I guess at least someone likes me." She glanced at Finn, who'd already begun walking over to the stable block so she came after him, Karl trotting along behind her.

"Any particular reason why you want me to see these horses?" she asked. "Especially when you don't seem to find my company particularly enticing."

Finn kept his gaze on the stables ahead of them. "You said you loved horses."

She rolled her eyes. "We both know that was a total lie. I just wanted to talk to you about Evan." At least, that was the ostensible reason.

"You can talk to me about Evan in the stables." He glanced at her all of a sudden. "Why did you want to stay in the truck?"

Beth opened her mouth to reply, then shut it, her face

feeling warm. She couldn't tell him the real reason, that she was finding him far too attractive for his own good and that she was rather overwhelmed. No, most definitely not.

"Perhaps I like the truck." She kicked at a stone. "Anyway, I'm a jewelry designer, not a horse person."

Finn said nothing to that as they approached the stables, a long, low wooden building with a corrugated metal roof. There were a number of stalls, each with an open front and a wooden gate and as the two of them came closer, one black horse put its head over the gate, nickering at Finn.

Clint, a tall man in his late sixties, whose weather-beaten, craggy face looked like it had spent decades being pounded by the elements, was already at the stall and he put a hand on the animal's long nose, smiling. "Seems like Jeff knows you're here."

"Jeff?" Beth murmured. "The horse's name is Jeff?"

Clint, who'd obviously overheard, gave Beth a narrow glance. "Nothing wrong with that name." He stepped away from the stall. "Horse just looked like a Jeff to me."

"Of course." Beth smiled at him. "I didn't mean anything by it. Just that a black horse is usually 'night' or 'shadow' or something more…poetic I guess."

Finn reached out and stroked Jeff's silky black nose, reaching into the pocket of his jeans with his other hand. The horse nickered again, pushing against Finn's hand. "Take no notice of her," he murmured softly. "Jeff's a good name for a horse, a fine name. And you're a very fine horse, aren't you, Jeff?"

Beth went very still. There was a coaxing note in his deep voice that she'd never heard before and it grabbed onto something inside her and held on tight.

Finn's attention was on the horse, the usually impenetrable expression on his handsome face relaxing into something much warmer, almost affectionate. It felt as if she'd made a profound discovery and she couldn't look away.

Jeff leaned further out of his stall, nosing down to where Finn's other hand was still in his pocket. "Oh, you know what I've got for you, don't you?" The lines of his face had softened completely now and then, much to Beth's shock, his hard mouth curved in a warm smile. "Demanding animal. I guess you can have this now." And he pulled a small apple from his pocket and gave it to Jeff, who crunched on it contently as Finn stroked his neck.

"You spoil that beast," Clint grunted, though he didn't look too unhappy about it.

Not that Beth was paying any attention to Clint. A bit hard to do so when Finn Kelly, whom she swore wouldn't know a smile if it bit him on the butt, was now smiling as the animal's soft mouth quested on his palm for more apple.

And what a smile...

Finn was a handsome man, she'd always known that, but his smile, lighting his face and the darkness in his eyes, took him from handsome to devastating in seconds flat. Now the only thing she could think of was what she could do to make him smile again. And at her.

Careful. You don't want to be getting too involved, remember? You're here for easy, for simple. Friends and a good time. That's it.

Oh, she remembered. But it was fine. All she wanted was to make a hot dude smile so she could enjoy the view, nothing more. Certainly nothing to do with the accelerated beat of her heart or the sudden heat that washed over her skin. Or the insane urge to follow the line of that smile with her fingertips, see if his mouth was as hard as it looked or whether it would feel soft.

And she was right in the middle of that thought when Finn looked over at her, that mesmerizing smile still in place, an echo of the heat she felt inside her gleaming in his dark eyes. "Don't tell me," he murmured in the same low, coaxing voice he'd used on Jeff. "You want an apple too?"

Acknowledgments

Thanks to: my agent, Helen Breitwieser, my editor Deb Werksman, and the team at Sourcebooks. Plus also New Zealand's South Island, which is a beautiful place and you should go there.

About the Author

Jackie Ashenden has been writing fiction since she was eleven years old. Mild-mannered fantasy/SF/pseudo-literary writer by day, obsessive romance writer by night, she used to balance her writing with the more serious job of librarianship until a chance meeting with another romance writer prompted her to throw off the shackles of her day job and devote herself to the true love of her heart—writing romance. She particularly likes to write dark, emotional stories with alpha heroes who've just gotten the world to their liking only to have it blown wide apart by their kick-ass heroines.

She lives in Auckland, New Zealand, with her husband, the inimitable Dr. Jax, two kids, one dog, and one cat. When she's not torturing alpha males and their obstreperous heroines, she can be found drinking chocolate martinis, reading anything she can lay her hands on, or being forced to go mountain biking with her husband.

You can find Jackie at jackieashenden.com or follow her on Twitter @JackieAshenden.

THE BEST OF ME

Warm and heartfelt Southern romance from *New York Times* and *USA Today* bestselling author Sharon Sala

Ruby Butterman and her husband, Peanut, cannot have children, but they're given a second chance at a family when six-year-old Carlie is left in their care by her dying mother.

It's a challenge for Carlie to adapt to a new town, a new school, and a new family, so Ruby and Peanut do their best to make her feel right at home. With the help of everyone in Blessings, Georgia, Carlie is settling in beautifully. Then someone from Carlie's mother's past decides he wants to take her away from her new life…if he can, that is…

"Sharon Sala is a consummate storyteller."
—Debbie Macomber, #1 *New York Times*
bestselling author

For more info about Sourcebooks's books and authors, visit:
sourcebooks.com

THE HONEYMOON INN

New York Times bestselling author Carolyn
Brown's Texas twang and inimitable sass shine
as close proximity leads to a fiery fling

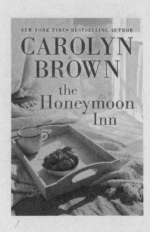

Pearl Richland left home as soon as she could and never thought
she'd look back. And she didn't, until she lost her job at the bank
and had to fall back on the only thing left to her name: the motel
her great-aunt Pearlita left to her. But with a winter storm coming
and some suspicious activity around town, Pearl hunkers down in
the motel with the only guest passing through town, a man named
Will Marshall. Luckily, he's a welcome distraction as the long, cold
days quickly turn to hot nights…

Previously published as *Red's Hot Cowboy*.

**"[A] fresh, funny, and sexy tale filled with
likable, down-to-earth characters."**
—*Booklist* for *Love Drunk Cowboy*

For more info about Sourcebooks's books and authors, visit:
sourcebooks.com

TO BE LOVED BY YOU

Hopeful contemporary romance where every person and pet gets a happily ever after, from author Debbie Burns

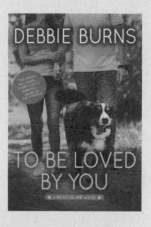

Jeremy Washington is always searching for new projects for the at-risk teens in his therapy program. At High Grove Animal Shelter—where his teens have been learning to train and foster puppies for adoption—he meets Ava, a yoga instructor with a big heart. After an unforgettable afternoon together, Jeremy knows Ava's the perfect person to help in his program, especially if it means he'll get to see her again...

"Burns is sure to win over dog lovers and fans of Kristan Higgins and Jill Shalvis."
—*Publishers Weekly* for *Head Over Paws*

For more info about Sourcebooks's books and authors, visit:
sourcebooks.com